Death in Bloom

Death in Bloom

JESS DYLAN

St. Martin's Paperbacks

First published in the United States by St. Martin's Paperbacks, an imprint of St. Martin's Publishing Group.

DEATH IN BLOOM

For information, address St. Martin's Publishing Group, 120 Broadway, New York, NY 10271.

www.stmartins.com

ISBN: 978-1-250-76951-0

Our books may be purchased in bulk for promotional, educational, or business use. Please contact your local bookseller or the Macmillan Corporate and Premium Sales Department at 1-800-221-7945, ext. 5442, or by email at MacmillanSpecialMarkets@macmillan.com.

Printed in the United States of America

St. Martin's Paperbacks edition published 2021

10 9 8 7 6 5 4 3 2 1

For Joanna DeVoe, a happy/hippie/witchy writer,
podcaster, and friend, who has inspired me
in so many ways. Thank you.

There are always flowers for those who want to see them.

—*Henri Matisse*

Chapter 1

I'm in the best shape of my life. I'm a Grammy-award winning singer-songwriter, blissfully married to my true love, an Italian model—

No, wait. Make that . . .

French actor.

No. Brazilian. Yes. That's it.

. . . my true love, a Brazilian actor and model who worships the ground I walk on. We live in a chalet on the coast of—

"Sierra?"

I gave a start and snapped my notebook shut, rattling the spoon next to my coffee cup. I was at my usual table in the corner, up against the turquoise-painted wall adjacent to the picture window. The bright wall featured a rotating display of local artwork, while the window supplied natural light and a view of the pink-petaled cherry tree on the street outside. White cursive lettering on the window announced the shop's name—*Coffee Art Café*—and conveniently hid me from any strolling passers-by. This spot usually afforded me a smidge of privacy for dreaming and doodling in my vision journal. Apparently not today.

"I thought that was you, Sierra Ravenswood! Still sporting short bangs and a bob, just like in high school."

I looked up at the stylish, well-dressed woman who had just entered the coffee shop. She fluttered across the checkered-tile floor, as light and graceful as a butterfly.

"Why, Deena Lee! What a surprise!" I plastered on a big smile, the kind you use when you run into an old classmate you haven't seen since graduation ten years ago—and you're wishing you'd worn anything but the overalls you'd grabbed from the bedroom floor that morning. She smiled in return.

Deena Lee was always nice enough back in the day, though we never ran in the same circles. I was a band geek—not that there's anything wrong with that. And when I wasn't practicing my clarinet or my guitar, I usually had my nose in a book. Deena, by contrast, was one of the popular, smart kids. If there was an academic team, she was probably on it—debate club, scholastic bowl, student council, you name it. Of course, she was pretty too and the only Korean-American in our school. When I last saw her, at our ten-year class reunion last summer, she'd been positively glowing with all her successes.

She flipped her long, black hair in a casual, carefree way. "What are you doing in Aerieville, Miss Sierra? Visiting your folks?"

I kept my smile firmly in place. "No, ma'am. I live here now."

She arched her perfectly-shaped eyebrows. "You do? I thought you moved to Nashville!"

"I did, a while ago. I moved back in January." *Four months ago, not that anyone's counting.* Before she could launch into the third degree, I quickly turned the tables. "How have you been? Last I heard you were working on your PhD—in Chicago, wasn't it?"

"Still am." She laughed gaily. "Perpetual scholar, that's me."

"You visiting your folks?"

"Mm-hmm. Daddy's birthday is this weekend. He doesn't want a fuss, but we'll have cake and ice cream."

"How long you in town for?"

Deena flinched, and for a second, I thought Miss "Perpetual Scholar" was offended by my grammar. Well, she grew up here too. In my opinion, when your conversation is colloquial, the usual grammar rules don't apply.

To my surprise, her lower lip began to tremble. She covered her mouth as if to hide it, but I could tell she was upset.

I hopped up and pulled out the chair opposite mine. "Sit," I said, touching her arm lightly. I didn't know if it was my upbeat personality or my sympathetic face, but folks tend to confide in me. They always have. My mom liked to say I could've been a therapist. I sat down across from her. "What's wrong, Deena?"

She heaved a great sigh. "I might be here for a while, that's what's wrong. Steve left me."

"Steve? I thought your fiancée's name was Troy."

"Troy? That's old news. He was two relationships ago." She sighed and shook her head. "I'm a smart woman, right? Why do I have so much trouble holding on to men? It's like I keep falling for the same type—the wrong type—over and over again."

An idea popped into my head, and I impulsively clapped my hands together. "Listen, I'm no psychologist, but I do know something that might help."

She looked startled, as if she hadn't really expected an answer. "You do?"

"Flowers."

Her surprise turned to confusion. "Flowers? What do you mean?"

"I mean pretty, sweet-smelling, cheerful flowers—and the mood-boosting art of arranging them."

"Um." Deena looked at me like I'd sprouted a second head. It didn't bother me. I was used to it.

"Listen," I said. "There's a bouquet-arranging class tonight at Flower House. Seven o'clock. You should come."

"Flower House? The old florist shop on Oak Street?"

"The one and only. I work there part-time." I had worked at the flower shop off and on during my high school years. Fortunately, the owner was happy to give me my old position when I returned to town. I checked my watch and scrambled to my feet. "Speaking of which, I gotta run. It was good seeing you!"

I waved at the kid behind the coffee counter and stepped outside into the springtime sun. As usual, my eyes were immediately drawn upward, from the flapping American and Tennessean flags on the green mound across the street to the redbrick clock tower (the tallest structure in town) to the misty-blue Smoky Mountains in the distance. Some say the mountains are Aerieville's defining feature, providing everything from resources and recreation to a sense of history and pride. For the Cherokee, the mountains were a sacred place, and I tended to agree. Of course, the tales my grandmother would spin—from my childhood to the present—surely influenced my thoughts on the matter.

Breathing in the magnolia-scented air, I took a moment to savor the warmth and beauty of the morning. Gratitude was key to a happy life. If you have a grateful heart, you're bound to attract more of what you're grateful for. With this in mind, I ticked off all my blessings, like the overflowing flower baskets hanging from the lampposts, as I walked down the sidewalk toward my car. *Good health. Loving—if quirky—family members. A cute house. A decent job.*

Positive thinking worked. I knew it did. I was a believer, through and through. A few years ago, I'd moved to Nashville with nothing but the guitar on my back, and within a week I'd manifested an awesome loft apartment, a steady gig, and a promising new boyfriend—all exactly like I visualized.

Unfortunately, it didn't last. One by one, I lost them all. But I didn't let it get me down. I told myself all those losses were the Universe's way of saying I had bigger and better things in store. I just needed to get clear on what I really wanted and set new intentions. That was all.

When I reached my car, a little two-door Fiat in bright electric orange, I patted the hood with a smile. This little baby was something else I'd attracted into my life. And, so far, I'd managed to hang onto it.

On the short drive across the village, from tiny Main Street to Old Town, I watched the scenery roll by. The dollar theater marquee advertised a second-run movie. An elderly gentleman twirled a cane outside the bank, and a young couple entered the Tasty Cone ice cream shop arm in arm. Near the ballfield, a red balloon rose lazily toward the treetops.

In my experience, signs were everywhere, if you only paid attention. Messages from the Universe, that's what they were. Sometimes just a wink and a nod, sometimes a warning. Sometimes an invitation. Heck, running into Deena this morning was probably no accident. I hoped she would drop by the flower shop later.

The instant the thought crossed my mind, a delivery truck caught my attention at the intersection in front of me. The placard on top read Friendship Pizza.

Ha. Come to think of it, I could stand to add more friendship to my life. Most of my peers had moved away, and I hadn't gotten out much since returning to Aerieville.

I should add "fulfilling friendships" to my vision journal.

I was still daydreaming when I parked my car along the street a block away from Flower House. My boss, Felix Maniford, wanted to save the parking spaces in front for customers. I didn't mind the walk. It was a nice day and a pretty, tree-lined boulevard. Mature oaks stood over a mix of residential and commercial buildings, including an antique store, a bakery, and the home of Aerieville's historical society (volunteer-run and almost never open). In no time, I was approaching the converted Victorian, an elegant if somewhat faded painted lady, long known as Flower House.

My eyes always went first to the picture window next to the front door. Since I was in charge of the display, I wanted to make sure it was attention-grabbing and tidy. We usually featured seasonal floral arrangements in the window along with a few charming gift ideas—mainly sachets, mugs, and vases. I liked to mix in little wooden signs featuring motivational word art whenever I could: Believe, Create, and Dream were my favorites.

Today, however, something distracted me. It was the Closed sign on the front door. My shift didn't start until ten o'clock, but Felix always opened by eight thirty. I tried the knob, and it was locked.

Wrinkling my forehead, I fished my keys from my purse and let myself in. It was possible Felix had closed the shop to make a delivery. But he usually waited for me before doing that. And from the looks of things, the shop hadn't been opened at all this morning.

I flipped on the overhead light and walked to the lone checkout counter in the center of the foyer-turned-storefront. Looking around, I hugged my arms to ward off a shiver. With its high ceilings and old windows, the Victorian was always a bit drafty. Fortunately, the abundance of colorful bouquets usually provided an inviting, homey warmth to the shop. At the moment, however, many of the fresh flowers were missing, undoubtedly still in the cooler in the back. And the refrigerated display case along the wall was dark. One glance at the cash register told me it was still empty from the night before.

Where was Felix?

I had just reached for the phone under the counter, when the front door burst open. *And there's my answer*, I thought. Standing on the entry mat, dropping papers from both hands, was my illustrious boss, Felix Maniford. As usual, his shock of white hair was in need of a trim and his plaid shirt in need of an iron. His jeans were rolled up at the cuffs. At five foot five (just a smidge taller than me), his pants were always on the long side—and he never bothered to have them hemmed.

"Oh, good," he said, his mouth twitching into a distracted smile. "You're here."

I crossed the room and picked up the fallen papers— which I now saw were fliers advertising tonight's flower-arranging class.

"Where have you been?" I asked. "Is everything okay?"

"Hmm? Oh, yes. Fine. Everything's fine. I just need to pick up something, and then I'm on my way."

"On your way?"

"Yes, I got a call just now. Well, a few minutes ago. It was the call I've been waiting for. Then I remembered—" He stopped himself, finally noticing my confusion. "I'm sorry, Sierra. I get ahead of myself sometimes. Now, where should I start?"

"How about with these," I suggested, waving a sheaf of fliers.

"Oh, right. Let's see. I was watering the garden this morning when I remembered your class—"

"*My* class?" I interrupted. It was true the class had been my idea, but Felix was supposed to lead it. He was the expert florist, not me.

"I knew there was something I was forgetting," he continued. "Then it hit me. I forgot to place an ad in the paper last week."

"Felix!"

"I know, I know. But then I had the idea to post some fliers around town. I printed off a bunch of 'em this morning."

"Did you hang any?" I asked.

"Well, yes. I hung one on the bulletin board at the library, and one at Bread n' Butter next door. I was gonna put up more, but then I got the call. The one—"

"The one you were waiting for," I finished. "Who from, Felix?"

His eyes darted past me to the checkout counter. "Excuse me, dear. I think I left my GPS here." He scuttled past me, as I shook my head in exasperation.

His GPS. That could mean only one thing. "Really, Felix? That's what has you so preoccupied? Geocaching?"

Ever since his wife, Georgina, passed away a dozen years ago, Felix had begun to spend less time on the business they'd created and more time on his hobbies: fishing and geocaching. He even moved out of the apartment on the second floor of Flower House to live in a little cabin in the woods, not far from his favorite fishing hole. But in recent years, he'd become especially enthusiastic about geocaching—the outdoor treasure-hunting game where players use GPS coordinates to find items hidden by other players.

"Here it is!" Felix announced, holding up a handheld navigating device. "Now, where's my flashlight?"

He headed for the workroom, with me close on his tail, then stopped so abruptly I almost ran into him. "Silly me. It's in the truck!"

"Felix, are you really going on a hunt now? When will you be back?" I followed him to the front door, feeling like a puppy dog. When he opened it, I had to resist the urge to grab his shirttail.

He paused long enough to turn back and give me a quick, fatherly nod. "Mind the store, will you? I could be a while."

"But, Felix! What about the class?"

"Class? Oh, yes. Have fun! You'll do great."

"But I've only been making bouquets for four months! I'm not ready to lead a class!"

My protests were futile. Felix was already scurrying down the sidewalk toward his pickup truck. He hopped in, slammed the door, and took off down the street—leaving me to shake my head in bewilderment.

Chapter 2

Flowers. Check.

Floral scissors, ribbons, vases. Check, check, check.

Refreshments. Check.

I ripped open a package of generic chocolate-chip cookies, selected a broken one, and crunched into it as I surveyed the room. When Felix and Georgina had purchased the house, many moons ago, they had big plans for their flower-themed business. They'd redone all the main-level flooring in a marble-looking porcelain tile and expanded the kitchen to serve as a workroom. In addition to showcasing Georgina's orchid collection—and selling flowers and related gift items—they had the idea to open a café inside the shop. They were going to feature a small menu centered on edible flowers they grew themselves.

And they certainly had the space for it. There was a large open room adjoining the front of the store, separated only by a built-in archway. Years ago, Felix brought in some small wooden tables and chairs and installed a glass bakery case and a serving counter.

Then, sadly, Georgina passed away. Felix naturally lost his enthusiasm for all their grand plans. He moved out of the upstairs apartment and scrapped the idea of opening a café. Now the bakery case held gardening supplies, and the countertop was piled high with seed catalogs.

Still, in spite of the clutter, the space was perfect for hosting workshops. When I talked Felix into teaching a bouquet-arranging class, he'd agreed it was a good idea. It would bring people into the shop and maybe even boost the store's image. Felix had to admit he didn't have as many customers as he used to. Most folks went to the florist in the grocery store or ordered their flowers online—which were then supplied by the larger, big-city florists. But Felix had something the larger stores didn't: years of experience and a vast knowledge of exotic plants. He always added a special touch to his arrangements, whether a unique sprig or an unusual blossom. I was looking forward to the class myself.

And then he went and bailed on me. I'd spent the last hour pushing tables together, clearing off the countertop, and generally cleaning up the place—all before hauling out buckets of flowers and gathering and setting out tools and supplies. The whole time I wondered if anyone would even show up. Part of me hoped they wouldn't.

After starting a pot of coffee (which I'd transferred from the kitchen workroom), I plopped myself into one of the wooden ladder-back chairs in the "events room," as I'd begun to call it. I needed to calm my nerves and set an intention for the workshop. I took a deep breath and closed my eyes. Then I popped them back open. The front door had jangled open. They were here.

"Yoo hoo!" called a male voice. "Anybody home?"

I scrambled to my feet and hurried out to the foyer. A tall, lanky guy in a polo shirt and pressed jeans flashed his dimples and raised a cake pan. "I come bearing brownies. Where should I put them?"

"Hey, Richard! How nice! Homemade is always better than store-bought." I led him to the counter in the events

room, then pushed aside my package of cookies and replaced them with the pan of brownies. "You're such a
sweetheart. The nicest guy I know." I had been acquainted
with Richard since high school, though he was two years
ahead of me.

"That's me," he said dryly. "Mr. Nice Guy."

"Nice, cute, single—and handy. I know you moonlight
as a fix-it guy when you're not working as a bank teller.
And come to find out, you bake too! If only. . . ." I trailed
off self-consciously, hoping I hadn't crossed a line.

He chuckled and patted my arm sympathetically.
"*You're* the sweetheart. But you know better than to lament
the things you can't have. It's always better to focus on the
possible—not the physically *impossible*."

I smiled. "You're right. What was I thinking?"

He reached for his wallet. "Shall I pay you now for the
workshop? Forty dollars is a steal for something like this.
Felix should really charge more."

"About that—"

The door jingled again, heralding the arrival of another
attendee: Letty Maron. Letty was a middle-aged schoolteacher with graying, dishwater blonde hair and a tendency
to wear cardigan sweaters all year round. She was also
a bit of a paradox. In her classroom, she displayed su-
preme confidence—everywhere else, she was extremely
reticent. I knew, because she sometimes invited me to
play my guitar for her second graders, and I was always
amazed at how different her demeanor was from the person I knew in the shop. The shy mouse would turn into a
queenly Mother Goose.

Today she was the mouse again. Timidly clutching
a foil-covered pie, she approached Richard and me with
downcast eyes.

"What have you got there, Letty?" asked Richard.

"Oh, nothing. Just a blueberry pie."

"*Just* a blueberry pie! Let's have a look."

As Richard took the pie from Letty, the door opened again, admitting a willowy African-American woman, followed closely by a pale, pudgy-faced man wearing tight jeans and a button-down shirt with one too many buttons left unfastened. I could smell his musky, incense-like cologne from several feet away. They both came straight to the snack counter, where the woman set down a tray of cupcakes and the man plopped down a bag of potato chips.

"Hi, Valerie. Abe," I said, nodding to each in turn.

I knew Valerie only slightly. She was some years older than me and ran a dance and gymnastics studio at the end of Main Street. I assumed she hadn't actually come with Abe. She fluttered her fingertips at me, then wrinkled her pert nose and turned her back to Abe. I noticed that both Richard and Letty also seemed less than pleased at Abe's presence. Whether this was due to his strong cologne or his generally obnoxious personality was hard to say.

As owner of the town's only garden center, Abe Ranker ran a booming business. But I'd heard tell of more than one resident who'd rather drive ten miles over to the next village just to avoid doing business with "Dishonest Abe." Though he'd never offended me personally, I was already beginning to worry about the negative vibes he was bringing to the workshop.

Before I could fret any further, the door opened again, and two more arrivals entered the store: Bill and Flo Morrison, owners of the bakery next door. Bill was tall and balding; Flo was nearly his height with long, silver-white hair, which she often wore twisted in a low bun. I was relieved to see them. An outgoing and friendly couple, they were fixtures in the Aerieville cultural scene, such as it was. There wasn't a concert, community event, or meeting they missed. Not surprisingly, they each carried a basket of treats. If I wasn't mistaken, it looked to be plastic-wrapped loaves of zucchini bread.

"More sweets!" groused Abe. "I guess I'm the only one with the foresight to realize not all snacks have to involve sugar."

A flash of annoyance crossed Flo's face.

"These look delicious," I hastened to say, as I took Flo's basket. "I didn't realize this was going to be a potluck."

"This is Aerieville," said Richard. "Throw a gathering, and folks bring food."

"Where's Felix?" asked Flo. "I brought extra zucchini bread just for him."

"Um, he's not here, so I'm filling in. Why don't we all sit down and get started?"

My nerves shot up again, as I took my place in front of the group. I longed to grab my guitar. I'd much rather play them all a song. My stage fright always took a breather whenever I shared my music. Public speaking was an entirely different beast.

All eyes turned to me as everyone settled into their chairs. I cleared my throat.

"Thank you all for coming. Uh, something came up and Felix can't be here. But I learned flower arranging from him, and I'm ready to show you everything I know." I glanced at their faces. If anyone was disappointed, they weren't letting on. Heartened, I continued. "So, there's a quote I like by the famous botanist, Luther Burbank. He said, 'Flowers always make people better, happier, and more helpful; they are sunshine, food, and medicine for the soul.'"

"Amen," said Richard. I looked up gratefully, and he gave me an encouraging wink.

"Springtime flowers are especially cheerful after the long, cold winter," I said. "So, I thought we should make—"

I broke off at the sound of the front door opening again. To my delight, I saw Deena step hesitantly into the events room.

"Oh, come on!" said Abe loudly. "If people can't arrive on time, they shouldn't bother coming at all."

Deena flushed a deep crimson, but a chorus of welcoming voices drowned out whatever else Abe had to say on the matter. Bill hopped up to make room for Deena at the table, and I rushed forward to grab her hand and pull her in before she could change her mind and flee.

"You made it!" I said. "And you're right on time. We're just getting started."

I resumed my opening spiel. "So, today we're gonna make a bouquet of spring flowers with peonies, hyacinths, tulips, and daffodils. There's a lot of room for creativity when it comes to flower arranging, but there are some basic rules to make sure you end up with a pretty result. I'll demonstrate each step, explaining as I go, while you all make your own bouquets."

I glanced around the table to gauge everyone's reactions. Most attendees seemed interested—or at least polite. Bill and Flo were already reaching for one of the clear glass vases I'd set out. Deena had a slightly bemused expression, like she still wasn't sure if she should stay. Abe was . . . staring at Valerie. She seemed to be aware of it, considering how she shifted away from him.

"Alrighty then," I said. "Everyone grab a vase. And be careful, 'cause I already filled them with warm water."

I'd thought I was being optimistic by setting out ten vases. Turned out I wasn't too far off the mark. I took away the extra two, then set the last one on the table in front of me.

"We're going to start with our greenery and make a base for the arrangement. There are many choices when it comes to the foliage. You could use fern leaves, dusty miller, seeded eucalyptus—you name it. Today we're going to use this nice leafy salal, also called lemon leaf." I held up a leafy twig and showed them how to trim the end to size. "Just set 'em in, one at a time, around the edge of the vase in a sort of crisscross pattern."

"I think I cut mine too short," said Letty. "It fell inside."

"That's okay," I said. "Just grab another piece. There's always gonna be some trial and error when you're first learning something." *Kind of like with me and teaching this class*, I thought, as I watched the group work. I realized I'd set the workstations too close together, and some folks were bumping elbows.

"Next we're gonna select our flowers. As you can see, we've got various shades of pink, peach, yellow, purple, and white. They all go well together. So, everybody come over to the buckets and pick out ones you want to use. Take about five to nine stems of each."

"It smells *luscious* in here," Richard remarked, as he walked by.

"That's the hyacinth," I said. "It has such a strong, sweet scent, it's used in a lot of floral perfumes."

"Where are the roses?" asked Abe.

"We're not using roses today," I said.

"Too expensive?" he asked, with a not-so-subtle smirk.

"It's not that," I began, about ready to offer to get some roses. Then I caught sight of Valerie glaring at Abe. He saw it too and dropped the subject.

As the students gathered their flowers, I quickly moved to make more space in the work area so they wouldn't be so crowded. Then I directed them to lay out their flowers within reach beside their vases.

"Lay them down?" said Valerie. "Won't that damage the petals?"

"No, they'll be fine. They're sturdier than you might think." I picked up a fluffy blush peony. "We'll start with the flowers with the largest blooms. Go ahead and clean off all the leaves. We don't want leaves in our water, growin' bacteria." I took my floral shears and trimmed the end, explaining that this would help the flower draw water. "Now feed your flowers in by the stem, spacing them more or less evenly. Turn the vase as you go, so you're always facing the side where you're placing a flower."

The group caught on quickly. The tables were soon littered with leaves and stems, as the bouquets took shape. I walked around, offering encouragement and guidance wherever I could. Now that the workshop was well underway, I was able to relax a little. And I was especially happy to see how much fun Deena seemed to be having. She was putting together a lovely bouquet, adding filler and additional greenery like a pro.

Suddenly, Letty cried out. "Ouch!" She dropped her scissors and brought her fingers to her mouth.

"You okay?" I asked, hurrying over.

She looked at the edge of her ring finger and winced. "I don't know how I managed to cut myself. I'm such a klutz."

Flo handed her a tissue. "Careful, honey. Those blades are sharp."

"Who knew floristry could be so dangerous," remarked Richard. "What with all the cutting and thorns and pointy stems."

I quickly found a Band-Aid for Letty and used a paper towel to wipe away a spot of blood on the table.

Abe pulled a face and made a gagging sound as I walked by him. "Next time keep your bodily fluids to yourself, Letty."

She pressed her lips together and didn't respond.

"Why don't you keep your comments to yourself?" snapped Valerie. "And your—never mind."

Your what? I wondered. *Hands? Eyes? Breath?*

I decided now was a good time for a break. I clapped my hands for attention.

"Okay, y'all. Let's set aside our flowers and dig into those yummy treats. When we come back, I'll give you some tips on how to make your bouquets last longer."

As folks swarmed to the snack bar, I walked over to Deena.

"You're good," I said, nodding at her bouquet. "I bet you've done this before."

She seemed pleased at the compliment. "I've always been creative. I was on the decorating committee in my sorority, and—"

A shout from the bar cut her off.

I rushed over in case I needed to play referee, then stopped short at what I saw. Letty was on her hands and knees trying to pick up a jumble of cookies and muffins scattered across the floor. Bill and Flo stood on the side-lines, apparently debating whether to intervene or flee. I couldn't blame them. Valerie, with a coffee stain spreading down the front of her dress, held a pie aloft. I was sure she was going to hurl it toward Abe, but then she seemed to reconsider at the last second. As she faltered, she wound up dropping the pie onto her own feet. She screamed in frustration. Abe laughed meanly.

"What's going on?" I yelled.

Valerie jabbed a finger toward Abe. "That man! He made me spill my coffee."

Abe's grin twisted into a scowl. "I didn't make you do anything."

Valerie flushed but held her ground. "You startled me,

and you know it. Trying to whisper in my ear or something. Richard saw you." She turned to Richard for confirmation. "Didn't you?"

Richard appeared sorry as he handed Valerie a napkin. "Actually, I didn't see that. But I did see Abe grabbing at the treats like a starving man. He must've knocked the cookies to the floor."

"I did not!" shouted Abe.

I looked him up and down. The crumbs on his face and shirt told another story.

"Everybody, please. Let's go sit down and finish up our bouquets." I leaned down and took Letty by the elbow, but she shrugged me off with surprising strength.

"Actually, we need to be going," said Bill. "Flo and I have another engagement. We're pretty much finished anyway."

"Me too," said Valerie. "I'm not staying in the same room as that lout for one more minute."

What's happening here? My workshop was falling apart before my eyes. And I hadn't even taken any pictures. At this point, the evening was more likely to end in a food fight than a group photo.

I was about to make one more plea for cooperation, when I noticed a strange look on Abe's face. He was making such a frightful grimace I took a step backward, bumping into Deena. I thought for sure he was gonna explode. Instead, he doubled over and fell to the floor.

Letty screamed, while Bill and Flo rushed to Abe's side. The rest of us just stared, too shocked to move.

"You alright, Abe?" asked Flo, giving him a gentle shake. Bill took the fallen man's pulse, then, to my dismay, began administering CPR.

"Call the paramedics," said Flo, remarkably calm under the circumstances.

I cast about for my purse until I realized Deena was already speaking into her phone. "Flower House," she said. "On Oak Street. A man has collapsed."

"It's too late," Richard murmured at my elbow. "I think he's dead."

Chapter 3

For a small town, Aerieville has an impressive emergency response team. Within minutes of Deena's call, an ambulance had arrived. And about a minute after that, the shop was swarming with police officers, technicians, and—most unfortunately—the county coroner. Richard had been right. Abe was dead.

I assumed he'd had a heart attack or a stroke. Or maybe an aneurysm. From the looks of him before he keeled over, he'd been feeling a mighty pain. I supposed he could've been choking, though it didn't look that way to me. More likely it was something internal. That's what I told Police Chief Walt Walden when he pulled me aside and asked for my account of things.

Actually, the chief's first question when he arrived was "Who's in charge here?" I looked around along with everyone else, until I realized they were all looking at me.

Oh, right. Dang it.

My skin prickled with heat under the chief's serious gaze. I didn't know him well, but we'd been acquainted since I was a little kid. Walt Walden was old friends with my dad, ever since their days as college football buddies.

From what I could tell, he seemed like an honest, decent sort of guy. He was tall and burly, with a straight-faced demeanor and a dry sense of humor—which could be intimidating when I was a child. But he always had a silly joke and a pack of bubble gum to share, which made him a welcome visitor whenever he showed up to see my dad.

At least, that's how it used to be. There were no jokes or packs of bubble gum today. Then again, we'd never met under such grim circumstances. For some reason, I couldn't help feeling this was somehow all my fault. Even though it most definitely wasn't.

Swallowing the dry lump in my throat, I told the chief about the flower-arranging workshop.

"Does anyone else work here?" he asked.

"There's Jim Lomack, who works in the greenhouse out back, and Francie Wilson, another part-time worker like me. But neither of them was in today. There's also the owner, Felix Maniford."

"Where is Felix?"

I lifted my hands in a shrug. "He asked me to lead the class."

"Alright. So, what happened?"

I told him everything I could remember, including the yelling, the spilled food, and Abe's collapse. "I don't know exactly what happened," I concluded. "I guess Abe was upset about something—maybe because Valerie accused him of startling her or because Richard accused him of grabbing at the snacks. He must've burst an artery or something."

The chief stared at me for a moment without saying anything. Then he nodded once and moved on to question somebody else. I exhaled and wiped my forehead with the back of my hand. I needed a drink.

The old kitchen, dominated by a large butcher-block table in the center of the room, served as both flower-arranging workspace and employee breakroom. I took a tall glass from a cupboard and filled it from the water pitcher in the fridge. After a big gulp, I leaned on the table and tried to get my nerves under control. My eyes slid to the back door. *Nah*. It wouldn't be right to run off. Nor was it right to keep hiding out in the kitchen. Clutching my glass of water, I slipped back into the front of the store and made like a wall flower while I watched the cops do their work.

Come to think of it, I was a little puzzled by their response. Why all the hubbub? Was police work so slow in this town that they had to throw all their resources into one man's heart attack? It seemed odd that they were being so meticulous with all their questions and photographs and notetaking, jotting down every little thing. It wasn't like this was a crime scene or anything.

Was it?

The second the thought crossed my mind—the terrible, terrible thought—I nearly dropped my glass. In the next instant, I raced around the shop, finally found my phone, and punched in Felix's number. Of course, the cops might have called him already. Everybody knew this was Felix's place. But Felix had a thing about law enforcement, so I wasn't too surprised if he wouldn't pick up. He darn well better pick up for me.

The call went to voice mail.

"Felix, where are you?" I hissed into the phone. "I *told* you I wasn't ready to lead a workshop, and guess what happened? A man has died! Right here in the shop!"

Before I knew it, tears sprang to my eyes. I gave a mighty sniff and ordered Felix to get here pronto.

An hour later, my boss was still a no-show. Chief Walden had finished questioning all the workshop attendees and told them to go home and hug their loved ones—or call them, as the case may be. Then he came over to me with a sober look on his face. The concern in his tired, brown eyes brought the lump back to my throat.

"You think of anything else I ought to know, Sierra?"

"No, sir. I told you everything that happened tonight." *The whole sordid tale.*

"Alright, well, we've got all we need for now. You're free to clean up, if you want to."

I glanced over at the floor where Abe had met his maker. It was still littered with cookie crumbs and glops of pie, as well as dirty napkins, paper plates, and other assorted trash. I could have sworn I'd seen a cop sweep up some crumbs into a plastic bag earlier. Evidently, they weren't helping me tidy up.

I turned back to the chief. "Are you gonna drive out to Felix's place?"

"Why, do you think he's there?"

"No. I thought you might want to wait for him or something."

"I don't have time for that. I'll give him 'til tomorrow to return my call."

I nodded and said goodbye. As I started to lock the door behind the last police officer to leave, I shot another glance at the mess over in the events room. "That can wait," I murmured to myself. Chief Walden might not be in a hurry to speak with the owner of Flower House, but I sure was. I needed to get this fiasco off my plate ASAP. For one thing, it was giving me the major heebie-jeebies. For another, I was beginning to worry about Felix.

After stashing the remaining flower arrangements in the cooler, I hurried out to my car. Fifteen minutes later, I pulled into the driveway of Felix's home. He lived in a log cabin on the edge of town, out near the Nolichucky River. It was nearly ten o'clock and dark as a crypt. With the engine still running and the headlights on, I climbed out of the car. Shivering against the nighttime chill, I ran up to the front door and gave it a good pounding. A deafening bark erupted from the other side of the door. I jumped back, clutching my chest.

Oh, yeah. I'd almost forgotten Felix had gotten a dog recently. There was no need to knock a second time—the barking pretty much raised the roof. Still, there was no sign of Felix.

For the heck of it, I tried the doorknob. It was locked, of course. So was the back door. Part of me feared Felix might be inside collapsed on the floor—just like poor Abe at the flower shop. But, come to think of it, Felix's pickup truck was missing. Thank the Lord. Obviously, he wasn't back yet. Then, where was he?

I tried to remember what he'd said earlier. He'd received a call, which made him want to go geocaching? And he said he could be gone a while. How long was "a while"? And why wasn't he picking up his phone? Knowing Felix, he'd probably forgotten it someplace. Or lost it. Or lost the charger. I could imagine any of those possibilities. Felix lived up in his head so much, he was prone to forgetfulness. *Which is why*, I suddenly remembered, *he gave me a spare key to his cabin.*

Maybe I should just go inside and wait for him. And keep the little yapper company.

I ran back to my car, took my keys from the ignition, and found Felix's house key. Using my cell phone as a flashlight to keep from tripping in the dark, I hurried back to the cabin and unlocked the front door. The second I stepped inside, the young dog launched himself onto my legs in one leap, his nubby tail wiggling with excitement. By the light of my phone, I could see that he was a Pembroke Welsh corgi and cute enough to melt anybody's heart.

"Hey, little guy," I said, scratching his ears. "Did Felix go away and leave you alone in the dark? What a meanie."

I flicked on the foyer light, then walked to the living room and turned on a lamp. The window shades were up, making me realize it wouldn't have been dark when Felix left. I wondered if he thought he'd be home before nightfall.

Just to make doubly sure the house was empty, I peeked in all the rooms. The bedroom was a pigpen, with clothes and books strewn all over the place. I paused at the doorway. Was it suspiciously messy? Or just absentminded-bachelor messy? I decided it was the latter and headed to the kitchen, where I found a dog leash on a peg by the door. As I hooked it to the pup's collar, I saw that his tag said Augustus.

"Augustus, huh? Do you go by Gus?"

The corgi barked once and scratched at the door.

"I'll take that as a yes." I took him outside to take care of business. When we came back in, I filled his water and food bowls, then wandered back to the living room. For the next hour and a half, I flipped through some of Felix's books, turned the television on and back off, and dozed in an easy chair. At around midnight, I decided I should go home.

I felt bad about leaving Gus. He sure didn't like it either. I left a lamp burning as a nightlight and promised him Felix would be home soon. *Surely he'll be home soon.*

My house was clear on the other side of town. Instead of skirting the village, I drove straight through the middle. It was a ghost town at this hour. I took a quick detour to swing by Flower House, hoping I'd find Felix's truck parked in front. No such luck. If anything, the shop seemed even darker than it should be.

I probably should've left a porch light on when I locked up earlier. Well, I wasn't about to do it now. The place might be haunted! If Abe was unpleasant in life, I could only imagine what kind of a spirit he'd make. I quickly crossed myself—a gesture I'd learned from my Catholic grandma, my dad's mom, who lived up north. Whether I did it out of guilt for thinking ill of the dead or for protection *from* the dead in question, I couldn't say.

I sped off and soon arrived, safe and sound, at my cozy cottage in the foothills on the south side of town. My mom called my cottage the "dollhouse" because of its diminutive size and gingerbread trim. But it was perfect for me: cute, functional, and affordable. That is, affordable with the monthly stipend I received from my parents. The monetary help was only temporary, of course—until I could manifest a higher-paying job. I was working on it.

After locking up and brushing my teeth, I headed straight for my bedroom. Right now I wanted nothing more than the oblivion of sleep. Then my cell phone rang, and I about jumped out of my pj's. Seeing it was my brother, Rocky, I sighed with relief.

"Hey, Rock," I said, upon answering. "Why are you calling so late? Is everything okay?"

"You're asking me? I was about to ask you the same thing!" His voice was raised a pitch higher than usual, either out of concern or necessity. There seemed to be a din of noise in the background. "One of my buddies just came into Cuties and said there was a ruckus at the flower shop tonight. Somebody got carted away in an ambulance?"

Ah, Cuties. The local pool hall. That explained the raised voices and intermittent clacks I heard. It was the sound of cues striking billiard balls.

I rubbed my forehead. "Yeah, there was a . . . ruckus, I guess. Abe Ranker had some kind of heart attack or something. And he, unfortunately, died. Right in front of me."

"Oh man. Hang on." The background noises faded as Rocky apparently stepped outside. "Are you okay?" he said, a touch quieter. "Have you told Mom and Dad?"

"No. I mean, yes. I haven't told Mom and Dad yet, but I'm okay."

"Do you want me to come over? Keep you company?"

I smiled at the offer. My brother the protector. Rocky was four years my junior but twice my size in pure muscle weight. People always assumed he was named after the fictional boxer from the Rocky movies, but that wasn't the case. In fact, we were both named after mountain ranges—the Sierra Nevadas and the Rocky Mountains. (Mom and Dad were big into rock climbing in their younger days.) Still, Rocky was built like a fighter. Maybe that explained why he often acted like he was older than me. That and the fact that he made more money. With his easygoing personality, plus a degree in kinesiology, he was a popular personal trainer.

"Are you at home?" he continued. "I can be there in ten minutes."

"You don't need to come over. I'm fine. I'm just gonna go to bed. I'm tired, that's all." *Exhausted was more like it.*

"You sure?" He sounded doubtful. "You know, you don't have to go it alone all the time. It's okay to lean on family sometimes."

"I know. And I'm sure. Thanks, Rocky. I'll talk to you tomorrow."

I sank into my feather bed and closed my eyes, as Rocky's words echoed in my mind. I knew I didn't have to "go it alone." My family was always supportive, even when they didn't understand me. Which they often didn't. Growing up, I was always a bit of a misfit, even in my own home. Whereas they were all sporty, athletic, and outgoing, I was more introverted and artistic. They'd watch football, and I'd write poetry. They'd lift weights, and I'd practice music. In fact, it was Rocky's guitar, a Christmas present he rarely touched, that I pickcd up one day and taught myself to play.

Mom used to say I had my head in the clouds.

Maybe I still did.

Chapter 4

Next thing I knew, I was blinking in the sunlight filtering through my lacy, white bedroom curtain. I'd had a surprisingly restful night's sleep, considering. But the minute the previous day's events came flooding back to mind, I grabbed my phone to call Felix again. I crossed my fingers, praying for him to pick up. He didn't. In fact, the recording this time told me that his voice-mail box was full. He hadn't even picked up his messages from the night before.

Where in the world is he?

I padded into the kitchen in search of breakfast and pondered what to do. I knew what I *wanted* to do. More than anything, I wanted to stay in my jammies and curl up on the couch with a cup of coffee and a good book. But that wouldn't be responsible. And given my track record the past few years, I always felt the need to prove I could be responsible—at least to myself, if not to my parents and everyone else.

So, I settled on a container of yogurt, then sprang into action. After a fast shower, I threw on some jeans and a blouse and hightailed it over to Flower House. Although the shop was generally open by appointment only on Sundays,

Felix was known to be loose with the "official" hours. If he was in the shop, he'd open up for folks no matter what time they happened by. The least I could do now was clean up the place and put a note on the door.

This time I parked right in front. As I walked up the sidewalk, a bird flew swiftly—and somewhat erratically—between two nearby trees. I knew birds were often omens of one sort or another, especially when they behaved out of the ordinary. I wasn't sure what this one meant. I'd have to ask Granny (my mom's mom) later. She would know.

I let myself in the shop, locked the door behind me, and went straight to the phone by the cash register. The first order of business was to change the store's recorded message. I dialed in and tried to keep my voice neutral as I spoke. "Flower House will be closed today. Sorry for the inconvenience."

Of course, everyone in town would know why. Come to think of it, it was kind of surprising that gawkers weren't already lined up outside.

Then the phone rang. My hand hovered over the receiver. I'd just said we were closed, but what if it was Felix calling? Or the police? I decided to answer.

"Flower House, Sierra speaking."

"Sierra? This is Francie. I just heard what happened. How awful! We're not open, are we?"

Francie was the other part-timer. I filled her in. "It's probably best not to come in," I added.

"Good," she said. "I was offered more hours at Manny's, and now I'm definitely going to take them."

Manny's was a flower shop in the next town over and, besides the grocery florist, our biggest competitor. I wondered if they expected to see an increase in business thanks to what had happened here.

"Okay," I said. "I'll let Felix know."

I'd just hung up the phone when there was a tap on the

front door. *Maybe I should ignore it.* I was in a hurry to get back to Felix's place.

"Sierra? You in there?"

It was Richard. *Whew.* At least he already knew first-hand what had happened. I had a feeling I'd be repeating my tale many times in the coming days and didn't exactly relish the thought.

"Morning, Richard," I said, as I let him in. "How ya doing?"

"Better than Abe," he retorted. "I saw your car out front and thought I'd pop in to commiserate. Where's Felix?"

"He hasn't come in yet."

Richard wandered through the archway into the events room. Surveying the mess, he made his way over to the snack counter, still littered with food. I followed reluctantly.

"No police tape, huh?" He picked up a muffin from the countertop, stared at it thoughtfully, and set it back down.

"Nope. I don't know why the cops were so zealous yesterday anyway. It seemed like they were making a mountain out of a mole hill."

Richard circled the bakery case, potato chips crunching under his feet. With the tips of his fingers, he flicked aside a wrinkled napkin, then rested his elbows on the counter. "You really don't know?"

"Know what?"

"Ol' Abe had been receiving death threats. I heard he filed a police report just a day or two ago."

"You're kidding."

"Scout's honor."

"So, he really *was* murdered? I think I need to sit down."

"It's intense, I know." Richard looked around again. "Got any gloves? I'll help you clean up in here."

"You're a sweetheart," I said automatically, still feeling a bit shell-shocked. I was having a hard time comprehending the fact that someone I knew had been *murdered*. And that someone else I knew had probably done it! I also couldn't wrap my head around how such a thing had even happened—and right here under my nose.

Rather than think about it too much, I gathered up some cleaning supplies and garbage bags and set to work. Besides the food mess, flowers, leaves, and trimmings littered the tables and floor, along with the flower-arranging supplies I'd so optimistically laid out the day before. Here and there, I also came across remnants of the crime-scene investigation: yellow plastic tape, empty evidence bags, and a suspicious-looking cotton swab. I wrinkled my nose and silently blessed Richard for his company, as much as for his help.

A few minutes later, the room looked less like a disaster area, if not quite sparkling. Richard stretched his back after tying off a garbage bag. "Not too bad," he commented. "But you'll need to bring a vacuum cleaner in here. It'll be the only way to get the powdered sugar out of the rug."

"Oh, we have a sweeper in the kitchen closet. I'll go get it." I took two steps, then paused. "Did you say powdered sugar?"

"Yeah, it's ground into the rug in a couple places. Must've been stepped on."

Frowning, I thought back to all the desserts folks had brought. I recalled brownies (plain), cookies, muffins, pie, zucchini bread. "What was the powdered sugar on?"

He leaned down and squinted at a spot on the floor. "Maybe it's creamer for the coffee."

I shook my head. "Couldn't be. I set out half-and-half, not powdered creamer. That stuff's nasty."

I walked over to see what he was looking at. Heads together, we bent down and stared at a white substance smudged into the burgundy rug. Then we looked at each other. After a beat, I laughed nervously.

"If this were the movies, somebody would lick their finger and taste the stuff."

Richard widened his eyes in horror. "Don't even suggest such a thing! Talk about nasty."

Before we could decide what to do, the front door jangled, putting a hold on our ersatz police investigation.

I pushed myself to my feet and turned toward the front door. Two women, one short and one tall, were gazing around the front of the store, gushing at how cute it was.

"Dang it," I muttered. "I should have locked the door behind you."

"Looks like tourists," murmured Richard behind me. "You might as well take their money, right?"

I glanced at my watch. "I guess so. Especially since I forgot to collect any money for the class last night."

We didn't attract a lot of tourists in our neck of the woods. But when we did, it was usually folks who had sought us out on purpose. I mustered up a smile and approached the pair. "Can I help you?"

With wind-swept hair, large sunglasses, and silk scarves tied casually around their necks, they looked like a couple of gals about town. A quick glimpse out the window showed me the cute red convertible that had brought them here. *Just a couple of carefree girlfriends, looking for adventure.* I felt a mild pang of jealousy. At the moment, I'd much rather be a shopper than a shopkeeper.

"We heard you sell exotic orchids," said one of the women. "Do you have the one called Golden Beauty? And a booklet on how to care for it?"

"We sure do. Follow me."

Before I could move, the door burst open with a clatter and another woman rushed inside. This one was a local, and one I knew well. Everyone knew her. Nell Cusley, owner of Nell's Diner, was the biggest gossip in town. I groaned inwardly.

"Oh, my goodness, Sierra! Is it true?" She patted her chest as she tried to catch her breath. Her cheeks were flushed, making me wonder if she'd run all the way here. Or maybe she was just excited. "Where's Felix, talking to the police? I just had to see it for myself. Where did it happen?" Her darting eyes fell upon Richard, still standing near the snack counter in the next room. "Was it in there?"

The out-of-town visitors appeared startled. "What happened here?" asked the short one.

"Um." *Do I have to answer?* I was about to redirect them to the orchid collection, when Nell spilled the beans.

"There was a death here yesterday! Poor Abraham. He breathed his last right here in this very shop. It happened while he was gobbling up all the treats, I believe." She looked at me with a question in her shining eyes. I pressed my lips together, as if they were stuck tight with superglue.

"Oh my," said the taller woman. "Shouldn't you be closed then?"

The shorter woman edged toward the exit. "I knew something was off the moment we entered this place. There's a bad energy in here."

My mouth popped open at that one. "Oh, come on!" There was no way they'd felt a "bad energy" in here.

"Let's go," said the shorter woman, grabbing her friend by the arm. Brushing past Nell, they were out the door as fast as they'd come in.

Nell slipped eagerly into the events room, as Richard sauntered toward me. "Not to worry," he said, nodding toward the window. "When one car leaves, two more arrive. No, make that three."

I followed his gaze. Sure enough, three more cars had pulled up.

"It's Deena!" I said, pleasantly surprised. She'd ske-daddled from the shop last night along with everyone else, and I didn't expect to see her again anytime soon. "But why isn't she getting out of her car?"

Out of the second car stepped a middle-aged man and a younger guy who resembled him. A father and son, I guessed, though I didn't recognize them. They started up the sidewalk, then halted and looked back at the third car, a brown sedan, which had parked behind them.

I would have halted too. Police Chief Walden had emerged from the sedan, and he wasn't alone. He was ac-companied by three people covered from head to foot in bright yellow hazmat suits. With their kits and bags and complicated-looking monitoring equipment, they were im-posing figures indeed as they marched up the path to the flower shop.

For the second time in twenty-four hours, I found my-self racing toward my boss's cabin by the river. This time I was even more rattled than before.

One look at the scary hazmat investigators had caused both Deena and the potential customers to reverse course lickety-split. At least Richard and Nell had waited with me on the sidewalk while the investigators did their work. Of course, I knew they were both eager to hear what the chief was going to say. When he gave the "all clear" a short while later, I nearly slumped in relief.

"There were no airborne contaminants," the chief said.

"Good to know," said Richard, plainly as relieved as me. Nell, on the other hand, looked almost disappointed.

"Why did you think there might be?" I asked.

"I didn't. But the mayor caught wind of folks whisper-ing about anthrax and such. I had to put the rumors to rest."

He turned to Nell. "Spread the word. There's no anthrax here, nor anything else that might endanger the public."

I almost laughed at Nell's status as the town busybody being used to let people know there wasn't anthrax at Flower House. Of course, then the fact that this was necessary at all almost made me cry.

She opened her mouth to respond, but the chief didn't give her a chance. He walked away, motioning for me to follow. "Can I have a quick word, Sierra? You too, Richard."

We dutifully followed him inside the shop and stood at the threshold between the front room and the events area. I glanced over and noticed that the trash bags Richard and I had filled were standing open in the middle of the floor. Other than that, nothing seemed out of place.

"Chief," I began. "There's a white powder on the rug."

"Not anymore," he said. "It's all been cleaned up."

"What was it?"

He shifted uncomfortably. "It appeared to be the same substance found on the deceased's clothing. Powdered sugar . . . laced with strychnine."

Richard and I gasped as one. "Strychnine?" I echoed. "Where in the world would someone get strychnine?"

"It's made from the seeds of a tree found in India and parts of Asia. But it's used in some pesticides. At least, it used to be. Not so much anymore."

"So, that's what killed Abe," said Richard.

"We don't have the autopsy report yet," said the chief. "But it does appear that Abraham ingested the poison. My guess is that the stress on his body triggered heart failure before the chemical had a chance to do its worst."

"Small blessing," I murmured.

Richard hugged his arms with a shiver. "You're sure it's safe in here? How much of that toxic stuff did you find?"

"There were traces on the carpet next to the glass case, but that's all. We did a sweep of the whole store. It's safe."

I was still hung up on the chief's news. *Strychnine.* Even the word sounded evil. And to think it had been right here, among all the snacks we'd been eating. Unless . . .

"Chief," I said. "Is it possible Abe was exposed to the poison before he even got here last night?"

He smiled ruefully. "Not likely. He would have been feeling poorly, and you all said he seemed fine until right before he collapsed. Anyway, the poison was definitely in the powdered sugar found on the floor."

"Somebody must've slipped him a mickey," said Richard. "Or whatever the equivalent is for laced food. I wonder how they did it without anyone noticing."

I thought back to the workshop and all the moments leading up to Abe's collapse. Could it have happened when everyone was up gathering their flowers? That didn't make sense. Abe didn't have any snacks yet. Maybe it was during the scuffle with Valerie, when she spilled her coffee and dropped the pie. Though, come to think of it, somebody had knocked over the cookies even before then.

In the midst of my ruminations, I became aware of the chief eyeing me closely. "Any ideas, Sierra?"

Slowly, I shook my head. "Not really. I can't believe any Flower House patrons would have intentionally poisoned Abe."

"Be that as it may, someone did. Give me a call if you think of anything else I ought to know." The chief headed for the front door, then paused with his hand on the knob. "By the way, don't go leaving town or anything silly like that. As long as this investigation is open, I'll probably have more questions for the both of you."

I fretted over the chief's words on the whole drive up to Felix's place. The implication was clear. I was a murder suspect!

Of course, Chief Walden didn't *really* suspect me. There was no way. He'd known me since I was a baby. The idea that I could be capable of hurting someone like that . . . it was preposterous.

Yet, as the Chief had said, "Someone did."

The moment I stepped out of my car, a spirited barking erupted from within Felix's cabin.

"Oh, poor Gus!" All at once, I dismissed my worries and rushed up the sidewalk, key in hand. I was scarcely in the door before the little dog pounced on my legs. He greeted me with so many wet puppy kisses, you would've thought I was his best friend in the whole wide world. It about melted my heart.

"Okay, okay, little guy. First order of business, let's take you outside."

As I walked through the front of the cabin to the kitchen in the back, I took a quick glance around. Nothing much had changed since the night before. The only signs of occupancy—a chewed house slipper and an empty water bowl—were clearly left by Gus. I dropped my purse on the kitchen table and took him out the back door.

As Gus sniffed every bush, tree, and flower, I bit my lip and stewed. What had I done to attract such a mess into my life? Almost immediately, I mentally kicked myself for the thought. First off, it was never productive to think of yourself as a victim. Secondly, I *wasn't* the victim in this case. I was still alive and kicking, with free will to boot. The problem was, I didn't know what to do.

A few minutes later, I finally coaxed Gus back inside with the promise of food. While he munched on his kibbles, I grabbed my phone from my purse. To my surprise, I'd missed four calls since stepping outside. I listened to the messages in order.

"Sierra, this is Mom." *Thanks, Mom. I think I know your voice by now, let alone your phone number.* "I heard about what happened at the flower shop. I hope you weren't involved. Call me."

Involved? Did my own mother think I was a suspect?

The next message was from my dad. "Give us a call, sweetie, or stop by the club. Walt hasn't called me back yet, and your mother is worried."

I should have figured he'd call his buddy, the police chief. What did it mean that Chief Walden hadn't called him back? Probably he was just too busy.

The third message was from Rocky. After our brief conversation last night, I expected him to check in on me. Only this time he wasn't acting alone. "Hey, Sis. Call Mom and Dad. People keep asking questions, and they're going crazy over here. Mom already made me try to find you at your house and the flower store, and you're not at either place . . . so, yeah, call them back."

"Tell her I'm worried!" hollered Mom in the background.

"Mom says she's worried. Later."

Well, shoot. I had already missed two other calls from my mom when I was cleaning up the shop. It figured that she'd ask Dad and Rocky to call me as well.

I moved on to the last missed call, fully expecting it to be another one from my family. Instead, it was from a strange number. I frowned until I recognized the voice on the other end. "It's Felix!" I said to Gus. "And it's about time."

But as I listened to the message, my excitement turned to confusion, followed by frustration.

"Hello, Sierra," he said, his voice sounding distant and crackly. "I hope you get this message. Forgot to charge my cell phone, and you never know with pay phones, so I'll make it quick. I've picked up a fantastic lead. Really incredible. I'll be gone quite a while, so you're in charge of

Flower House. You can close it or not—it's up to you. Talk to Byron. He'll fill you in."

I squeezed my eyes shut as I listened to the message. Did Felix just say he put *me* in charge of the flower shop? Why not Byron? Byron Atterly was Felix's longtime, trusted bookkeeper. He paid the bills and issued the paychecks. If anyone should run the shop in Felix's absence, it should be Byron.

Felix paused in his message as a tinny announcement played in the background. I couldn't make out the words.

"That's my flight," Felix said, half to himself. "Oh! One more thing. I left a voice mail for Abe, asking him to pick up my new pup and take him home. He has plenty of room and, besides, he owes me one. He probably already reached out to you—I told him you have a key to my cabin. Alright, then. I think that's it. Just remember: 'To be idle is a short road to death.' Bye, Sierra."

When the message ended, I pressed the button to save it. Beyond that, I could scarcely move. This was all too perplexing.

Gus barked once and jumped on my legs. I leaned down to scratch the top of his head.

So, Felix intended Abe to take care of Gus. Abe, who is now dead.

After a minute, I forced myself to get a move on. I looked around for a grocery bag, which I then began to fill with puppy food and other supplies. Gus followed me around like a child with serious separation anxiety.

"There's a lot I don't know right now," I told him. "But I do know one thing. You're coming with me."

Chapter 5

Rays of sunshine streamed through newly-budded trees, making for a pretty picture as I drove the winding road into the mountains. The drone of the car lulled Gus to sleep. Or maybe he was just content now that he wasn't alone anymore. Poor little guy. I still couldn't believe Felix up and left his new pup like that—not to mention leaving me in charge of his business! Whatever he was after, it must be pretty darn important.

Before long, my worries took a back seat to the view out my window. As I climbed steadily higher, the terrain grew wilder and wilder. One turn offered a breathtaking glimpse of the fertile valley below; the next brought me face-to-face with the rising peak of Mount Jay. I shifted into a lower gear and took the curves slowly, as much for safety as for gawking.

Fifteen minutes later, I came to the narrow lane leading to my grandmother's house. As always, I admired the bird-filled trees and abundant wildflowers that seemed to welcome me to her land. I had many happy memories roaming the woodlands here as a kid. The two-story farmhouse looked just the same as it always did, if a little faded: white siding, forest-green shutters, hanging baskets of flowers and plants, and a rusty iron horseshoe nailed above the front door.

Growing up, I often found I clicked more with Granny than with my own parents or brother. She drew me out of the house and into the garden, taught me the names of flowers and trees, and told me stories of days gone by. I picked vegetables and herbs with her, and helped her snap beans, shell peas, and shuck corn. All the while, she'd prattle on about various mountain traditions. One of my favorites was: "When a waxing moon shines, plant above-ground crops; when it's on the wane, plant crops below. Take a rest from planting on the quarter moon; same for the dark and full."

She also said, "Always leave a house by the same door you entered, else bad luck'll follow you out." Most of her sayings hadn't rhyme nor reason. They were enchanting nonetheless.

I parked at the end of the driveway and let Gus out of the car. He promptly announced himself with a full-throated yap, causing an orange tabby to dart under an azalea bush. Granny Mae stepped out onto her front porch, shaking a jingle ball.

"Hello!" she called. "This is Tiger's toy, but she won't mind if the puppy wants to play with it."

"Hi, Granny." I scooped up Gus and followed her inside, through the living room and into the sunny kitchen. I had phoned ahead, so she knew to expect us. I was welcomed by the mouthwatering aroma of sautéed onion and peppers mingled with the savory scent of herbs, spices, and mixed greens.

"Come and have some tater soup and a mess of poke salad," she said. "The bread will come out of the oven in a few minutes."

I set Gus down on the braided rug and tossed him the toy, then turned to give Granny a hug. She seemed shorter every time I saw her, though no less strong. She worked from sunup to sundown and had the vigor and calluses to show for it.

"It smells wonderful in here," I said. "What can I do to help you?"

"Not a thing. Set yourself down and tell me what's new."

I smiled as I watched Granny bustle about, from the stove to the table and back again. She looked just the same as she always did, gray hair cut short to keep it out of her face, and a gingham apron to keep the flour off her clothes. She would put on a dress for church and occasional trips to town, but around the house she usually wore blue jeans and a plain cotton shirt.

"You've been in the garden this morning," I said, noting the dirt on her knees.

She laughed and looked down at her pant legs. "This is dirt from the woods. I was digging up roots. Betty's gout is acting up, so I'm goin' to make her some sassafras tea."

Betty was a neighbor who lived down the road a piece. In fact, all Granny's neighbors lived "down the road a piece," some of them miles away. But they'd still trek through rain, sleet, or snow to see Granny for her home remedies. She was well known in these parts.

She sat down across from me, and we chatted about this and that. At one point, Granny said, "I knew I was goin' to have a visitor today, even before you called."

"How'd you know that, Granny?" I asked, thinking I already knew the answer.

"Why, because I dropped a dish towel on the floor as I was drying off the breakfast dishes." She had a twinkle in her eye, but I knew she was being sincere.

"And why should that be, Granny?"

"I don't know. It just is."

"Hmm." I sipped my soup and pondered Granny's inherited superstitions. In some ways, we were a lot alike, with our beliefs in signs and omens. Except I liked to think I only put stock in the ones that made sense.

I helped myself to another slice of warm bread. "How are you getting along, Granny? Anything I can do to help you out while I'm here?"

She narrowed her eyes with a hint of suspicion. "Did your Ma tell you to come up here and look after me?"

"No, ma'am. But even if she did, so what?"

"Hmph. Never mind."

For more than a year now, my mom had been trying to convince Granny to leave the mountain and move into town. Granny adamantly refused. I couldn't blame my mother. It didn't seem right that Granny should be way out here all by herself—especially when the place used to buzz like a beehive, with all the folks running around hither and yon. She and Grandpap raised eight kids on this land, six girls and two boys. Of course, all the kids grew up, as kids do, and moved away—some near, like my mom, and some far. A while back, more than a decade ago, Grandpap passed away. Then Granny's sister, Aunt Dottie, moved in. It was just the two of them holding down the fort, until Aunt Dottie passed away a couple of years ago.

"Mom's a worrier," I said, with a pang of guilt. At least I'd sent her a quick text before driving up here. I let her know I was fine and would talk to her later.

"Worry is like a snipe hunt," said Granny, pushing herself to her feet. "Pointless. Now, how about some rhubarb pie?"

I smiled again, as Granny cut the pie and served me a generous portion. She also brought out some chicken from the refrigerator and fed little bits to Gus, who had tired of the ball.

In spite of her age, I had to admit Granny seemed just

as fit and capable as ever. And when she sat back down, propped her elbows on the table, and leaned forward, I realized she was sharp as a tack too. She fixed me with a penetrating gaze.

"Alright, missy. Out with it."

"What?"

"No more beating around the bush. Who died?"

I swallowed a bite of pie and opened my eyes wide. "Died?"

"You heard me. I had not one, not two, but *three* calls from townsfolks this morning, informing me about dogs howling in the night. Everybody knows that means death. I didn't see any portents around here, so I figure it wasn't any friend or kin of mine. But it *was* somebody in the community. And here you are, bustin' at the seams with your untold news. Let's hear it."

"Alright, Granny Mae. You're right."

I'd told myself I was coming up here to clear my head and, at least for a little while, escape the burdens that seemed to keep piling up on me. But part of me must've been after Granny's advice all along. I shared with her everything that had happened.

She was a good listener, keeping quiet except for occasional exclamations of "Land sakes!" and "You don't say!" When I finished, she patted my hand and hopped up, once again bustling about her kitchen. Only this time she wasn't gathering food.

"I've got just the thing," she said. "If you want to keep that flower shop a welcoming place, you've got some work to do."

In no time flat, Granny had filled me a basket of tools and supplies. Besides candles, oils, and salt, there was dried basil to hang over the doors and windows and a jar of cloudy ditchwater to sprinkle around the "murder room." For my personal protection, she made me a special sachet by filling a square of flannel with bits of herbs, roots, and dirt. She tied it off with a piece of red twine, instructing me to keep it in my pocket by day and under my pillow by night. This was one of her famous "herb bags." She made and sold them to customers all over the county who sought her help. Folks used them for various purposes— whether to attract love, money, or luck, or to get rid of whatever was ailing them.

I stood up and took my bowl to the sink. "Thank you for all this. I don't know if Abe's resting in peace, but I'm willing to try anything to cleanse the place."

As Granny walked Gus and me to the door, I noticed her hold her hip and limp a little. I hesitated and looked at her, concerned. "Granny, are you okay? Is your hip bothering—"

"Hush now," she said, raising a hand to cut me off. "There's something else I need to say to you."

"What is it?"

"From what all you told me, I have a feeling salt and basil ain't going to be enough. There's really only one sure thing to do."

"What's that, Granny?"

"Catch the killer."

Granny Mae's words rang in my ears the whole drive back down the mountain. And I didn't like it. I didn't like it one bit. I'd much rather follow Granny's folk traditions any old time than try to catch a killer. I shuddered at the thought.

With my basket full of supplies and my mind made up, I went straight to the shop to get started. First I let Gus sniff around the sidewalk and entrance to Flower House, and then I took him to the kitchen. I opened the interior back door, so he'd have a view through the glass storm door, and set out a bowl of fresh water. He'd be fine in the kitchen, with plenty of room to move about. In spite of my efforts, he didn't like being left alone. He whimpered and scratched at the door, making me feel like a heel.

"Oh, you're alright in there!" I said through the door. "I just can't look after you right now. Maybe you'll be good, but maybe you'll get into the flowers or chew up the merchandise. I can't take the chance."

It wouldn't matter if he chewed on the table legs in the kitchen. They were already all scuffed up. After a minute or so, he quieted down and I went to work. I had the basil hung and the salt scattered, and was just fixing to sprinkle the ditchwater, when a furious barking from the kitchen made me about jump out of my skin.

"Jeez Louise, Gus!" I hollered. "What'd you see, a squirrel?"

I figured if I ignored him, he'd quiet down again. But then I heard another noise: the slam of the storm door, followed by the scrape of a chair and a human voice. Someone was in the kitchen.

With the jar of ditchwater still in hand, I skittered to the kitchen and swung open the door—and found myself face-to-face with a stranger. I froze in my tracks, thrown by the guy's unusual attire as much as his sudden appearance. He seemed to be about my age and was kind of cute, in a boyish sort of way. But the most striking thing was his clothes. From his buttoned-up plaid shirt and high-water pants to his horn-rimmed glasses and bow tie, he looked like he could've played the part of "stereotypical nerd" in a school play.

We spoke at the same time.

"Friendly pup."

"Who are you?"

"Oh, my bad." He wiped his palm on his slacks before

extending a hand. "I'm Calvin." As if that explained any-thing.

I ignored his hand. "What are you doing in here? Why did you use the back door?"

He glanced at the door as if it would answer for him. "Well, I thought it would be less disruptive to the business if I move my stuff in through the back."

"What stuff? What are you talking about?"

"Didn't Felix tell you? We signed the lease a couple of weeks ago. I'm moving in today." He pulled some papers from his back pocket and set them on the table. "Here's the lease and a check for my security deposit and first month's rent. Do you work here? What's your name?"

I stared, at a loss for words. It was just like Felix to rent out the upstairs apartment and not tell me. He was so for-getful and distracted—especially lately.

Calvin blinked owlishly behind his glasses and looked around. "Where is Felix anyway?"

I sighed. I really wished people would stop asking me that. "He's not here, and he may not be back for a long time. You might need to find someplace else to live."

His face fell. "You're kidding! But all my stuff is in a rental van, and I have to return the van tonight. Plus I don't have any place else to stay. Can't you just take my check and give me the keys?"

Take his check. That reminded me, I still needed to talk to Felix's bookkeeper, Byron Atterly. Maybe he could reach Felix and find out when he'd be back.

Gus was alternately jumping on the new guy's legs and scratching at the back door. Calvin took it in stride, reaching down to pat Gus's head whenever the pup would hold still long enough. He also looked curiously at my jar of ditchwater, gray and dirty with bits of twigs and stones. Before he could ask me any questions, I grabbed Gus's leash from the table and handed it to Calvin.

"Can you do me a favor? Take Gus outside. I need to make a phone call and figure out what to do."

"Uh, okay. Sure."

As soon as the door closed behind them, I glanced at the papers on the table. "Calvin Foxheart," I read. According to the address on his check, he'd lived in Knoxville. I wondered what brought him to little ol' Aerieville and how he'd met Felix, until I remembered I had more pressing concerns. I scooted to the front of the store and found Byron's phone number in a booklet next to the cash register.

He answered on the first ring. "Atterly here." His distinctive voice, raspy from so many years of smoking, wavered slightly. He must be pushing eighty, I mused, if he was a day.

"Hello, Byron. It's Sierra."

"Ah, Sierra. Just the person I wanted to speak with."

"Really? Is it about Felix? Where *is* he anyway?"

"I don't know where he is at the moment, but I can tell you where he *was*. As of eight a.m. this morning, he was at an Internet café in Nashville. That's where he sent me an email that concerns you."

"Nashville? Was the café at Nashville International Airport? He left me a message around eleven saying he was about to get on a flight. Where was he going? More importantly, when is he coming back?" Surely, he wouldn't be gone too long. After all, he must have left his truck in an airport parking lot.

"I'm afraid I can't answer those questions. Here, let me read you the part that pertains to you."

Byron cleared his throat, mumbled through what I presumed was the opening of the message, then said, "'I've decided to retire and take a long-awaited trip. Since I'll be away for an indefinite period of time, I would like to convey Flower House, including the building, the business, and all its assets, to Sierra Ravenswood, for the amount of one dollar. Please draw up the papers. If Sierra declines, please convey the greenhouse to Jim Lomack and shutter the store.'"

You could've knocked me over with a feather. A couple of seconds passed before I could form any kind of response. "Wowee," I finally said. "That is *not* what I was expecting."

Byron chuckled softly. "I, of course, have power of attorney over Felix's business matters. I will consult a real estate lawyer for guidance, but I should have the papers ready for you to sign by the end of the week. Of course, if you're not interested, I'll go ahead and start the process of closing up shop, canceling the utilities, and whatnot."

"This is crazy," I muttered. "I can't even think straight."

"Well, you don't have to decide right now. But let me know as soon as possible."

He hung up, and I wandered the store in a daze. Everything was happening so quickly. Yesterday morning I was a part-time flower-shop employee, biding my time here until I could figure out how to manifest my big-time music career. And today I was offered the opportunity to *own* Flower House all by myself, lock, stock, and floral.

I lightly touched some of the flowers on display as I strolled, inhaling their earthy, sweet scents. Sometimes I drew strength and encouragement from the botanical world, feeling sure I'd tapped into the "secret power of plants," as some folks called it. And other times I felt completely lost in the dark. If only I would receive a sign, telling me what to do.

Suddenly, there was a noise at the front door. I had made sure to lock it behind me earlier, and I knew the Closed sign was still prominently displayed. Maybe Calvin was trying to come back inside. I headed to the foyer and immediately noticed a piece of paper on the floor beneath the mail slot. Only this clearly wasn't mail. It was a folded sheet of lined notebook paper. I glanced out the window and didn't see anyone walking away, so I picked up the paper and opened it. I read the handwritten message once, and then a few more times to make sure I wasn't seeing things. There was only one line:

You better get out of there if you know what's good for you.

I frowned, thinking at first that it was from a concerned customer, worried about my safety. But the tone of the message definitely sounded more like a threat than a friendly tip. What in the world did this mean?

All at once, I started to laugh. The Universe sure had a fine sense of humor. This note wasn't exactly a road sign, but it did give me an important bit of information. Granny Mae was right. Nothing would be settled until I got to the bottom of this mystery.

Chapter 6

I stepped outside the front door of Flower House and shielded my eyes against the late afternoon sun. Where had that new guy gone? For a second, I felt a pang of worry for Gus. How distracted must I be to let a total stranger take off with the little corgi? *Jeesh!*

Then I spotted them down the sidewalk, and I had to laugh. If anyone was being dragged away, it was Calvin by Gus. I could hear Calvin chuckling from a block away. "Wait up, buddy!" he said, trotting to keep up. Gus was pulling him toward Melody Gardens, a small, grassy park, catty-corner across the street.

Another voice drew my attention right next door. A woman and two young children had just emerged from Bill and Flo's bakery, Bread n' Butter. The kids, clutching cookies as big as their heads, left a trail of crumbs in their wake. This gave me an idea. Who better to ask about the source of the powdered sugar on the floor than our resident bakers? I should go talk to Bill and Flo.

For some reason, my feet wouldn't follow through on this plan. I stood rooted in place, biting my lip. The truth was, I was feeling kind of shy about facing the Morrisons after my disastrous turn at leading the workshop. I also imagined they'd be none too happy to learn about Felix's retirement. A vacant shop on the block wouldn't be good for their business. And the prospect of having *me* in charge surely wouldn't inspire much confidence. I knew it didn't in me.

What I needed was a peace offering. Not that we were at odds, but it couldn't hurt to soften their feelings about me. If I'd learned anything from my days working at a florist, it was the power of flowers to lift spirits and mend fences. I went back inside and made a beeline for the workroom.

"Let's see," I muttered to myself. "Which flowers to use?" Floriography might not be as well-known as it used to be, but most folks still knew a little something about the language of flowers. Everyone knew red roses symbolized romantic love. And most people associated daisies with cheerfulness or innocent children. Beyond that, I'd found that different flowers could evoke different moods, even if you didn't know their traditional Victorian meanings. Some were weightier and more formal, while others were lighter and more whimsical. Some were lush and sensuous, and some were simple. It all came down to what message you wanted to impart.

Something white, I thought. *The color of peace and good will*. I opened the case containing a rainbow of tulips and reached for the white ones. According to tradition, white tulips represented forgiveness. *Perfect*.

And yellow, I added, reaching for another bucket. *The color of friendship*.

It didn't take long for me to put together a pretty bouquet of white and yellow tulips, interspersed with healthy green leaves. I arranged the flowers in a large clear, glass jar. The result was elegant and cheerful, without being too fancy. Now I was ready to face the neighbors.

Bread n' Butter was empty of customers when I pushed

through the front door, flowers in hand. The bakery had a downhome appeal, with gingham curtains, two little wooden tables, and cutesy kitchen art hanging on the brick walls. It smelled like hazelnut coffee and oven-fresh bread. Inhaling deeply, I took a second to appreciate the warm, welcoming aroma.

Though, now that I looked around, I noticed the place was a little less tidy than usual. Besides a smattering of crumbs on the floor, the tables were unbussed and a puddle of spilled coffee dripped from the edge of the countertop. I pulled some paper napkins from a metal dispenser and was about to dab at the spill, when Flo shouldered through the kitchen door, a cell phone in one hand and a cleaning rag in the other. From the looks of her drawn face, she was perturbed about something, and maybe slightly worried.

I offered up a smile and showed her the flowers. "Hello, Flo. These are for you and Bill."

"Oh?" Her eyes flickered in surprise. "Why, whatever for?"

"Just because."

Her forehead was still wrinkled in confusion, so I quickly fessed up. "It's my way of saying sorry. You know, about yesterday . . ." I trailed off, uncertain. *Was this a mistake? Callous, even? A man has died, and I think I can smooth it over with tulips?*

"Aren't you sweet," said Flo, and I breathed a sigh of relief. She pocketed her cell phone, took the flowers, and placed them next to the cash register. Then she used her rag to clean off the countertop.

"How's Felix holding up?" she asked. "He was one of the few people who actually got along with Abe Ranker."

Ugh. More questions about Felix. I didn't know what to say. As far as I knew, my boss (former boss?) still didn't know what had happened.

Flo must have taken my silence as disapproval at her lack of respect for the dead. "Such a terrible thing to happen to anyone," she said quickly. "Bill and I plan to order flowers for the funeral as soon as there's a date set. Will Felix open back up soon? At least for online orders?"

"Um. That's to be determined. I'm not really sure."

"Well, it's understandable to be closed today, but flowers don't last forever. Of course, Felix knows that. He'll be mindful of his inventory."

"Right." I smiled weakly and backed toward the exit.

"Pastries for the road?" she asked.

"Another time." I waved and left the bakery before she could ask any more questions about Felix. I was halfway back to Flower House when I remembered my original purpose for wanting to talk to Flo—to ask her about the powdered sugar. *Boy, am I scatter-brained, or what?*

When I returned to Bread n' Butter, the tabletops were clean, but Flo had disappeared again. I peeked inside the bakery case while I waited. Maybe I'd order a pastry after all.

After a few minutes, I decided to call out. "Hello? Flo? I'm back!"

Another minute passed, and I was starting to get impatient. Where had she gotten to? I walked to the side of the counter and pushed open the door to the kitchen. I opened my mouth to holler for her again, but the words got caught in my throat. I saw something that made me freeze in my tracks: a skull and crossbones. It was printed on a cardboard box sitting on a cluttered metal cabinet along the wall. The box was labeled Rodenticide.

Rat poison? Didn't Chief Walden say the poison that killed Abe was found in some pesticides?

A scraping noise made me jump. It sounded like a door opening—probably that of an office or closet around the corner. Then I heard voices. It was Bill and Flo, and they seemed to be arguing. With one hand still on the kitchen door, I craned my ears to listen.

"I don't see why we should wait," said Flo. "We've been waiting for years. Now that he's gone, we're free to move ahead."

"Come on, Flo," said Bill. "It wouldn't look right. People will talk. We need to bide our time."

"I'm tired of waiting!"

"I am, too! But we need to be smart about this."

The shuffling of footsteps broke my momentary paralysis. I slipped out of the kitchen, gently closing the door behind me. Then I fled the shop once more. This time I ran across the lawn and up the sidewalk, not stopping until I was safely back inside Flower House. I leaned back on the closed door and shut my eyes. *Bide their time? What in the heck was that all about?*

"Peony for your thoughts."

I about jumped out of my skin as my eyes flew open. Calvin and Gus were walking in from the back room, Calvin with a goofy grin. "*Peony.* Get it? Since this is a flower shop?"

Ugh. "Yeah, but jeesh! Don't sneak up on me like that." My nerves were frayed enough already.

Gus barked once and launched himself toward me, dragging his leash on the floor.

"Sorry about that," said Calvin. "I thought I had a hold of him."

I sank to the floor and let the puppy jump in my lap and lick my hands. "Okay. It's alright," I cooed, as I scratched his furry head.

Calvin stuffed his hands in the pockets of his slacks and smiled crookedly. "He's got more energy than any dog I've ever known."

"Known many dogs?" I asked.

He laughed, though it came out as a snort. "Yeah, actually. I've known a canine or two in my time." He removed his hands from his pockets and tried to rest his elbow on the checkout counter—but somehow missed. Laughing awkwardly, he crossed his arms in front of his chest. I raised my eyebrows, half-amused and half-fascinated.

My cell phone trilled in my purse. I pushed Gus off of me and looked to see who was calling. It was my mom. Sighing, I stood up. Instead of answering, I'd just go see her in person.

Calvin cleared his throat. "So, have you, uh, heard from Felix? Can I start moving my stuff in?"

I walked over to the cash register to make sure it was locked up. "I hate to break it to you, dude, but Felix has gone on an extended trip. He won't be back anytime soon."

"Where did he go?"

I glanced over at him. "What does it matter where he went? The point is, the future of Flower House is up in the air right now. There are a lot of things I have to figure out."

"You? So, you're in charge?"

"Why not me? You think I'm too young? Do I look incapable?" I was feeling extra defensive for some reason.

"No, no," he said hurriedly. "I just meant, if you're in charge, then you could give me the keys to the apartment."

My eyes fell to the piece of paper I'd set on the counter. It was the mysterious note.

"Hey, when you were out with Gus, did you happen to see anyone standing outside the front door to the shop? Maybe crouching down?"

"Uh, no. I don't think so. Why?"

I handed him the paper. "Someone slipped this under the door."

He lifted his glasses up to read the note. *Guess he's nearsighted*, I thought irrelevantly. I also couldn't help noticing how much the chunky glasses altered his appearance.

Frowning, he returned the note to me. "I don't get it."

"Didn't you hear about what happened here yesterday?"

He shook his head. "I just got to town this afternoon."

As much as it pained me to repeat the story, I knew I had to do it. I gave him the abbreviated version. I thought surely it would scare him away. What was scarier than murder? Instead, he only seemed curious.

"Did the victim have a wife or any other family? It had to be someone close to him, right? Crimes like that are almost never random."

I stared at him in wonder. No fear? Well, he didn't witness it all, like I did.

"No wife or kids," I said. "Not that I know of anyway." My phone rang again. "Speaking of family, I really need to go and see mine."

"You're married?" asked Calvin. Was it my imagination, or did I detect a hint of disappointment in the question?

I suppressed a smile. "No. I'm talking about my parents." I looked around. "Where's Gus?"

We found him by the front door, chewing on the entry rug. He'd managed to unravel one whole edge, and in only a few minutes. I picked up his leash.

"I'll take him with me. As for you . . ." I turned to look at Calvin. He gazed at me with pleading eyes, baby blue behind those thick hipster glasses, and clasped his hands together like a supplicant. Any second now, he was liable to drop to his knees and kiss my feet. And for all the wrong reasons.

I shook myself. "Look, I suppose it's probably not a bad idea to keep this place occupied for the time being—"

"I can help you keep an eye on things!" Calvin interjected, his eyes bright with eagerness. "I can even help you out with the business. I'm really good with plants. Dogs too."

I smiled in spite of myself. "I just might take you up on that. But, listen, this is gonna have to be a trial situation. I really don't know what's going to happen to this building."

"Understood. It's a month-to-month lease anyway. Just so I have someplace to stay tonight." He glanced at his watch, no doubt thinking about his rental van.

"Alright. Let's see if I can find the apartment keys." With both Gus and Calvin at my heels, I headed to the small office next to the workroom.

I sure do hope I'm doing the right thing.

It was prime time for the after-work crowd at Dumbbells, the small health club my parents owned. Hal and Mandy Ravenswood had always been fitness buffs. It was what had brought them together back in college, where Dad played football and Mom led the cheerleading squad. They'd bonded over team spirit, rock climbing, and working out. It was only natural that they'd turn their passion into a business. As a kid, I'd spent a good chunk of time tumbling on the gym mats here and, later, minding the front desk, while Dad trained the lifters and Mom taught Jazzercise. But I was never interested in taking over the business.

And if I'd been old enough to have a say, I definitely would have vetoed the name they chose. To this day, it still embarrasses me to tell people my parents run a business called "Dumbbells."

Luckily, Rocky was the complete opposite. He was more than happy to spend all his waking hours sculpting his muscles and helping others do the same. That took at least a little bit of pressure off of me—and placed it on him to find a significant other with similar interests.

The front desk was unattended when I entered the lobby, but the glass door to the weight room was open. I peeked in and was met with the familiar sound of clanging barbells and grunting lifters. The thump of hip-hop music drifted in from the adjacent fitness studio. Gus tugged on his leash, no doubt attracted by the exciting odors of body sweat mingled with shower soap. I was trying to get my dad's attention when the office door flew open and my mom rushed at mc like a tiny, leotard-clad linebacker.

"Sierra! It's about time! Where have you been?"

"Sorry, Mom. It's been a busy day. I thought you were leading an aerobics class?"

"I asked Charlene to cover for me. I've been too worried to do anything."

Gus jumped on my mom's legs, his nubby tail wagging. I was beginning to realize he jumped on everyone. I was going to have to enroll him in doggie etiquette school.

"Sorry," I repeated. "Mom, meet Gus— my new dog."

"You got a dog?"

"Well, Felix got him, but he's mine now."

"Oh? Dogs are a lot of work, you know."

"I know. But he's real smart. He knows his name, and he comes when he's called." I struggled to hold onto the leash as Gus tried to steer us toward the weight room. "Sit, Gus. Sit!" He ignored me.

Mom laughed shortly, then turned to me with a serious expression. "Listen, hon. I assume you're not going back to the flower shop, so you can work here. I've already started the paperwork to put you back on the payroll. Swimsuit season will be here soon, and we're getting busier already. We'll be adding on another Jazzercise class—"

"Wait a minute," I said, trying to interrupt. She kept talking.

"You can cover the desk and phone, while I'm teaching or working in the office. I have some ideas for a new spring ad campaign, which you can help out with. Of course, if you want to take a class, Dad or Rocky can sit up here for an hour."

I could feel my face tightening up like a celebrity on Botox. "Mom—"

She held up her hand. "Don't worry about any interference with your music career. We can always cover for you if you get a gig or any guitar students."

Ouch. I knew she didn't mean to be hurtful, but I could've done without the reminder of my stalled music career. (*Stalled*, not failed.) It was flip comments like these that drove me out of the family business in the first place. As soon as I turned sixteen (way back when), I'd started looking for part-time work elsewhere. During breaks from high school, I tried my hand at every opportunity I could snatch, from mowing lawns to flipping burgers. Then Granny recommended me to Felix and Georgina at Flower House. They hired me to deliver flowers and do odd jobs around the shop, eventually teaching me how to arrange flowers myself. Flower House had been good to me over the years.

Mom was still prattling on about Dumbbells, telling me her plans to spruce up the gym for the spring campaign. I finally had to raise my voice.

"Mom! I don't need a job. I need to look after the flower shop."

"You don't have to do that, hon. Why should you do that? Besides, won't they be closed for a while?"

Before I could answer, my dad ambled in from the weight room, wearing his usual gray sweatpants and blue Dumbbells T-shirt, with a towel draped around his neck.

He was followed closely by a younger, taller version of himself—my brother, Rocky.

Mom immediately sought reinforcements. "Hal, Rocky, tell Sierra she doesn't need to go back to that flower shop. She should work here instead."

"Listen to your mother," said Dad, pulling me into a brief one-armed hug.

"She probably doesn't want to abandon Felix," said Rocky, taking the leash from me and leaning down to accept kisses from Gus.

I flashed him a grateful smile. "That's true," I said. *Even though it kind of feels like Felix abandoned me.*

"The place is a crime scene!" said Mom. "Nobody's going to want to do business there now, at least not until the murder is solved. I heard some people wondering whether it could've been a poisonous plant that did ol' Abe in."

"What?" It was on the tip of my tongue to ask who had said such a thing, but I thought better of it. There was no stopping the gossip train in this town, and all that was really beside the point anyway. I sighed. "Actually, the future of Flower House is kind of in flux right now."

"What do you mean?" asked Dad.

I maneuvered behind the reception counter, so I could plop down on the tall stool. Rocky crouched on the floor, giving Gus a belly rub, while Mom and Dad gave me their undivided attention. I told them everything, from Felix's unusual trip and Abe's collapse at the workshop to the message from Byron and the sudden appearance of the new guy, Calvin. Mom kept asking me questions, most of which I couldn't answer.

"The thing is," I concluded, "I don't know what I want to do yet. But it might be kind of cool to own my own business. What do you think?"

For a fraction of a second, my question hung in the air,

as my parents seemed to process the information. Then they pelted me with objections.

"That house is so old," said Mom. "It's got to be a money pit!"

"Is the business in the red?" asked Dad. "You get his assets, you get his debts too."

"It's too much responsibility!"

"It'll eat up all your time."

"It sounds like a bad idea."

"The timing is not good."

I could feel my face heating up and my muscles clench. Every negative point pushed me that much closer to accepting the offer just to be contrary. Instead, I took a deep breath and forced myself to smile. "Why don't you tell me how you really feel?"

Mom reached across the counter to smooth my hair. "We're concerned, honey."

"We don't know if it's even safe for you to be there," said Dad.

My mind immediately jumped to the note that had been slipped under the door at Flower House. I swallowed. "I'm sure the police will catch the murderer soon."

Dad crossed his arms in front of his chest, reflexively tightening his biceps. "I wouldn't be so sure. I've left a couple messages for Walt, and he hasn't called me back yet. Hasn't even sent a text."

I tossed a look at Rocky, who had been quietly scratching Gus's head and neck, like he was a dog whisperer or something. My brother had been on the receiving end of our parents' *smotherly* love plenty of times. *Why isn't he defending me?*

He finally spoke up. "Sierra's not a dummy," he said. (*Gee, thanks, Rocky.*) "Give her some credit. She didn't say she was gonna take Felix's offer. She'll at least sleep on it. Right, sis?"

"Of course, I'll sleep on it. I won't make any snap decisions. I'll think it through, list the pros and cons."

"I'd say being the scene of a murder is a pretty big con!" said Mom.

A customer passing through the lobby halted at Mom's words. He turned back, mouth agape. Dad stepped forward and clapped him heavily on the back. "Good workout, Joe. Have a good evening now."

"Uh, yeah. Thanks, Hal."

As soon as Joe left, I stood up and moved to take the leash from Rocky. Gus hopped eagerly to his feet. "I'm sure this will all blow over in no time," I said. "Chief Walden is probably out questioning people, closing in on a suspect as we speak. That's probably why he hasn't called you back, Dad."

Rocky looked thoughtful. "I wouldn't want to be questioned by Chief Walden, innocent or not."

"Why not?" asked Mom. "You've never committed any crimes." She said it as a statement, but there was a note of questioning in her tone.

Rocky chuckled. "No, Mom. I haven't. But still. Walt Walden is intimidating. Wasn't that his football nickname in college—the Intimidator? You've told us stories about those days."

I recalled how small the chief had made me feel and realized Rocky was right. I turned to my dad. "Does he have a partner? Someone to play 'good cop' to his 'bad cop'?"

Dad narrowed his eyebrows. "Walt is a good cop."

"You know what I mean," I said.

"He doesn't have a partner," Dad said. "But I'm sure the whole Aerieville police force is working on this case. I'll give him another call tonight."

Mom took her place behind the counter and shuffled through some papers. "Come home for supper, Sierra? I have a roast in the crockpot."

Deena Lee was one of them. Of course, she was a marvelous dancer.

Letty rubbed her finger along the rim of her mug. "It almost didn't open. I'm not sure how Valerie ended up getting the approval she needed. You'd have to ask her about it."

Yes, I thought, as I set my cup down and stood up. *I definitely* will *have to ask her about it*. I thanked Letty for the tea and cookies and left her house, thoughts swirling in my mind.

Before picking up Gus, I went back to Flower House to put Valerie's bouquet in the cold-storage case until tomorrow. While I was there, I realized I'd better check and see if we'd received any online orders. Just because the shop was closed didn't mean folks couldn't visit our website. Usually, Felix was the one to download the orders each evening. Now it was up to me.

As I sat at Felix's old chestnut desk and waited for the site to load, I looked around his small cluttered office. If I was going to be the new proprietor, I'd definitely want to make a few changes. For starters, I'd remove the mounted fish hanging on the wall above the computer. *Blech*. The poster of Victorian salmon flies, featuring brightly-colored exotic bird feathers, was kind of neat, but not really my style. The vintage wildflower chart, however, I'd probably keep.

Swiveling in the chair, I couldn't believe how messy the room was. An overstuffed bookcase contained a jumble of old books and trinkets. *That might be fun to look through—if I can ever find the time.* Beyond that, stacks of newspapers and magazines covered every available surface. So did a thick layer of dust.

I turned back to the computer and saw that we actually had three orders. I printed them out, mentally running through what I'd need to put them together in the morning. Too bad I'd told Francie not to come in.

I was about to double-check the inventory file, when I heard a creak from somewhere within the shop. I paused, staring at the open door into the dark hallway. Of course, it had to be Calvin. Both doors, front and back, were locked.

Still, it was starting to feel strange to be here so late. *I should get going.* I shut down the computer and grabbed my purse. Flipping off the light behind me, I emerged from the office and stepped into the hallway, where I stood for a moment, listening. Had I heard another noise? The office was in the rear of the building, across the hall from the kitchen workroom. To my left was the closed door leading to the upstairs apartment. I turned right and made my way toward the front of the store. Halfway there, I stopped again. This time I definitely heard a strange noise. It was a scraping sound, like something scratching on a window. It was coming from the orchid room.

Without thinking, I reached my arm into the room to feel for the switch on the wall and flipped on the overhead light. Nothing seemed out of place. Tall tables and shelves displayed half a dozen varieties of orchid, some in pretty, ceramic pots, along with a wall of books on all things orchid: growing guides, history books, pictorial books featuring colorful photos, and more. The south wall was dominated by a large picture window. The curtains were open, revealing only blackness on the other side.

I crossed the room and made sure the window latch was secure. Then I cupped my hands to the pane to peer outside. It was too dark to see anything. *Weird.* I told myself it must have been a branch scratching against the window, but I knew this was unlikely. There were no trees outside this window.

After a moment, I pulled back and drew the curtains.

Then I turned around—and came face-to-face with a tall man standing silently right behind me. I screamed.

"Sorry to startle you," he said.

"Bill!" I exclaimed. "What are you doing here?"

Bill Morrison gave me the barest of smiles. "Just being neighborly," he said mildly. "Everything okay?"

"Uh." I was still so surprised I couldn't seem to form words.

He nodded once, then turned and left the room. I followed him into the hallway and watched as he walked to the front door and let himself out.

I was still staring after him, when Calvin appeared at the end of the hall.

"Oh, hello," he said. "I didn't know you were here. I thought I should make sure everything was locked up." He started for the office door and stubbed his toe. "Oopsie-daisy!" Then he laughed his goofy, snorting laugh. "Well, I guess you can do it. Lock up, I mean. Since you're here."

I overlooked his awkwardness. "Why was Bill here?"

"Bill? He helped me carry up my furniture earlier. Then he came back a little while ago and brought muffins. He also helped me hang some shelves. Nice guy."

I was feeling uncommonly irritated, probably due to tiredness and shot nerves. With my hands on my hips, I leaned in. "Listen, I'm glad you had help and all, but you gotta be careful about who you let come in here. Bill is a murder suspect, you know."

Calvin's eyes got big as saucers. "What? No way!"

It sounded ridiculous, even to me. Yet I knew it was true. "Yes way. I told you what the police chief said. Somebody poisoned a man at my flower-arranging workshop. Everyone who attended is a suspect."

"Wow. Sorry. He seemed nice. He came over when he saw me unloading the van and offered to help. He was kind of a lifesaver."

"Yeah, well, most murderers don't go around acting all murdery. Haven't you ever heard the phrase *It's always the one you least suspect*?"

As the words came out of my mouth, I was hit with another realization. The killer really could be anyone . . . even a shy schoolteacher who lives alone and serves you tea and cookies.

It seemed preposterous. Still, maybe I should rethink my plan to go and question all the witnesses. At least, not by myself. Like Rocky said, I was no dummy.

Not usually.

Chapter 8

I wasn't sure where I should have Gus sleep, but he made the decision himself when he jumped onto the foot of my bed. With his short, little legs it took a couple of tries to get up there. Once he settled in, I didn't have the heart to make him move. At least my feet wouldn't get cold overnight. I put Granny's sachet under my pillow and soon dropped to sleep like a stone in water.

In the morning, we awoke early and went for a short walk around the block before heading into work. I was glad Gus was an easygoing pup. He handled car rides well and seemed friendly with everyone.

On the other hand, he was not exactly a tranquil little guy. As I set about making bouquets in the work kitchen at Flower House, bustling from case to table, snipping stems and stripping leaves, I found Gus constantly underfoot. Once, when I dropped a leaf on the floor, he snatched it up in his mouth before I even realized what had happened.

"Let go of that, you little scamp!" I chased him around the room, until I finally cornered him by the tall metal trash can. "Drop it, Gus." He didn't drop it. But at least he didn't bite me when I pried open his mouth and pulled out the wet, mangled greenery. I tossed it in the trash, then washed my hands, wondering if perhaps a flower shop wasn't the safest place for a young, curious dog.

There was a tap on the kitchen door, and Calvin stuck his head in. I noticed he'd parted his hair on the side, but his gel wasn't holding. Little pieces stuck up, calling to mind a grown-up Dennis the Menace.

"Everyone decent?" he asked, with a silly grin. I gave him an arch look, and he chortled, causing his glasses to slip down his nose. "Just kidding. Why wouldn't you be decent? Of course, I don't know you very well. And there's more than one meaning of the word—"

"Hey," I said, cutting him off. "Do you know anything about which plants are poisonous to dogs?"

He dropped his grin and came inside, pushing up the sleeves of his striped sweater. "Did Gus eat something he shouldn't have?"

I picked up one of the leaves that littered the worktable. "He tried to eat a rose leaf," I said.

Calvin relaxed his shoulders. "Oh, that's okay. Roses aren't toxic to dogs. Unless they've been sprayed with pesticides."

"Most are, but not these. These came from our greenhouse. Felix tries to follow eco-safe practices where possible."

Calvin walked to the back door and peered outside. "I'd love to take a look at the greenhouse sometime. I'm kind of a botany nerd."

I raised my eyebrows. *Is that the kind of nerd he is?* I decided to let it go, as I stepped around Gus to pick up my shears.

"Jim should be back today. He was off for a few days, which is rare for him. As long as I've been here, Jim has always been back there taking care of the greenhouse. He's not a very talkative guy, but he probably wouldn't mind showing you around."

I wondered if Jim knew anything about Felix's departure. Come to think of it, the old gardener was probably close to retirement age himself. If Jim were to bail on me too, there was no way I could keep the business running.

Calvin turned around and nodded at the worktable. "Why so many roses? I thought they were mainly for Valentine's Day."

"Roses are associated with matters of the heart, which makes them appropriate for almost any occasion," I said. "I'm adding a couple of pink ones to these magenta gerbera daisies and alstroemeria for a birthday bouquet. The red roses will be a nice accent among the purple and pink carnations for a get-well bouquet. And these ivory roses are going in with the lilies for a sympathy arrangement." I talked as I worked, again strewing cuttings all over the table and floor.

Calvin held Gus back. "Well, those are all real pretty. But you should know that lilies are not good for dogs. Maybe I should take Gus for a walk."

"Oh, would you? I've got to deliver these, but I won't be gone long."

"Happy to. Take your time." He paused with one hand on the doorknob and looked back at me. "Take your thyme, and your sage and rosemary too. Take all your fragrant herbs!"

"Good one," I said, trying not to roll my eyes.

After they left, I put the finishing touches on the bouquets and wrote out the message cards as specified in the orders. That done, I stuck the cards in plastic floral picks, which I added to the arrangements, and wrapped the bouquets in floral tissue paper, before quickly cleaning up the kitchen. One at a time, I carried the bouquets to my hatchback and placed them in a special box for safe transporting. At the last minute, I decided to bring the tulips I'd made for Valerie as well. Just in case.

My first stop was a dentist's office, where one of the hygienists was celebrating her birthday. This reminded me that Deena had mentioned her father's birthday was coming up. Maybe that was why she came to the shop yesterday—until she was scared off by the hazmat crew. I shuddered at the memory. Too bad I didn't have Deena's phone number. I'd like to make her a friendship apology bouquet too.

After the dentist's office, I dropped off the get-well flowers at the senior center. My last delivery was at the Feder Family Funeral Home. Margie Feder, the director, answered my knock and greeted me with surprise.

"Are these from Flower House?" she asked. "I thought y'all were closed. I've been telling people to order from someplace else."

"Oh, don't do that!" I said, as pleasantly as I could. "We closed temporarily for a day or so, but we're still taking online orders."

"I'm sorry, dear. I'd heard Felix Maniford left town after what happened."

I forced myself to keep smiling. I wanted to ask her where she'd heard it, but I knew that was beside the point. "Sure, he left, but not because of what happened. He went on a little trip, that's all. The timing was coincidental."

She raised a doubtful eyebrow.

"It's true! He left me in charge. We're still open." *At least for now.* I gave her a cheerful wave, as I backed away. "Spread the word!"

On my way back to Flower House, I drove by Light Steps Dance Studio, arguing with myself as I slowed the car and pulled into an empty space along the curb.

Remember last night, Sierra? When I vowed I wouldn't

go on questioning murder suspects all alone, like some kind of clueless scary-movie victim? That is one resolution I really should keep.

But . . . I also wagered I could get folks to open up better than Chief Walt "the Intimidator" Walden. And I got such a great lead from Letty!

Anyway, I rationalized, as I got out of the car and headed to the dance studio, *what could happen in broad daylight in a place of business full of people?*

I ignored the voice in my head that tried to remind me Abe had died in a place of business full of people.

The dance-studio lobby was a welcoming space, with lavender-painted walls and minimal furniture. Simple black-and-white waiting chairs lined the wall facing the tall reception counter, which was also lavender. The wall behind the receptionist featured a large decal with the studio's name and logo: a pair of elegant pointe shoes with a fluttering ribbon. To the right was a small shop selling ballet shoes, tights, and leotards in all sizes. And to the left, next to the door to the rest of the studio, was a glass case featuring an impressive number of trophies. They were clearly serious about dance here.

I approached the slender teen-aged girl at the front desk. In her baggy sweater and leggings, and with her ballerina bun, she certainly looked like a dancer.

"Hi!" I said, setting the flowers on her desk. "Is Valerie around?"

She pointed to the side door. "She's rehearsing, but she should be finishing up soon. You can go on back."

"You sure it's okay?"

"Oh, yeah. She likes an audience."

"Cool! I'll just leave these flowers here."

Following the girl's directions, I walked down a short hallway until I found a grouping of chairs facing a wall of glass windows. The chairs were empty now, but I imagined they would be filled with parents later, when the after-school classes began. Now, at ten in the morning, the studio was quiet, except for the muffled strains of classical music—some waltz I should probably know but couldn't quite place.

Through the windows, I could see a spacious dance floor—and Valerie, prancing, leaping, and twirling like a spinning top. I watched her, mesmerized. She was dressed all in black from her tights and leotard to her ballet shoes—except for fluorescent green leg warmers, which flashed like a hummingbird's wings as she extended her legs from one arabesque to another. For a woman in her thirties, she was in exceptionally good shape. Heck, for a woman of any age, she was in great shape. I found myself seriously thinking I ought to sign up for one of my mom's Jazzercise classes.

When the song ended, I clapped loudly. My enthusiasm was real, but I also hoped she'd hear me through the glass. She looked up and gave me a little curtsy, then waved me in.

"Wow!" I said, as I approached her. "Valerie, that was amazing! So, so beautiful."

"Thanks," she said, a little breathless.

"Do you have a show coming up? I'd love to get tickets."

She picked up a water bottle from the floor near the wall and took a swig before answering. "My students are preparing for a competition. I like to run through the choreography myself so I can coach them better. Plus, it's fun."

"I bet. And good exercise too."

She wiped her brow with a small towel, before pulling on a sweatshirt. "Are you thinking about signing up for dance lessons?"

For a second, I almost said yes, simply to be agreeable.

After all, my purpose for being here was to get her to open up. But then I came to my senses.

"Maybe someday. Ballet is such a lovely art form. But, no, I just stopped by to drop off some flowers, so I thought I'd come back and say hi."

She looked up sharply. "Flowers? From who?"

"From me. I felt bad after what happened the other night. I think it was kind of traumatic for all of us."

"Oh." She seemed to visibly relax, leading me to wonder who she'd thought had sent her flowers. "That's sweet of you. Any word from the police?"

I leaned on the ballet barre as Valerie stretched her legs. "Yeah. Chief Walden stopped by the flower shop yesterday. He told me they found traces of strychnine on Abe's clothes."

She stopped mid-stretch. "Strychnine? That sounds bad."

"I'll say. I guess it was mixed in with some powdered sugar. Do you remember seeing any powdered sugar on any of the treats at the workshop?"

"No. I don't think so. I brought cupcakes with pink and white frosting. No sprinkles."

"Well, whoever did it must have really hated Abe, don't you think? To go to such an extreme measure. Hated his guts."

Valerie's eyelids fluttered slightly before she nodded. "I guess so."

"Did you know he'd been receiving death threats?"

Now she looked really surprised. "No. You're kidding. What did they say?"

"I don't know. It's just a rumor I heard. I probably shouldn't have said anything. I'm just so creeped out by the whole thing." I hugged my arms to ward off a shiver. Talking about all this really was giving me the heebie-jeebies.

Valerie patted my shoulder. "That's understandable. It's a lot to handle."

"I'm just glad no one else is in danger. Abe was clearly targeted. He must have made an enemy out of someone."

A bitter laugh escaped from Valerie's lips. "No doubt. I'm sure there are quite a few people who felt poorly toward Abe."

"You mean, because of how he used his position on the zoning committee?"

"Yes," she said shortly.

"Well," I ventured, "at least he approved Light Steps."

She straightened suddenly and looked at her watch. "Someone has this floor reserved at eleven o'clock, so we need to get out of here. Thanks for stopping by."

"Of course. I hope you like the flowers. I left them at the front desk. They're tulips. I think you used tulips in your arrangement the other night."

"I did, yes. It was a nice class. Until the end." She started walking to the door, and I followed, wishing I could come up with a way to keep the conversation going. "I probably wouldn't have gone," she continued, "if I'd known Abe was going to be there."

And there's my opening. "I don't blame you," I said. "It almost looked like he was harassing you. What did he say when he made you spill your coffee?"

She didn't answer at first. We passed the spectator chairs and proceeded down the hallway, past the restrooms and locker rooms. Finally, she paused next to a large bulletin board.

"He didn't have a chance to say anything. I jerked away when he invaded my space. But I know what he was *going* to say."

I faced her expectantly.

She shrugged. "He was probably going to ask me out. He's been trying to get me to go out with him for years.

Ever since . . ." She trailed off, reaching out to straighten a poster on the bulletin board.

I lowered my voice. "You can tell me, Valerie. I won't blab. I promise."

I could tell she was wrestling with something in her mind. Finally, she sighed. "Oh, what does it matter, anyway? I did go out with him, once or twice, several years ago. I had to. He wouldn't approve my business license if I didn't."

Whoa. I hadn't seen that coming. "Jeez, Valerie. That's terrible."

"I should have reported him, but I was young and naïve. I didn't think I had a choice. I lost a boyfriend over it too." She shook her head, clearly still hung up on the memory. "The worst part is, even after I told Abe I didn't want to date him anymore, he continued to hold it over me. He said if I told anyone about us, my business license would be revoked. He implied that I had committed some kind of crime."

"What a jerk!"

"I resented him ever since. I always thought he'd have to pay someday, that there would be justice—" She broke off, seeming to catch herself. "That sounded bad. Don't misunderstand."

The young receptionist poked her head into the hallway. "Val, there's a phone call for you. It's Carly's mother."

"I'll be right there," she said. After the receptionist left, she turned back to me. "Thanks for listening, Sierra. I've never shared this with anyone. I guess I needed to get it off my chest."

"Of course. I'm glad I could be here for you." I shook my head, still digesting the fact that Abe had been able to get away with such unethical behavior. "Hey, do you suppose Abe did the same thing with any other young women?"

She seemed to consider it, then shook her head. "No. He flaunted his power and probably got all kinds of kickbacks. But I never heard of any other women he was involved with. For some reason, he was just obsessed with me." She laughed without humor. "In fact, if not for me, Abe probably wouldn't have been at the bouquet-arranging class."

"What do you mean?"

"He heard me talking about it at Bread n' Butter that morning. That's where I saw the flyer."

"Had he followed you to the bakery?"

"No. He was already there. I think he was just coming out of a meeting with Bill when I arrived. But I know he heard me mention the workshop to Flo. And he was looking at the flyer when I left."

Of course. For the killer to be prepared with the poison, he or she would have to know Abe would be at the class. And this proved Bill and Flo knew.

"Was anyone else in the bakery at the time?" I asked.

"I don't think—no, wait. Yes. Letty Maron was sitting at one of the little tables. She's so quiet, I almost forgot."

"She must have seen the flyer too."

"I suppose. Also, Richard Wales was coming in the door as I left."

"Huh." *So, everyone at the class—except Deena and me—would have known Abe planned to attend.*

Which meant everyone was still a suspect.

Chapter 9

Means, motive, and opportunity. That was what detectives looked for, wasn't it?

On my way back to Flower House, I kept running ideas through my head, thinking about what I knew and what I didn't. There was much more in the latter category.

Let's see. The means for murder. That would be the poison. Who had access to strychnine? It wasn't like you could just go buy it at the local hardware store. I assumed. On the other hand, if it was an ingredient in some pesticides, it probably wouldn't be too hard to come by.

What about motive? From what I gathered, lots of people didn't care for Abe, but who would want him dead? What would drive *anyone* to murder? Revenge? Was someone holding a grudge for past wrongs . . . like Valerie? Or did someone want to get him out of the way. Maybe he was blocking someone's big plans, like those of . . . Bill and Flo?

As for opportunity, everyone at the workshop had access to the treats, though how the killer managed to get the laced powdered sugar onto Abe's food and no one else's, I couldn't imagine.

"And why do it at Flower House at all?"

"Excuse me?"

I looked up into the confused face of the guy behind the counter at Bluebird Café and laughed at myself. I'd been so absorbed in my thoughts, I barely noticed I'd stopped off for lunch.

"Never mind," I said. "What's the special today?"

"It's meatless Monday, so we have a special on our grilled-vegetable paninis." He pointed to a sign on the counter next to him.

"Sounds good. I'll have that. And, you know what? Make it two, plus two bags of chips and two bottles of lime seltzer. To go, please." I was starting to feel guilty about leaving Gus with Calvin for so long. Surprising him with lunch seemed like a nice gesture.

As it happened, when I walked in the front door of Flower House, Calvin wasn't the only one to be surprised. It was like I'd entered a whole new flower shop. Furniture was rearranged, and new display tables had been brought in from the storeroom. Potted plants, buckets of eucalyptus, and fresh-cut flowers, which had previously been on the floor, were now on the tables. The wall shelves had also been elevated. And the welcome rug had been moved outside.

Calvin had puppy-proofed the place.

"Where did you get this?" I asked, touching a short wooden gate that spanned the arched opening to the events room.

"From the pet store," he said, stuffing his hands in his jeans pockets. "Gus and I took a little trip. I bought him some toys too."

Gus ran up to me and jumped on my legs, letting me know he still loved me best.

"Aren't you the lucky little fellow," I said, scratching him behind the ears.

"I was thinking," said Calvin. "It's probably best to

keep the door to the kitchen workroom closed. You know, to keep Gus out of trouble. We should nip it in the bud, so he doesn't *nip* any *buds*."

"Ha ha," I said. "Actually, you're right. That's a good idea."

"Same for the office. At least for now. I started moving things around in there, but there's so much stuff. It's going to take a while."

I stopped petting Gus and frowned. "You were in the office?"

"Was that off-limits? I'm sorry. I should've asked first. I was just trying to help. Sometimes I go too far. I—"

"It's okay. Don't worry about it." *Jeesh*. I raised the bag from the café and gave it a little shake. "Have you had lunch yet?"

We ate in the events room at a table near the window— as far as possible from the place where Abe had keeled over. Gus was nearby, happily chewing on one of his new toys. I grinned as I watched him, realizing that the pup's joyful energy was probably doing more to clear the air here than Granny's ditchwater could ever do.

Calvin sat stiffly across from me, gazing out the window as he chewed his sandwich. He wasn't a bad-looking guy, I realized. Beneath the glasses and the aw-shucks attitude was quite an interesting face, actually. Almost like a young Leonardo DiCaprio—or a Harry Styles, minus the pop-star hair. He was something of an enigma, though. One minute chatty and full of silly puns, the next quiet and distant—like now. *Maybe I can do something about that.*

"So, did anybody stop by this morning?" I asked.

"Uh-uh. The Closed sign is on the door."

"I know," I said good-naturedly. "I thought somebody might have knocked."

"No. There was a call, though."

"An order?"

"I don't think so. It was somebody named Francie. She said, 'Tell Sierra to mail me my last check. I'm going full-time at Manny's.'"

"Terrific," I muttered. First Felix and now Francie. How was I going to keep this shop going by myself? Suddenly, I was feeling more fretful than flirty.

Calvin looked out the window again, thoughtfully crunching on a potato chip. After a moment, he said, "Any word from Felix?"

"Nope."

"Where did you say he went?"

"I didn't." Now it was my turn to gaze out the window. Where *was* Felix? Had he really just picked up and left his entire life behind? His home, his business, his new puppy? It was so bizarre.

"Did he—" Calvin began, at the same time I said, "What brought you—"

Calvin snorted his nervous laughter. "You go first."

"What brought you to Aerieville?" I asked.

"I wanted a change of pace, something smaller and closer to nature. I was tired of living in a big city, and I heard Aerieville was nice."

"What did you do in Knoxville?"

"I was an adjunct at UT, but I also did some consulting. I'm actually in the middle of a pretty big consulting project right now, which has allowed me to take a break from teaching."

"What kind of—"

He interrupted to ask, "Are you from here?"

"Uh, yeah. Born and raised."

A knock sounded at the front door, causing Gus to bark in response. I jumped up, grateful for the interruption. Having lunch with Calvin was turning out to be way more awkward than it should have been. To my delight, I found Deena standing on the stoop.

"Hey, you!" I grabbed her hand and pulled her inside. "I was just thinking of you this morning. Come on in! Care for some coffee?"

"No, thank you. I just wanted to give you this." She pulled a check from her purse and held it toward me. "This has been weighing on me since Saturday. I arrived late to the workshop, and then left without paying."

I waved away the check. "You don't have to do that. After what happened, I wouldn't feel right charging anybody."

"No, really. Take the check. You provided all the flowers and supplies, and showed us all the steps for making a bouquet."

Gus gave a yip and scratched at the gate, no doubt longing to jump on Deena's legs. Calvin walked up behind him. "Hello," he said.

I introduced Calvin to Deena, as she tried to press the check into my hands. "I invited her to the workshop," I explained to Calvin. "I'm not taking her money."

"This is still a business, isn't it?" she asked.

"In theory," I answered. Then I relented. "Fine. If you're going to be so stubborn." I took the check to the cash register and popped it open. It was empty. Which made sense, since I'd neglected to stock it this morning. Not that it mattered.

Deena leaned over the gate to let Gus sniff and lick her fingers. I was impressed. I would have thought she'd be too fastidious for doggy germs.

"Well," she said, straightening up. "I should go."

"Do you have to?" I asked. "I was hoping we could have a chat."

She glanced at the snack counter behind Calvin. "Are you sure it's safe to be in there? I happened by yesterday and saw people wearing protective gear."

Calvin raised his eyebrows and inched away.

"It's fine," I said. "The cops gave us the all-clear. But that is kind of what I wanted to talk to you about."

Just then, there was a sound at the front door, and we all turned to see who would enter. For a second, I thought we might actually have a customer, but it was only Richard.

"Hello, hello," he said cheerily. "Are y'all open?"

"That's the million-dollar question," I said. "I know the bank's open, though. Shouldn't you be at work?"

"Lunch break." He wandered around the shop, sniffing flowers and testing the sturdiness of the rehung shelves. "You've redecorated."

"Yeah, thanks to our new mascot," I said. "The little fur ball begging for your attention is Gus."

Richard walked over and held out his hand to Calvin. "Nice to meet you, Gus," he said.

Calvin blinked. "Oh, I'm not Gus. I'm Calvin."

"Kidding," said Richard, stepping over the gate and crouching down to greet Gus. "Come here, little pooch. Show me some love. What a good dog."

Deena smiled. "How have you been, Richard? We didn't get a chance to catch up the other night."

"That's right. For some reason the evening was cut short. I forget why." He made an ironic face. "But, seriously, it's all anyone's talking about. I just came from Nell's Diner and, hoo boy, talk about gossip central. Lips were flapping so fast, I got whiplash trying to keep up."

"I'm afraid to ask," I said.

"I don't have time to get into it right now anyway. I gotta get back to work. But I was wondering if you'd like to grab a cuppa with me later. Say, four thirty? At that new little tea room, Tea for You?"

"Sounds good. I've been wanting to check out that place. Can Deena join us?"

"The more the merrier."

She checked her watch. "I can do that."

"And I can hang out with Gus here, if you'd like," offered Calvin.

"That would be great," I said. "I'll owe you lunch again, I guess."

After Deena and Richard left, I checked the computer and the answering machine, to make sure there were no missed calls or orders. There were none. Either people assumed we were closed (a good bet, considering the sign on the door and the outgoing phone message I had recorded), or else the shop had a pall on it. Probably both.

Next I changed the water in the buckets Calvin had moved and removed all the flowers with brown petals. There were so many, I had to make three trips to the garbage can in the workroom. As I was tying up the trash bag, Calvin came up behind me.

"Would now be a good time to see the greenhouse?"

I glanced out the kitchen window. "Yeah, sure. I'm kind of surprised Jim hasn't come in. I haven't noticed his car outside either."

I made sure Gus was happily occupied with a bone in the gated events room, then found the key to the greenhouse. Calvin grabbed the garbage bag on our way out, and I led him to the dumpster in the alley.

"We have to keep the lid closed tight," I said, as I pushed it open. "Sometimes bears like to come down from the mountains."

"Yikes. I'll remember."

We proceeded to the greenhouse and were welcomed by warm, humid air, fragrant with a woody, sweet scent. Entering the greenhouse always felt like a mini-vacation, like a trip to a tropical paradise. I made excuses to come out here frequently in the wintertime, but I hadn't been out here lately.

It was a large structure, about the size of a three-car

garage, divided in two. One half contained several varieties of orchids, along with a few ferns. The other side contained rose bushes. Felix sourced most of the flowers we used from wholesalers around the world, as well as local flower farms when the season was right. But it was nice to have a few fresh flowers year round right here in the backyard.

Calvin and I began our walk-through in the warmer, orchid side of the greenhouse. As we strolled up and down the concrete aisles, he touched some of the plants, checking the moistness of the moss in which they grew. "They seem a little dry," he commented.

"I think the sprinklers are on a timer," I said. "Maybe the supplemental grow lights and temperature level too."

I slowed my steps and took a look around. The flowers appeared healthy and the glass walls were clean. Still, I couldn't help feeling a sense of neglect in the quiet greenhouse, as if it had been abandoned. Maybe it was simply the knowledge that Felix had left his entire life's work so abruptly. Or maybe it was Jim's absence. The old gardener had been away for only a few days, attending to some personal business, according to Felix. But I'd really thought he'd be back by now.

Then we came upon the workbench, and I realized that something truly was amiss. The table was completely empty. No tools, no pots, no soil. No seed packets or gloves. Not a single piece of evidence that this was a working greenhouse.

"That's odd," I said, running my hand over the table.

"What's the matter?" asked Calvin.

"Jim's tools and supplies are all gone."

He looked under the bench. "There are some pots and bags of soil under here," he said. "The tools are probably put away. Is there a tool chest or shed someplace?"

"There's a shed in the yard, but why would he take

everything out there when he was only supposed to be gone for a few days? No, I'm telling you, this is weird."

Calvin wiped his hand over the bench too. "Is he not normally a neat person?"

"Not this neat. It looks like he purposefully cleared the table for some reason." I circled the workbench, trying to figure out why this bothered me so much. It wasn't like the surface was spotless. There were some grains of dirt and specks of dust. He hadn't poured bleach over it or anything, as if trying to erase something terrible. *Why is your mind going there, Sierra?* No, it was more like he needed the surface to lay something out on. Maybe something like blueprints or a map. And then he packed up all his stuff and left.

Calvin was eyeing me like I might be a little bit loony. I tried to laugh. "I've been told I have an active imagination," I said. "It seems to be getting away from me."

He crinkled his eyes and nodded gravely. "That's okay. This is quite a *thorny* puzzle. It *rose* out of nowhere. It could be something—*orchid* it be nothing at all?"

"Alright, alright," I said, raising both hands in surrender. "Enough."

Half groaning, half chuckling, I turned to walk on— and inadvertently kicked a tall trash can at the corner of the aisle. On a whim, I looked inside.

"Huh," I said.

"What is it?" asked Calvin, coming up behind me.

"There's a bunch of crumpled-up papers in there." I reached in and pulled out a handful. "They seem to be letters," I said, as I carried them over to the workbench and dropped them in a pile. "Or the start of letters."

I smoothed one of the papers and read it out loud. "'Dear Angela, I'm sorry I couldn't wait to tell you this in person.'"

"Is that it?" asked Calvin.

"Yep. That's it for this one. The next one is just as short. 'Dear Angela, by the time you get this letter, I'll be long gone.'"

Crap.

"Who's Angela?" asked Calvin.

"If I'm not mistaken, Angela is the name of Jim's ex-wife." I opened another crinkled paper. "'Angela, I hate to leave so suddenly, but I don't have much time. I need to catch up with Felix.'"

Catch up with Felix? Shaking my head, I reached for the last piece of paper. Calvin, meanwhile, had overturned the trash can and was now shaking it vigorously.

"For someone in a hurry, Jim sure took his time to get his letter right," I said. "Listen to this one. 'Angela, I have a once in a lifetime opportunity. I can't explain now. But when Felix dropped by to borrow my folding shovel, and said he was leaving right away, I knew he'd finally found it.'"

Calvin came over and plucked the letter from the table. Pushing his glasses to the top of his head, he peered closely at the paper, as if there might be more to find beyond the few short sentences I'd read.

"Geocaching," I said, with a note of disgust. "That's what this is all about. Felix was bitten by the geocaching bug, and apparently it got Jim too." I looked over my shoulder at the overturned trash can. "Was there anything else in there?"

"Just a broken pen and a receipt from Bread n' Butter Bakery," he said, handing me the receipt. "It's for coffee and a muffin, on Saturday at twelve ten p.m."

"Saturday! He was here on Saturday? Wait, twelve ten—that's about the time I was out buying cookies for my workshop. I can't believe I missed him."

"Are you sure Jim's the one who tossed all these things?"

"Has to be. To confirm, I'll ask Flo, but I've no doubt it was Jim."

Calvin flipped through the letters, then put both hands on the table and gave me an earnest look. "*Now* will you tell me where Felix went?"

"I can't," I said. "Because I don't know. He didn't tell me. He took a trip and planned to be gone a long time. That's all I know."

Calvin stared at me for a moment, apparently trying to decide if I was telling the truth.

"Actually," I said, "there is something else I know."

"What?"

"I know this business is in trouble."

Chapter 10

Richard and Deena were already sipping chai lattes and nibbling on butter cookies when I joined them at Tea for You. They made a smart pair: Richard in the light blue dress shirt, pressed trousers, and skinny tie he'd worn at the bank, and Deena in the ruffled blouse, pleated skirt, and high heels she'd worn for no apparent reason. As usual, I wore jeans and comfortable boots. At least my top, a dark-pink, fitted sweater, was one of my newer ones. I had no regrets.

After ordering a ginger tea at the counter, I slipped into the chair next to Deena and across from Richard. "Howdy, gang. What did I miss?"

"Richard was just asking me about Chicago," said Deena. "I think he'd like it there, but he's skeptical."

"I'm sure I'd love the museums and the shows, but I'm a country boy at heart," said Richard, passing me the plate of cookies. "Maybe I'll give it a try sometime—maybe sooner than later, the way people are talking. I'll have to go someplace when the villagers run me out of town on a rail. We all will."

"What do you mean?" I asked. "What did you hear at Nell's?"

"Not much. Just that Abe was poisoned at Flower House and one of us did it."

Deena's hand flew to her chest. "One of us three?"

"One of us seven," said Richard. "Though, some people figure Felix did it, and that's why he skipped town."

"Felix left *before* Abe died," I pointed out.

"People don't know what they're talking about," said Richard, with a wave of his hand. "I've decided not to pay attention to gossip anymore."

"Good luck," said Deena.

Richard turned to me. "Have the police been back to Flower House since yesterday morning?"

"No. But I did learn something interesting about Abe. Besides owning a garden center, he was a member of the town zoning board."

"I already knew that," said Richard. "I read the newspaper."

"Did you know he used his position to benefit himself?" I shared what Letty had relayed—that Abe was known to withhold his zoning approval if he didn't like the applicant. Without naming Valerie, I also mentioned that I'd heard Abe would sometimes ask for special favors.

"That doesn't surprise me," said Richard. "That man was a slime ball."

"Do tell," said Deena, leaning forward.

Richard finished chewing his cookie before answering. "I just mean he was unpleasant. I never actually interacted with him myself. But you saw how he was at the workshop. Disagreeable for no reason."

Deena sipped her latte thoughtfully. "I can't believe what happened was simply someone's reaction to Abe's disagreeableness."

"Same here," I said. "The murder had to be premeditated. I've been trying to figure out where the powdered sugar came from." I told Deena about the white substance

Richard and I had found, which the chief's people had tested. "Which treat was it on?" I asked, rhetorically.

"It wasn't on any of them," said Deena.

"How can you be sure?" I asked.

"Simple. I felt bad for showing up empty-handed. I looked at that table of snacks and counted them. Then I counted the number of attendees, to figure out if I was the only one who hadn't brought anything."

"Aw, you poor thing," said Richard, reaching over to pat Deena's hand. "That's precious."

She made a face at him. "I know it's silly, but etiquette is important to me. Anyway, I remember for certain that nothing was sprinkled with powdered sugar. If there had been, I would have made a point to avoid it to make sure none spilled on my dress."

"Powdered sugar is messy," Richard agreed with a nod.

I thought about what this meant. "So, the killer was carrying the powder somehow, and applied it directly to Abe's food. How were they so sneaky?"

"Or bold," added Deena.

Richard tapped his spoon on the table absentmindedly. "What I want to know is what are the police doing? I don't know about you ladies, but I don't particularly relish being a murder suspect. People at the bank are looking at me funny, and my handyman business is taking a hit. Two customers cancelled on me in one day."

I gave him a sympathetic look. "Business at Flower House is suffering too."

"Doesn't your dad know Chief Walden?" asked Richard.

"Yeah. But as of yesterday, they hadn't spoken. I'm sure the chief is busy. He's probably looking into Abe's background."

"I wonder what will happen to his garden center," mused Deena. "Did he have any family?"

"I don't know," I answered. "He had employees, though."

I hadn't been to Abe's garden center in ages. In fact, the last time I could remember going there was when I was a teenager, helping my parents pick up landscaping supplies. As I thought about it, another memory popped into my mind.

"Richard, didn't your mom work at the garden center, years ago?"

He nodded. "Yes. Part-time. Before she got sick."

We all fell silent, and I felt like a heel. It had been over a year since his mother had passed away, but that didn't mean it wasn't still a sensitive subject. The last months of her life were especially hard on Richard, as he was her sole caretaker. As I recalled, he'd started doing handyman work shortly after her death. He needed the extra money to pay off her medical debts.

Deena changed the subject, and we finished our tea. A short time later we said goodbye, promising to keep one another posted if we learned anything about the investigation. Richard walked back to the bank where he'd left his car, and Deena and I headed to our cars along the curb.

"Was it wrong of me to bring up Richard's mother?" I asked. "I hope I didn't upset him."

"I don't think so," she said. "People usually like to remember their loved ones and appreciate it when others do too. He may have felt sad, but you didn't do anything wrong."

I stopped at my orange Fiat. "This is me," I said. "Hey, let's exchange numbers so we can keep in touch."

"Alright." She took her cell phone from her purse and handed it to me so I could input my number.

"You know," I said, as I returned her phone, "something Richard said struck me as a little odd."

"What's that?"

"He said he'd never had any interaction with Abe. And, I don't know, that just seems unlikely in a town this size. Especially since his mother had worked for Abe. I swear I even remember him mentioning going to his mom's work-place back in the day. Don't you?"

Deena appeared doubtful. "Yeah, maybe. But that doesn't mean he would have talked to Abe, necessarily. I'm not sure what he said was that unusual."

"You're probably right. Never mind."

I got into my car and waved at her as I drove away. All this murder talk was making me paranoid. I was seeing evasions and deceptions where there were none. I needed to get a grip and stop being so suspicious.

After picking up Gus from Flower House, I went home to my little cottage and settled in for the night. I prac-ticed my guitar, did a load of laundry, and made myself some pasta for dinner. Sitting at the kitchen table, with Gus hovering at my feet hoping for a crumb, I flipped open my vision journal. Just for kicks, I paged back to the beginning.

This was going to be the year, I thought. *My year.* I was going to save money, get my act together, and make things happen. One of my biggest goals, I noted, was to "embark on a fulfilling new career."

"I guess I should have been more specific," I said rue-fully. "Taking on sole responsibility for Flower House was not exactly what I had in mind."

Gus barked in reply.

"And get this," I said with a laugh. "I wrote down a goal to 'meet an exciting new man.' And who have I met? Nerdy Calvin Foxheart."

Gus jumped up, placing his front paws on my knees. I scratched the top of his head. "I know," I said. "Calvin has been good to you. And I don't have anything against nerds, per se. Maybe I'm a nerd too. He's just so goofy."

I closed my journal and pulled my laptop across the table. My plan was to search Calvin's name, but I stopped myself. *Why am I thinking about him, anyway? I have more important things to worry about.* Instead of typing Calvin's name, I typed *Abe Ranker Aerieville.*

A list of search results filled the screen. I skimmed them, then clicked on the website for Ranker's Garden Center. It didn't take long for me to realize it wasn't exactly the small business I'd thought it was. Evidently it was part of a franchise. I wasn't sure how franchises worked, but presumably the business wouldn't close. Maybe the parent corporation would keep it running.

Next, I clicked on the website for the Town of Aerieville and read about the Zoning Board of Appeals. There were five members, three elected and two appointed by the mayor, all of whom served two-year terms with no term limits. They hadn't updated the page yet; Abe was still listed as one of the members. Apparently, he was the longest-serving member, having been appointed by the mayor twelve years ago, then reappointed every two years. The job was voluntary, I learned. Maybe that was why he was reappointed so many times. Probably not many people would be willing or able to put in the time for free.

I grabbed a notepad and jotted down the names of the other four zoning board members. One of the names I recognized as a neighbor of my parents. I wasn't sure what I was going to do with the information. It might be interesting to talk to them and get their impressions of Abe. I wondered if they would attend his funeral.

Clicking back to the search results, I opened on a link

to the Feder Family Funeral Home. The memorial service was scheduled for Wednesday evening, with the funeral and burial the following morning. I opened Abe's obituary and read that he was survived by a sister and some nieces and nephews in Florida, and a stepson in California. He was preceded in death by his parents, a brother, and a wife of fourteen years. Reading this last part gave me a twinge of sympathy for old Abe. Maybe it was those losses that turned him into such a curmudgeon.

I scrolled down to the comments section to see if anyone had left any messages of condolence. There were more than I expected, maybe ten or twelve. Most were pretty generic, including brief notes from the "Garden Center family" and the mayor, plus one from one of the zoning board members. There were at least two from church-related organizations. The rest were short messages from names I didn't recognize. I skimmed them, half wondering if anyone would allude to the circumstances of his death or say anything about seeking justice. That probably wouldn't be appropriate. Then again, propriety didn't always seem to apply when it came to public comments on the Internet.

I scrolled to the end and almost clicked out of the page when I read the very last message, and froze. I had to read it twice more to be sure I'd read it right. It started out innocuous enough, but then took a decidedly dark turn.

Abraham,

Gone but not forgotten. Thinking of you with sorrow and remembrance. Where you caused pain, you called forth your end. You reaped what you sowed. You shall suffer no more than what you rightly deserve, eternal flames your reward. Proverbs 11:21

The poster was "Anonymous" and the message was unsigned. I quickly opened a new webpage and looked up the Bible verse: *"Assuredly, the evil man will not go unpunished, but the descendants of the righteous will be delivered."*

Goose bumps prickled along my arms. Was this a message from Abe's killer?

Chapter 11

The next morning, I awoke before dawn with the nagging feeling I had forgotten to do something. I took Gus out, then gave him some fresh food and water before hopping in the shower. It wasn't until I poured myself some coffee and a bowl of cereal that I remembered: I'd forgotten to check for online flower orders the night before. Come to think of it, I'd also neglected to call Byron—though, I was sure he'd soon be calling me to get my answer to Felix's offer. If I had any sense, I'd take a hard pass. The thing was, I wasn't ready to make a final decision yet. Because where would that leave me? Back to work at Dumbbells, that's where. And with a store full of dead and dying flowers—not to mention a homeless Calvin—on my conscience.

Dressed in army green cargo pants and a pale pink blouse (my version of serious work clothes), I jangled Gus's leash by the door. He came running, always ready for adventure.

"Alright, Augustus. Let's see what this day will bring."

The sun was just breaking over the mountains as I made the drive to Flower House. All was quiet and peaceful on sleepy old Oak Street. I imagined Bill and Flo were probably in the kitchen at Bread n' Butter, whipping up pastries, muffins, and rolls. I'd have to drop in on them later.

I let myself in the front door of the flower shop and flipped on the light in the foyer. Before I had a chance to unhook Gus's leash, he stiffened beside me and let loose a low, rumbling growl.

"What's the matter, buddy?"

All of a sudden, he lurched forward, pulling me with him. He made a beeline for the events room—where a male voice called out.

"Keep him out of here!"

"Calvin?" I tightened my grip on Gus's leash, as he led the way through the open gate. Then I gasped. The room was a wreck.

Tables and chairs were overturned. Catalogs, garden magazines, miscellaneous supplies and books—everything that was once on a counter or shelf—was now strewn all over the floor. Flowerpots were tipped over, adding dirt and leaves to the mess. And, worst of all, the bakery case was on its side, its glass front shattered.

Incredulous, my eyes roved over the disarray, falling at last upon Calvin, wearing striped pajamas and moccasin slippers, sitting as calm as a Buddha statue in the midst of it all. He held an open book in one hand.

"What did you *do*?" I exclaimed, spouting the first thing that came to mind.

"Me? I didn't do this. I found it this way."

"What? When?" I was so confused.

Still holding the book (which seemed to be something about Tennessee trees and shrubs), he carefully pushed himself to his feet. "About half an hour ago. A loud noise woke me up. I thought it was something outside, like a garbage truck maybe. But then I remembered what you said about bears, and I figured I better investigate. And it's a good thing too. I found the back door standing open."

"Are you saying a *bear* did this?"

"Huh? No. Somebody broke in—somebody human, I'm pretty sure. But I'm glad I got the door closed before any bears could get any ideas, you know?"

"Did you call the police?"

"Not yet. I was looking around first. I don't think anything was stolen."

I rubbed my temple to ward off an impending headache. I had so many questions . . . like, how would Calvin know if anything had been stolen? And what was he thinking trampling all over a crime scene? And did he really not hear sounds of destruction *inside* the house?

And, was he actually reading that book about trees—which he now seemed to be flipping through, cover to cover?

"What are you *doing*?" I asked.

He looked up at me and gave an embarrassed laugh. "Looking for clues?" Setting the book down, he tried to step over a chair lying on its side—and tripped, falling right into me.

"Jeez!" I yelled, falling backward.

Gus let out a loud string of excited barks. Whether he was defending me or trying to join in the fun, I couldn't say.

"I'm sorry!" panted Calvin. He steadied himself on the wall then grabbed my hand to pull me to my feet. "Are you okay?"

"I'm fine," I said, through clenched teeth. I handed him the leash. "Here. Take Gus outside, please. I'm calling the police."

Calvin looked down at his pajamas, then shrugged and took Gus out the front door. I pulled out my cell phone and made the call. While waiting for the cops, I walked through the shop to see for myself if anything else was damaged. From the looks of it, the cash register was undisturbed, as was Felix's office. (It still didn't feel natural to call it *my* office.) I noticed Calvin had moved things off the floor and raised a lamp cord out of a curious puppy's reach, but that was all that was out of place. The orchid room, the bathroom, and the kitchen were similarly devoid of clues—except for the busted lock on the back door. Someone had pried the strike plate right out of the door-jamb.

"Dang," I muttered.

Turning around, I scanned the floor, hoping to spot a muddy footprint or dropped business card. No such luck. My eyes fell upon the closed door to the cellar. I hadn't been down there in ages. As I recalled, it was unfinished, with a cracked concrete floor and crumbly stone walls. Felix had used the basement as a woodshop at one time. There were probably still tools down there, along with old flower shop paraphernalia, a monster of a boiler, cobwebs, and who knew what else. I had my hand on the knob when a loud banging made me jump.

I hurried to the front door and admitted two police officers: Officer Dakin, a young male cop I recognized from the night of Abe's death, and an older female officer who introduced herself as Officer Bradley. Her yellow blonde hair was pulled back in a short, tight ponytail, and her demeanor was blunt but courteous.

"You called about a break-in?" she said.

"Yes, unfortunately." I showed them the mess in the events room and told them what I knew. They looked around, paying special attention to the busted bakery case with the aid of a flashlight.

"I don't see any prints," Bradley said. "Whoever did this either wore gloves or wiped it clean afterward."

She sent Dakin outside to interview Calvin, then took a walk through the shop and inspected the back door. After again checking for prints, she confirmed what I'd already deduced: somebody had used a tool, probably a screw-driver or crowbar, to bust the door open.

"Do you think it was a pro?" I asked. "Somebody who's done this before?"

"Not necessarily," she said. "Anybody could have seen that this wood was old and soft and figured out how to bust through it."

"But *why*? It's not like we're a jeweler or a cell phone store. They didn't even touch any of the expensive orchids."

"Looks like the purpose was vandalism," said Officer Bradley.

I thought about this and wasn't at all satisfied. There had to be a reason behind the act.

"What's in *there*?" the officer asked, pointing at the basement door.

"Oh, yeah," I said, opening the door. "I was hoping you'd take a peek at the cellar."

I followed her down the creaky, wooden stairs and found the basement just as dank and dirty as I'd remem-bered. She shined her light in all the corners. Thankfully, there were no signs of any intruders.

A few minutes later, Bradley and Dakin reconvened in the front of the shop and began filling out paperwork. I leaned on the checkout counter, wishing that Felix were here to take care of things.

Bradley looked up from her report form. "You're sure nothing was taken?"

"Yes," I said. "There was no money to steal anyway."

"What about flowers?" said Dakin. "Would you know if any flowers were missing?"

"Oh, yeah," said Bradley, as if this reminded her of something.

I glanced at the buckets of cut flowers, noting a few more had brown petals. "I suppose I might not notice if one or two stems were gone," I said. "But I don't think that's the case. It looks to me like the intruder was more interested in making a mess than stealing flowers."

"What about any black ones?" Dakin pressed. "Do you carry any black flowers?"

"Black roses, in particular," Bradley added.

I looked from one to the other of them, wondering if they might be joking. They seemed perfectly serious. "Uh, not at the moment. Occasionally, a customer might ask about black roses for a fortieth birthday gag gift, and we'll place a special order. And we might stock some around Halloween. But we don't have any now. Why?"

The two officers glanced at each other, and Dakin shrugged.

"The timing isn't right anyway," said Bradley. "That lady filed the harassment report yesterday, and this B and E happened this morning." She turned to me and smiled. "Never mind. We thought there might be a connection here with another case, but it's just a coincidence."

Dakin took another look around the events room, while Bradley finished up her report and handed me her business card.

"We'll question the neighbors before we leave. Give us a call if anything turns up missing. And be sure to get the door fixed."

"Right. The door." The responsibilities just kept piling up.

As the officers were leaving, Calvin and Gus walked across the front yard. At the same time, an old Subaru Outback pulled up to the curb, and I broke into a relieved grin. It was Granny!

Granny Mae bustled up the sidewalk, laden with bags on each wrist and a pail of herbs and wildflowers under one arm. Leave it to Granny to bring flowers to a flower shop. I rushed down to meet her.

"Granny Mae! What a surprise."

"I came as soon as I could," she said, handing me the pail. "And not a moment too soon, I see."

The officers nodded at Granny, and I shuffled her to the front door with Calvin and Gus at her heels. Once inside, she set down her bags and pulled out a piece of chicken, which she gave to Gus.

Calvin hovered nearby. "This is your grandma? Nice to meet you, ma'am. I'm Calvin Foxheart."

"Any friend of Sierra's is a friend of mine," she said, handing him a sandwich wrapped in cellophane.

"He's not—" I began, then shut my mouth. I didn't want to be rude for no reason. "What do you mean you came as soon as you could?"

"My maw always said, 'A dream out of season means trouble out of reason.' And I had a dream last night where it was snowin' and icin' like the dead of winter. You were there, stuck in a drift. I knew it meant trouble." She peered through the archway into the events room. "Now, what happened in here?"

"We had a break-in, Granny. I haven't had a chance to clean it up."

Granny looked up at the ceiling and toward the front windows. "I see you hung the basil. Did you sprinkle the ditchwater?"

"Yes. Well, a little, anyway."

Granny removed her jacket and rolled up her sleeves. "Fetch me a broom, will you?"

For the next hour or so, the three of us worked to put the events room back together. I looped the end of Gus's leash to a window latch to keep him safely out of the way, and gave him a bone to chew on. Calvin and I turned up the furniture, while Granny dusted, vacuumed, and swept, muttering prayers as she went.

Once the tables and chairs were back in place and the cracked bakery case upright, Calvin gathered up the scattered books and papers, rifling through them as he went. I picked up a collection of metal vases and replaced them on the shelf they'd been knocked from.

Why would anybody wreck this room? I wondered. Could it be someone upset over Abe's death, wanting to get back at Flower House?

Something on the floor next to the baseboard caught my eye. I crouched down to get a better look and saw that it was a brown button, about a quarter of an inch in diameter. I picked it up and turned it over in my fingers. It could have been here forever. It could have been lost by anyone. But I had never noticed it before, and I'd just cleaned in here with Richard two days ago. Could it have been dropped by the intruder?

I glanced at Calvin. His pajama top had brown buttons, but none were missing that I could see. As if sensing my gaze, he looked up, and we locked eyes. I gave him a brief smile and looked away, pocketing the button.

The next moment a crash sounded behind me, and I whirled around. The shelf had fallen off the wall, dropping all the metal vases to the floor.

Gus barked and Granny came running over. "Land sakes!" she said. "What happened now?"

"I don't know," I said. "Maybe the burglar shook it loose and the screws just now decided to give in."

Still barking, Gus pulled his leash free and bounded over. Calvin scooped him up and took him out of the room.

Granny narrowed her eyes. "It's been said that dogs and cats won't go into a room where spirits and ghosts are present. Little Gus feels something here."

"He barks at everything, Granny."

She surveyed the room, including the broken shelf. "This is where it happened, isn't it? Where Abe was murdered?"

"Well, yes. But—"

"That's why you're having all these problems. His spirit is not at rest."

I tried to smile, portraying a confidence I didn't really feel. "It wasn't a spirit that broke the door."

"I don't care," she said, stubborn as always. "This place is goin' to be a magnet for trouble until that man's spirit finds peace."

I knew there was no point in arguing. "His funeral is tomorrow. Maybe that'll do the trick."

"Good," she said, nodding. "Here's what you have to do. Find something that belonged to Abe, something small. Place it in a hollowed-out tater and pin it shut. Take it to the cemetery at midnight tomorrow and bury it next to Abe's grave. That'll help draw his spirit where it should be and keep it out of here."

I stared at her for a beat before responding.

"Oh, is that all?"

Before Granny left, she made Calvin find a ladder and hang more basil above the entry to the events room. In return, she gave him an acorn for good luck. With my help, she also moved the fallen vases to a table in the front window and used them to display the wildflowers she'd brought—bloodroot and dogwood blossoms, both white-petaled flowers that symbolized protection to the early Native Americans of our area. She left us with chicken sandwiches, a container of potato salad, and a jar of molasses-sweetened Spicewood tea, then set off to "look in on your mama" at Dumbbells.

"Your granny is awesome," said Calvin, as soon as she'd gone.

"Yeah, she's somethin' else," I agreed.

He eyed the jar of tea, where bits of twigs had settled

on the bottom. "You sure this isn't more of her ditchwater?"

I chuckled. "Fair question. But, no. Those are spicebush sticks. Spicewood tea is one of Granny's favorite spring tonics. It's good for what ails you."

"If you say so," he said doubtfully. "Maybe I'll try it later. Gotta get dressed now." He grabbed another sandwich and headed upstairs.

After putting the rest of the food in the fridge, I sent Richard a text, asking if he could come by and fix the back door. Luckily, he got right back to me and said he could. He had a toolbox in his car and would come straight from work this afternoon. In the meantime, I went into the office and, with Gus at my side, sat at the computer to check for online orders.

There was only one, an order for a simple spring bouquet. I made a sour face when I saw who had placed the order: Nell Cusley, of Nell's Diner.

"How do you like that?" I said to Gus. "What do you want to bet Nell just wants to pump me for gossip?" I decided I'd ask Calvin to make the delivery.

I turned back to the computer and began poking around Felix's files. There wasn't a whole lot to see, since Byron did the bookkeeping. But I did come across an employee contact list that went back for more than a decade. I skimmed through the names. It looked like Felix cycled through part-timers at a fairly rapid pace. He'd hired Francie for the first time when I left for Nashville after high school, but he let her go when business slowed down, only to rehire her again later. During the busy seasons—around Valentine's Day and Mother's Day especially—he took on extra help. I recognized a few names here and there, including Letty Maron's son, Trent, who worked here one spring while I was away. *So, that's his name. Trent, not Troy or Trey.*

Not surprisingly, Jim Lomack's name was constant on the roster from the very beginning. I clicked on his file and noted the name of his emergency contact: Angela Lomack. I jotted down her number, thinking I'd give her a call later. I was curious to know what Jim's final letter said, if he ever did finish it, and whether or not he planned to come back.

I clicked out of the employee list and opened the inventory file. There was a calendar noting the standing orders for supplies we received weekly, as well as a list of routine orders for special holidays. Mother's Day was less than a month away, I noted. In fact, we should be getting orders already. I really needed to decide if we were staying open or not.

Another file contained ads Felix had placed in various newspapers and bulletins. In a stroke of inspiration, I realized that was what I ought to do. I needed to run a clearance sale. Whether we stayed open or not, there was inventory that needed to move.

I set to work mocking up an ad for discount flowers. As I worked, my mind wandered to the strange condolence message I'd come across the night before. Was it really as sinister as I'd imagined? To find out, I opened a browser and pulled up the website again. *Yep. It's just as sinister.*

Using my cell phone, I snapped a picture of the computer screen and forwarded it to Deena, with a short note: *Check it out. This is weird, right?*

A minute later, she replied with one word: *Creepy.*

I was about to text her again, when I received a message from Richard. He'd left work early and was on his way to Flower House. I hopped up and took Gus outside, then relegated him to the events room once more with toys and treats. He didn't protest, so I took that to mean there were no spirits to speak of.

Even though Granny, Calvin, and I had given the room a thorough cleaning, I walked through again, just to triple check that we'd missed no shards of glass. Gus helped, making sure no corner went unsniffed. I had my back to him while I was scrutinizing the floor. When I turned around, I found that he had something in his mouth. It appeared to be made of cloth.

"Whatcha got there, buddy?" I reached for the object, but he was too fast. He ran a few steps away, then stopped to look back at me.

"Oh, it's a game, is it? Alrighty, then." I chased him around the room, until I finally cornered him beside the gate. With a handful of treats, I finally managed to get him to drop his prize. It turned out to be one of Granny's flannel herb bags.

"Oh, jeez," I said. "Who knows what was in there?" Fortunately, the drawstring was pulled tight and the bag was flat. It must have fallen from one of Granny's many satchels. Leaving Gus in the events room, I found my purse where I'd left it by the cash register and stuck the herb bag in a side pocket. I'd return it to Granny next time I saw her.

The front door opened then, and Richard let himself in. "Is it safe?" he said, peeking into the events room. "This place is becoming crime central."

"Tell me about it."

I led Richard to the kitchen workroom. He followed, taking in everything with blatant curiosity. In the kitchen, he ran his hand over the counter, and opened and closed some of the cabinets. "Is this the original cabinetry?" he asked.

"I don't know. Probably. But check out the door. Can it be fixed?"

"Everything is fixable." He pulled the door open and

examined the damage. "No problem. I just need a new piece of wood."

"There might be some scraps in the basement."

Richard found what he needed and set about repairing the door, while I made Nell's bouquet.

"Did you see Abe's obituary?" I asked. "The memorial service is tonight."

"Is that so?"

"Yeah. I was thinking of going. Want to come along?"

He made a face like he'd swallowed spoiled milk. "No, thanks. Why do you want to go? You hardly knew him."

"I just thought it might be interesting, you know? A chance to learn more about Abe—and get some insight into who might have wanted him dead."

"Well, look at you, Miss Nancy Drew. Are you really going to play detective on this case?"

"Why not? You said yourself the whole town thinks we're suspects. Don't you want to solve this thing?"

"I want it solved, yes. But not by me."

He was being sensible, of course. But I still wasn't convinced the Aerieville police force was making any progress.

I put the finishing touches on the bouquet, as my mind continued to ponder the Abe situation. "Hey," I said, remembering something. "Who told you Abe had been receiving death threats?"

Richard didn't answer right away. "I don't recall."

"What? Come on."

"I wasn't supposed to say anything." He closed the door and tried out the new lock, turning the latch back and forth. "But if you think about it, I'm sure you can come up with a name. Who's the one person in this town who always has the inside scoop?"

"Nell?"

"Bingo."

I looked at the flower arrangement and wondered at the coincidence. *Guess I'll be making this flower delivery myself after all.*

It was as if the Universe wanted me to.

Chapter 12

Nell's Diner was a 1950s-era eatery, complete with vintage Coca-Cola signs and red vinyl booths that ran the length of the small prefab building. Matching vinyl-covered stools lined the long sit-down counter facing the kitchen. Officially, the restaurant was open for breakfast and lunch only, but its hours were loose. When I arrived at three fifty, there was no indication that closing time was in ten minutes. Two older gentlemen sat in one of the booths, playing checkers and nursing coffees. A teenage girl sat in another booth poring over homework and swigging soda. As soon as I entered the place, Nell herself came out from behind the counter and greeted me like a long-lost friend.

"There's my flowers! I was wondering if they would come today. Folks are saying Flower House is closed, but the website didn't say so." She wiped her hands on the apron straining across her ample midsection.

"We're partly open," I said, handing her the flowers. "Things are kind of in a state of limbo right now."

"Well, of course they are! Sit down and take a load off, why don't you? Have some pie and coffee, on the house."

I looked at the pie case sitting on top of the counter. "Is that banana cream?"

"You bet it is." She returned to her place behind the counter and set the flowers down. Then she grabbed the coffee carafe and poured me a cup. "Cream and sugar?"

"Yes, please." I sat down at the counter. "I don't want to keep you, though. I know it's almost closing time."

"Never mind that. Those old coots don't like it when I kick them out anyway."

"We heard that," called one of the old men, without looking up.

Laughing heartily, Nell set down a piece of pie in front of me. "Felix back yet?"

I considered my words carefully before answering. *Give a little, get a little,* I decided. "Felix took an extended retirement trip. He was already well on his way when Abe passed, otherwise I'm sure he would've come back."

"Of course, he would've. And where exactly did he go?"

"Oh, you know Felix. He's on one of his geocaching adventures out West." *Probably.*

"Is that so? He left rather suddenly, didn't he? What about Flower House?"

"It wasn't that sudden. It was in the works for a while." *This must be true,* I rationalized. *After all, he told me he'd been waiting for the call he received.* "As for the shop," I continued, "he gave Byron instructions and left me in charge. I'm holding down the fort for now. I don't want to make any major decisions until Abe's death is resolved." *Sure. That sounds good.*

"That's wise," said Nell, nodding sagely. "It's a puzzler, alright. Abe was arranging flowers, when he up and died?"

I took a bite of pie before answering. I needed to start asking some questions of my own.

"No," I finally said. "We were pretty much done with our flower arrangements and had taken a snack break. Say, did you hear anything about Abe receiving death threats?"

"Why, did he mention it?" she asked.

"No, not to me. I heard about it later. I was just wondering. Where did you hear it from?"

"I couldn't say. I expect it was common knowledge." She lifted the carafe. "More coffee?"

"No, thanks. I don't want to be up all night." I put my hand over my cup. "I coulda sworn somebody told me they heard it here."

"That's not surprising. Folks like to talk here."

"Hm. I just wish I knew what the threats said exactly."

"What they said?" Nell wrinkled her forehead. Evidently, I'd stumped her.

One of the old men snickered behind me. "Miss Nell's big ears have their limits," he said.

"Mind your business," Nell snapped, "before I toss you out on *your* big ears."

"I don't understand," I said, looking from Nell to the old man.

"Nell gets most of her information secondhand," he explained. "Or second *ear*, I should say."

Ah. Now I get it. Nell was an eavesdropper.

"I remember now," she said, without a trace of embarrassment. "There was a clerk from the police department in here for lunch one day last week. She must have mentioned the death threats—loud enough for all to hear, I'm sure."

"Sure," I said, disappointed. So much for getting any useful information from Nell. At least the pie was good. I polished off my slice and took another sip of coffee.

Nell took a rag and wiped down the counter. "I could

tell something was bothering Abe," she said. "He seemed worried last time he was in here."

"When was that?" I asked.

"Must've been last Tuesday or Wednesday, two or three days before he was killed. He was having lunch with Valerie."

I snapped to attention at that. "Valerie Light? Are you sure?"

Nell chuckled. "There's no mistaking Valerie Light. How many other leggy African-American ballet teachers live in this town?"

I frowned. Valerie had told me she hadn't gone out with Abe in years. As much as she disliked the man, why would she be having lunch with him? Part of me wanted to ask Nell if they seemed to be arguing, but I realized how that might sound. The last thing I wanted to do was to appear like I was accusing anyone of anything. All this gossiping was leaving a bad taste in my mouth.

"They had their heads together," Nell volunteered. "And they were kind of whispering. Hard to tell what they might've been discussing, but Abe sure looked worried, like I said. Makes you wonder."

My cell phone rang, and I fished it from my purse. It was Calvin.

"Sierra, can you come back to the shop soon?" There was a note of urgency to his voice.

"Yeah, I can be there in ten. What's up?"

"Well, we've had a string of customers ordering flowers for a memorial service tonight. Deena and I are doing our best trying to fill the orders, but it turns out it's a lot harder than I thought it would be."

"Deena's there?" I stood up, shouldering my purse. "Wait—did you say *you're* arranging flowers?"

"I'd say 'trying' is the operative word," he said. "You

know, you should really have gloves back here. I've already pricked myself twice."

"I'm on my way."

I dropped my phone back into my purse and thanked Nell for the pie and coffee as I headed to the door.

Nell had been watching me closely. "Everything okay?"

"It's great," I said. "We have customers!"

Calvin and Gus both ran up to greet me when I came through the front door at Flower House, Gus's nails clicking happily on the porcelain floor. "Thank goodness you're back," said Calvin, handing me several slips of paper. "I found a price list under the counter, but I didn't know how to operate the credit card machine or the cash register, so I took checks from two people and IOUs from the others."

"IOUs?" *Good grief.* Luckily, it was a small town. Sorting through the papers, I recognized all the names, including Flo's from next door.

I put the checks and notes in the cash register, then trailed Calvin back to the kitchen. He tied Gus's leash to the knob of the door leading upstairs and left the kitchen door open. This way Gus could sit in the hallway and still keep an eye on what was happening in the kitchen.

"He likes to see where we are," Calvin said, as I scratched Gus behind the ears.

"I can't blame him," I said. "Corgis are herding dogs, aren't they? He wants to know where his pack is."

"What do you think?" asked Deena, gesturing to a large bouquet of lilies and roses in the center of the work-table. "I followed the instructions you gave us in class the other night."

"It's beautiful," I said, turning the vase to view it from all sides. "Great job."

"Thank you." She beamed proudly.

"One of the customers asked for a standing wreath," said Calvin. "I was hoping you'd know what that means, 'cause I sure as heck don't."

"Not to worry," I said, opening a low cabinet next to the fridge. "You just have to start with one of these wire frames, some bendy twigs, and compact moss. We used to use floral foam, but it contains some nasty chemicals and isn't biodegradable. We've had to get creative."

"If you get it started, I can probably finish it," said Deena. "This is fun."

I put both Deena and Calvin to work as my assistants, and together we completed all of the arrangements in less than forty minutes—which was a good thing. Abe's memorial service was scheduled to begin at six. I had less than fifteen minutes to get them to the funeral home.

"Want me to help deliver these?" asked Calvin.

"Thanks, but I was gonna ask Deena if she'd come with me," I said. "I thought maybe we could pay our respects together."

Deena looked down at her dress, a navy blue wrap-around with purple flowers. "I suppose this will do," she said, smoothing the unwrinkled fabric.

"It's perfect," I said. "Better than what I've got on, but I don't have time to go home and change." I was just happy my pink blouse was still unstained and fairly wrinkle free.

Calvin helped us load up my Fiat and said he'd take Gus for a walk. With Deena at my side, I headed the car for the Feder Family Funeral Home.

"I'm so glad you were here to help," I said. "I meant to ask—how did you happen to drop by in the first place?"

"I couldn't stop thinking about that message you forwarded me, the supposed condolence." She pulled her phone from her purse and tapped open our text conversation. "This sentence in particular: *'You shall suffer no more than what you rightly deserve, eternal flames your reward.'"*

"I know, right? It totally implies Abe got what he deserved."

"It's so sneaky, though," she said. "I mean, I think of an eternal flame as a sort of memorial to honor a fallen hero. But 'eternal flames'—in this context—it sounds like the person is alluding to hellfire."

"It also said he reaped what he sowed, didn't it? It was definitely written by somebody who didn't think much of Abe—to put it mildly. Maybe even his murderer."

"Right. Richard or Letty or Bill or Flo or Valerie."

I braked at a stop sign and glanced over at Deena. She looked grim. "Or you or me," I said, trying to lighten the mood.

"I don't think it was you," she said. "You were with me during all the scuffling around the snack table."

"Gee, thanks," I said. "For what it's worth, I don't think it was you either. You're the only one who didn't bring a dish."

She gave me a sharp look, which I returned with a goofy grin. "Plus, you're a sweet, upstanding citizen who wouldn't hurt a fly," I added.

"Not to mention the fact that I barely knew Abe and certainly didn't know he would be at the workshop."

"Which, by the way, everyone else knew." I filled her in on what Valerie had told me, about seeing the flyer at Bread n' Butter that morning.

"Interesting," she said.

We arrived at the funeral home, and I pulled up to the side door. As we got out and walked to the rear of the car, Deena touched my arm. "Sierra, you still want to stay after dropping these off?"

"Well, yeah. That was the idea."

"To pay your respects?"

"Uh-huh," I said.

"And?"

I met her eyes. "And . . . maybe to do a little looking and listening too, you know? Maybe even pick up a clue or a lead."

"Good," she said, with a quick nod. "We're on the same page."

Margie Feder met us at the door and held it open while we brought the flowers inside. "Cutting it a little close, aren't you?" she said pointedly.

"I had some last-minute orders," I said. "I'm impressed we actually made it before folks started arriving."

"Some folks are here already," she said. "The family is anyway."

Deena and I exchanged a glance. "The family?" I echoed.

"Abraham's sister and nephew," Margie said with a nod toward the viewing room. "Her name is Bette Sampson, and her son's name is Cort."

Margie directed us to place the flowers on a table next to the open coffin, which was centered on a dais at the front of the room. I couldn't help glancing inside. As with other viewings I'd been to, the body in the coffin bore little resemblance to the former man. His frame seemed small in a loose brown suit, and his smooth, impassive face was unnaturally tan.

Deena and I made three trips to the car and back before returning to the viewing room as guests. I was nervous about speaking to Abe's sister, but I knew I had to do it. I nudged Deena to come with me and she nodded. We approached the woman and her son. She was in her fifties, with gray-blonde hair pulled back in a low bun, and he was in his early twenties, blond and stocky. They sat in straight-backed chairs at the end of the first row facing the coffin and didn't raise their bowed heads until we were standing in front of them—and I could see that they were both looking at their phones.

"Hello, Mrs. Sampson," I said quietly, holding out my hand. "I'm so sorry for your loss."

She covered her phone with one palm and looked up. "Thank you. It was a real shock." Her hand was cool, I noticed, and her grip loose.

Swallowing my nerves, I proceeded to introduce myself. "I'm Sierra Ravenswood. I work at the flower shop where Abe passed away. This is my friend, Deena."

Deena held out her hand. "I'm very sorry for your loss."

"Thank you," she repeated, shaking Deena's hand.

For a few seconds, we looked at each other without saying anything. Then Deena offered her hand to the young man, murmuring words of condolence.

"Thanks," he said.

I bit my lip, wondering at the sister's lack of interest in who I was or my connection to Abe. "So, you're from Florida?" I said. "Did you fly in yesterday?"

"We flew into Knoxville and rented a car this morning," she said. "We'll be heading back after the funeral tomorrow."

"Oh," I said, surprised. "That's, uh, a quick trip."

"Yes. I didn't want to miss a lot of work, and Cort is in school at Florida State. He's got finals next week. We'll come back after his summer break starts in a few weeks, you know, to sort through Abe's house and see what we can sell."

Cort scoffed quietly. "Can't think of a better way to spend my summer."

"It won't take all summer," Bette said to her son, in a tone that indicated they'd already had this conversation.

"Have you been to Aerieville before?" asked Deena.

Bette shook her head. "No. Abe and I weren't especially close. After our parents died, years ago, I used to invite him to Florida for the holidays, but he never came. Last time I saw him was at our brother's funeral two years ago." She sighed, turning her phone over in her hands. "You can only try so much with some people. We lived our separate lives. I just hope he had enough in assets to cover the cost of the funeral."

"I suppose—" I began, but stopped myself as other guests began filing to the front of the room. I was going to say something about the police investigation, but I thought better of it. Now wasn't the time.

Deena and I moved to the edge of the room and spoke in low voices.

"That wasn't as bad as I thought it would be," I said.

"She was a bit detached," Deena said. "This whole thing probably seems unreal to her."

"That's understandable."

The room began to fill up, with a line forming from back to front along the side. Deena and I decided to split up and quietly mingle and/or eavesdrop. *I'm turning into Nell*, I thought, with a twinge of guilt. All for a good cause, though. I maneuvered past chairs and people, nodding at an older lady who wore a badge that said Church Volunteer and murmuring quiet hellos to a couple of shop owners I recognized from around town. No one seemed inclined to strike up a conversation. I made my way to an adjacent room, where refreshments were laid out on a table. After helping myself to a glass of water, I strolled through the opposite door and wound up in the front hall, where I spotted Margie standing near the guest book.

"I didn't know you were still here," she said, as I approached her.

"Yep. I wanted to offer my condolences to the family."

"It's a nice turnout," she said, holding out a pen. "Sign the guest book?"

"Sure." I scribbled my name in the book, then glanced

at the other names. Bill and Flo Morrison were among the first to sign in, as well as some of the zoning board members.

I handed the pen back to Margie. "Speaking of condolences, who maintains the online condolences page on your website? Do you have a web administrator?"

"Debbie, our office clerk, posts the obituaries. Is that what you mean?"

"Does Debbie monitor the comments?"

"Monitor?"

"Hang on. I'll show you what I mean." I took out my phone and brought up the screen shot I'd sent to Deena.

Margie squinted at my phone. "I don't understand. What's the problem?"

"Did you read the whole thing?"

She peered at my phone again, her lips moving as she silently read the comment. "Oh," she said, as the words sank in. "Oh, dear."

"Is there any way of figuring out who left that comment?"

"Let's find out," she said, turning on her heels. I followed her down the hallway and into a room marked Private. It was a good-sized office, with two desks and several filing cabinets. Margie sat at one of the desks and shook the computer mouse.

"Debbie isn't here, but I think I can access the website builder."

I stood behind her and watched as, with a few clicks of the mouse, she brought up the back-office version of the funeral home's website. She scrolled down the comments until she came to the one we were looking for.

"There's an IP address," she said. "And, let's see. The stats page says it's from the Aerieville area. I can't get any more specific than that."

"Mind if I take a picture of the I.P. number?" I asked,

already opening the camera in my phone. Not that I'd know what to do with it.

"I guess not. But hurry up. I'm going to delete this comment. I don't think the family would appreciate it."

I snapped the picture and made sure it was clear before dropping my phone back into my purse. "Is there any way you can hide the comment without deleting it?"

"I don't think so."

"I'm just not sure you ought to delete it yet. It could be important. Don't you want to show it to the police?"

"I guess you're right, but it will have to wait." She pushed away from the desk and stood up. "I need to get back to the visitation and make sure the reverend is here. It's almost time for the prayer service."

As we exited the office, Chief Walden walked up the hallway. He gave me an inquisitive look, and I turned to Margie. "Here's your chance to talk to the cops."

"There's no time now," she said, looking at her watch. She split off from me and darted into the viewing room.

Chief Walden was still eyeing me, with a mixture of curiosity and disapproval. At least, that's the way it felt to me. I flashed him a polite smile and ducked into the ladies' room. Margie could fill him in when she had time. Somehow, I didn't think the chief would appreciate any assistance from me.

There was a woman standing at the sink in the powder room. On second glance, I saw that it was Letty Maron. She was scrubbing her hands so intently, she didn't notice me come in. From what I could tell, she seemed to be trying to remove a black stain from under her fingernails.

"Hi, Letty," I said.

She jumped, then laughed self-consciously. "Hello, Sierra. I didn't see you there. I, uh, did an art project with my students today, and this ink won't come out. It's so embarrassing."

"It's not that noticeable," I assured her.

"That's good." She turned off the water and grabbed a paper towel. "It gives me an excuse to get a manicure, anyway."

"That's the spirit." I shook my head after she left. *What a skittish lady.* Always so jumpy.

When I returned to the viewing room a few minutes later, the prayer service was underway. I stood in the back and subtly looked around the room. There were several familiar faces—including Chief Walden again. He stood against the wall and, like me, was also observing all the guests. His eyes locked on mine, and I quickly looked away. Why did that man make me feel so nervous?

Letty had taken a seat at the end of a row about half-way up. Bill and Flo were in the front row. I didn't see anyone else from my bouquet workshop, which wasn't a surprise. I didn't expect Richard or Valerie to be here.

All of a sudden, someone grabbed my arm, causing me to squeak. I turned to see Deena, her face a mask of concern.

"Sierra, can we go?" she hissed. "I have something to tell you."

Chapter 13

"Okay, let's go over this again," I said. "Tell me *exactly* what you heard."

The minute we left the Feder Family Funeral Home, Deena relayed a conversation she'd overheard between Bill and Flo Morrison. She was so worked up, I had a hard time making sense of what it all meant. I told her we'd probably both think better over a loaded pizza and a bottle of wine, so we called in an order for delivery. Then we picked up Gus and Deena's car from the flower shop, and she followed me home to the dollhouse.

"Your place is so cute!" she'd said, momentarily distracted from our purpose.

"Thanks," I said, opening a bottle of red wine. "It's the perfect size for now—not too much to clean." I poured two glasses of wine and handed her one, then filled Gus's food bowl.

Deena took a sip of the wine and read the notes I'd posted on my refrigerator. "'I am a creative soul.' 'I create my reality.' 'I am abundant.' What is all this?"

"Affirmations. You know, positive thinking?"

"Interesting. I didn't realize you were into this sort of thing. It's kind of woo-woo, isn't it?"

"Call it what you will; it works regardless." I cleared papers and books from my small, round kitchen table and pulled out a chair for Deena before taking a seat myself. "Haven't you heard the saying 'Energy flows where attention goes'?"

"I can't say that I have," she said, sitting down.

"Really? How about 'What you focus on grows'?"

"Is that a saying? I mean, I guess it makes sense."

It always kind of surprised me when people didn't appreciate the power of their own attention. I was a teenager when I first had this realization. I was at the library one day (as usual lifting books instead of weights), when I came across a self-help guide on positive thinking and the "law of attraction." It rang so true to me. Happier people attract more happiness. Miserable people attract more of the same. Everything depends on your perspective.

Gus had finished off his dog food and was now pawing at my legs for my attention. I got up to fill his water bowl. "Of course, it makes sense," I said. "I use affirmations as reminders of what I want to increase in my life. It helps direct my focus, which in turn brings energy to my goals."

I sat back down and smiled. "So, if we focus on this mystery, we'll open ourselves to more opportunities to pick up on clues and figure it all out."

She hugged her arms and shivered. "I thought I wanted to figure it out, but now I'm not sure I want to be involved."

"You're already involved," I pointed out. "Besides, you're the only one who heard what Bill and Flo said. That probably wasn't an accident."

"You mean they wanted me to overhear them?"

"No. I mean in a bigger sense. You were meant to receive that clue."

I could tell she wasn't convinced, but it didn't matter. The doorbell rang, signaling the arrival of our pizza.

I paid the deliveryman, while Deena found plates and napkins, then we resumed our places at the table. After we'd each had one slice of pizza and refilled our glasses, Deena was ready to repeat what she'd heard—this time more calmly.

"It was right after you left the viewing room," she said. "I started talking to a man named Vernon, who said he was a regular customer of Abe's garden center. He seemed nice. Said he just wanted to make an appearance and meet Abe's sister. I noticed Bill and Flo speaking to another couple, and I asked Vernon if he knew who they were. He said, yes, they were on the town's Zoning Board of Appeals."

"Was there something about their conversation that caught your attention?" I asked.

Deena nodded. "Yeah. Bill and Flo both seemed exceptionally pleased. Flo, especially, had this gleeful expression that seemed out of place, considering she was standing only a few feet away from Abe's dead body."

"Then what?"

"As I watched, Flo poked Bill and they excused themselves from the people they were talking to. I saw them slip into a side hall, which led to the other viewing room. After a minute, I left Vernon and followed them. The other viewing room was dark and empty, but Bill and Flo were in there, sitting in a pair of chairs beside a fireplace."

"I didn't see that room," I said.

"It was quite nice, sort of furnished like a living room, with upholstered furniture and end tables. Anyway, their backs were to the door, so I was able to sneak in without being seen. I crouched down behind a sofa to listen."

"Wow! That's so gutsy. I'm impressed."

"I didn't feel gutsy," Deena said, rubbing her knees. "I felt like I was doing something crazy—especially considering I was wearing a dress."

"What were they saying?"

"Flo said something like, 'We're so close. We're almost there.' Bill sounded like he was being more cautious. He said the zoning board was 'in the bag,' but there was more to do. He said Flower House needs to close."

"Those were his exact words? 'Flower House needs to close'?"

Deena nodded. "Flo kind of laughed and said that wouldn't be a problem."

I narrowed my eyes. "I don't like the sound of that."

"I didn't like the sound of any of it. After that, Flo said she was more worried about what they gave to Abe."

"What does that mean?"

"I have no idea. Whatever it was, Bill said it was probably still at Abe's house. He said the police wouldn't have thought anything of it. Flo said they could probably get it back tomorrow, while everyone is at the funeral."

"They're going to break into Abe's house?"

"Flo sounded like she wanted to, but Bill said no, it was too risky. He said they should talk to Mrs. Sampson and get her to let them in. They decided they'd offer to help her sort through Abe's things, so they could freely look for whatever it is they're after."

"Gosh, how sleazy is that? I had no idea the Morrisons were so deceitful."

"I was so scared at that point, I was shaking. They got up, and I thought for sure they'd see me. I had to crawl around the couch, so I'd be on the other side when they walked past. I must have stayed there on the floor for five minutes after they left, just frozen." She cupped her wine glass with both hands and took another sip. "I'm really not cut out for this sort of thing."

"You did great. This is fantastic information."

"But what does it mean? It doesn't prove anything."

"It proves Bill and Flo are up to something."

We lapsed into silence, nibbling on our pizza, each absorbed in our own thoughts. Gus was lying on the floor near our feet, attentive to our every move. It was as if he sensed our serious mood. Or maybe he was just waiting for one of us to drop a crumb of food. I broke off a tiny bit of crust and tossed it to him.

"I'm going to call Chief Walden," I finally said.

"Good," said Deena. "You can tell him what Bill and Flo said and let him figure out if it means anything."

"Right. I also want to make sure Margie Feder told him about the weird fake condolence."

I used my phone to look up the number of the Aerieville police station and placed the call. Unfortunately, Chief Walden wasn't available. I left a message, asking him to call me back, then set my phone next to my plate. Maybe he'd get back to me right away.

I took a peek into the pizza box. *Might as well finish it off.* As I doled out the last two slices, I asked Deena how much longer she thought she'd stay in town.

"I'm not supposed to leave while the investigation is pending, remember?" she said.

"Are you missing a lot of work or school in Chicago?"

She hesitated a moment, then sighed. "No. There's not really a deadline on my dissertation, and I told my advisor I'd be away for a while. And I don't have a job right now. Steve paid for everything. Our lease was in his name, so he may still be paying the rent for all I know, even though he moved out." She curled her lip in a snarl. "He moved in with another woman, the jerk."

"I'm sorry," I said. "I haven't had very good luck with men either."

She raised her eyebrows a smidge and waited for me to go on. I wavered for a moment. This was an embarrassing topic and a memory I didn't love to revisit. Still, Deena had opened up to me.

"His name was Josh," I finally said. "He was my flame in Nashville."

Deena reached for the wine bottle and poured the rest of the contents into my glass. "Go on."

"He was a writer—or wanted to be, anyway. I thought he was so cool. He was opinionated and intense, but also charming. Kind of a sexy, starving-artist type, if you know what I mean."

"Mm, not really," said Deena. "I usually go for rich, professional types: bankers, lawyers, businessmen. I don't see the appeal of a 'starving artist.'"

"Fair enough," I said, with a rueful smile. I thought about my fantasy lover—an artist who happened to be wealthy, like a movie star. As if there were hordes of those passing through Aerieville.

"So, things fizzled with Josh the writer?" asked Deena.

"More like crashed and burned." I took a sip of wine, cringing at the recollection. "We had moved in together and started sharing everything—including my credit card. I thought things were getting serious. Turns out I was seriously deluded."

"Let me guess. He was unfaithful?"

"Big-time. He was taking off in the evenings, right after dinner. I thought he was building a set at the theater where I performed. Instead he was having a fling with my understudy."

"Ouch," said Deena. "Wait, you mean *at* the theater?"

"Yep. Backstage. I walked in on them, uh, getting busy. Right there among the props and costumes."

"Oh, that's awful." Deena gave me a sympathetic look, and I could tell she meant it.

"That's not the worst of it," I went on. "I was so stunned and flustered, I turned heel and ran . . . and tripped. I fell right off the stage and broke my leg."

Deena clapped her hand over her mouth. "What? No way!"

I nodded and, perversely, found myself grinning. In retrospect, the whole thing was so ridiculous—from my incredible naivety to the sorry conclusion. "To this day, I can't stand to hear anybody tell an actor to 'break a leg' before going on stage."

That made Deena laugh, and I joined in. It felt good to finally be able to see the humor in one of my worst moments. And the more we laughed, the funnier it seemed. Gus barked excitedly, probably wondering what was wrong with us.

"I'm sorry," Deena gasped. "Did that really happen? I can't believe it."

"Well, it was actually just my ankle," I admitted. "But it makes for a better story if I say it was my leg."

Deena threw a napkin at me, making me giggle even harder. "Between the broken ankle and my broken heart, I couldn't perform anymore," I explained. "The understudy got both my man and my job!"

"That has got to be the saddest thing I've ever heard." Still chuckling, she reached for the bottle again and found that it was empty. "Do you have any more wine?"

I uncorked another Merlot, and we each had half a glass more. Deena told me how she'd been spurned in prior relationships (always by slick and shallow players, it seemed), and I told her about the one awkward date I'd had since returning to Aerieville. It was an arrangement my mom had set up. The guy was an overly-tanned protein-powder salesman, with biceps that rivaled my brother's.

"Sounds like a far cry from your starving-artist type," Deena joked.

"Yeah, maybe even *too* far. The whole date was one big sales pitch."

Deena laughed. "You weren't impressed?"

"Oh, I was impressed alright—by his single-minded focus. He was good too. I'm still not sure if he just wanted to make a sale—or if he genuinely wanted to help me tone my muscles."

"You're so funny." Deena stood up and took our glasses to the sink. "I never knew you were so funny."

We switched to water and continued chatting, as she helped me clean up the kitchen. In truth, I was kind of surprised at how much fun I was having with Deena. We'd run in different circles in high school and never really had the chance to get to know one another.

After a while, Deena checked her watch and said she should be going. "My parents will be wondering where I am."

"I can relate to that." I walked her to the door and told her I'd fill her in if Chief Walden ever called me back.

However, I couldn't keep my eyes open much longer. It had been a long day, and the wine had made me sleepy—not to mention all the laughing. Plus, I remembered there would be a flower delivery at the shop early tomorrow morning. I took Gus out one more time and got ready for bed.

Despite my sleepiness, it turned out to be a fitful night. I had strange dreams of being chased through a dark, cavernous building. Felix was there, talking in riddles, and then he was gone. Then the scene shifted and I found myself standing before Flower House—and it was on fire! I stood frozen, helpless, as flames shot through the windows and roof.

I awoke with a start, relieved it was only a dream.

After the troubled night's sleep, I decided to go ahead and get up extra early. I took a fast shower, threw on some jeans and a thin green sweater, and hustled over to Flower House with Gus in tow. It was still dark out when we arrived, but, thankfully, all was quiet and peaceful. As soon as we went inside, Gus ran for the door to the apartment, evidently looking for Calvin.

"He's probably still sleeping," I whispered.

I put on some coffee in the kitchen workroom, then went to the office to check for orders. A few minutes later, there was a knock at the back door. It was a young man with three boxes of fresh flowers, our standing weekly order. I thanked him and immediately unpacked the boxes, pulling out bundles of carnations, gerberas, gladioli, tulips, and birds of paradise. Working quickly, I cut open the plastic wrap and snipped the rubber bands, then cut each stem and placed all the flowers in clean pails of fresh water with powdered flower food. Finally, I placed the pails in the cooler and was just cleaning off the worktable when Calvin came downstairs. I was happy to see he had gotten dressed, though his hair was sticking up as usual.

"Morning, glory," he said, helping himself to some coffee. "I've been thinking."

"About what?"

"About Felix's house. You said he left you in charge of the shop, but is anyone looking after his house? I assume he has plants to water and mail to bring in. I could do that."

I stared at him for a moment without answering. He'd been nice and helpful in the few days I'd known him, but did that mean I should give him the keys to Felix's cabin? I didn't think so.

"Thanks, but that's not necessary," I said. "I've got it covered."

"Oh, okay. You sure? 'Cause, I don't mind."

"Yeah, I'm sure. But, actually, I've been thinking too. I could really use some help around here, especially in the greenhouse. I don't know what kind of extra time you have, considering the project you're working on. But, if you're open to it, I could let you live in the apartment rent-free next month in exchange for a few hours of work each day. What do you say?"

"I say . . . I'd *lilac* that very much. You've got a deal!"

"Great," I said, smiling in spite of myself. His puns were starting to grow on me. "I have some phone calls to make now. Maybe you could go check on things in the greenhouse and cut a few long-stem roses?" I handed him a clean pail and some shears. "Try to make them all about twenty-five inches if you can, and be sure to cut the bottoms at an angle. There should be some gloves out there somewhere. Check in the shed."

I spent the rest of the morning in the office on the phone. After calling the newspaper to place the ad, I dialed the number for Angela Lomack, Jim's ex-wife. I wasn't sure how receptive she'd be to my call, so I was pleasantly surprised when she was willing to talk.

"Yeah, I got a letter from Jim," she said. "He always did have a flair for the dramatic. Of course, he's a chicken too. Couldn't just tell me in person he was going to go chasin' after Felix on some dern fool treasure hunt. He knew I'd try to talk him out of it."

"Did he happen to say where exactly he was going, and when he planned to come back?"

"Nope. That's another reason he left me a letter—so he wouldn't have to answer any questions. Like I said, he's kind of a chicken. That's partly why we didn't stay married."

"I'm sorry," I said.

"Oh, don't be, honey. We got along better after we ended the marriage than before." She chuckled, then paused. "Of course, I'm sorry he's gone too—not least because that's the end of my alimony checks!"

"Sorry," I repeated. "Have you tried calling him?"

"Oh, he doesn't own a cell phone. He's old school, through and through. Frustrating as heck."

"I can imagine," I said. Jim sounded worse than Felix. "Say, did you happen to know Abe Ranker? Or did Jim know him?"

"Dishonest Abe? Yeah, we knew him. Jim did some work out on his farm a long time ago, back when we were first married."

"Why do you call him 'Dishonest Abe'?" I'd heard the nickname before, but I wanted to hear what she'd say.

"I probably shouldn't speak ill of the dead. I heard he passed away. But the truth is, he was an opportunistic, greedy sort of person. He would shortchange his workers, skimming hours off their pay. He'd cheat customers too, when he thought he could get away with it."

"Did Jim have any contact with him recently?"

She laughed again. "What you really mean is 'Did Jim hold a grudge and slip him some poison?'"

I was glad our conversation was over the phone, so she couldn't see me turning red. Evidently, I wasn't being as subtle as I thought. "I didn't mean—" I began.

"It's alright. Jim's not the sort to hold a grudge. I'm sure he hadn't given that man a second thought in twenty years or more. He's too busy chasing rainbows and playing 'adventure.'"

"Thanks for talking with me, Angela," I said. "If I happen to hear from Felix, I'll ask about Jim."

"Oh, I don't think Jim is with Felix."

"You don't?" Now I was confused.

"He's *competing* with Felix. They're in a race to see who can find the treasure first." She scoffed. "Dern fools."

"Maybe so," I said. "Well, thanks again—"

"You know," she said, "I was kind of surprised when you said you were from Flower House. Somebody else from the shop already called me two days ago."

"Was it Byron Atterly, the bookkeeper?"

"No, it was a young man. He said he was the manager. A Calvin something or other."

Calvin? The manager? "Oh, really?" I said, playing it cool. "And he asked you the same questions as I did?"

"Pretty much."

"Sorry about that. Mixed signals, I guess."

I hung up and stared out into the hallway, frowning. *That was odd.* Before I could consider it further, my phone rang, and I saw that it was none other than Byron the bookkeeper.

"Hello, Byron," I said. "I was planning on calling you today."

"You've made a decision, then?" His voice was low and raspy as always. I pictured him sitting at an ancient desk, wearing bifocals to peer at his ledgers. In my mind, I also imagined him writing by oil lamp, using a fountain pen and inkwell. Admittedly, I had a fanciful imagination.

"Not exactly," I said. "I was going to let you know that both Francie Wilson and Jim Lomack have quit. You can issue their last paychecks and remove them from the payroll."

"Very well. So, you'll be shuttering the store, then?"

"No." Either he wasn't hearing me, or he assumed I would do the logical thing. He obviously didn't know me very well. "I haven't decided yet. Can I have a couple more days?"

There was a pause on the other end of the line before he answered. "I noticed there have been no cash deposits the past two days. You won't be able to stay open for much longer if there are no proceeds."

"There will be some proceeds. I—I'll get to the bank today."

"Alright, then. Keep me posted."

As soon as I hung up, I went to retrieve the IOUs Calvin had collected, and grabbed the last of Granny's potato salad from the fridge. Like any good multitasker, I sat at the computer eating and preparing customer invoices. I'd have to go to the post office later to get some stamps and mail the invoices—except for Bill and Flo's. Theirs I could hand deliver, and perhaps weasel some more information from them while I was at it. From what I gathered, Flo was eager to carry out some sort of plan. Maybe I could capitalize on that eagerness and get her to spill the beans.

In the midst of my daydreams, I became aware of Gus staring up at me.

"Do you need to go out, bud?"

He barked once.

"Okay. I'll take that as a yes."

I found Gus's leash and took him out the back door. As we crisscrossed the yard, Calvin emerged from the greenhouse. He spotted us and came over, carrying a pail full of pink, yellow, and peach roses.

"A rose by any other name would . . . still have sharp thorns. Do you happen to have any Band-Aids?"

"Uh, yeah. I think there's a first aid kit in the house. Didn't you find any gloves?"

"Yes, but they were pretty worn out. That toolshed is a wreck, by the way."

"What do you mean? A wreck, like the events room was a wreck?"

Calvin's eyes got big. "Gee, I didn't even think of that. Maybe you'd better take a look."

I handed Gus's leash to Calvin. "Those roses need to be put in some fresh water with flower food and placed in the cooler right away. You can leave them on the worktable, and I'll take care of it in a minute."

I jogged over to the shed, a small wooden structure with a single barn door held closed with a rusty latch. I stared at the latch for half a second. Had there been a padlock here before? I thought there had been, but maybe that was a long time ago. I didn't have much cause to come out here very often. Jim and Felix always took care of the yard work.

I pulled the door open wide, allowing the sun to light up the dim interior. At first blush, I wouldn't have called the shed a wreck, though it was far from tidy. "Dusty" and "cluttered" were more like it. Besides the expected push lawn mower, weed eater, and garden hose, there was a stepladder, an old card table, and assorted tools. In one corner, a bag of potting soil had spilled its contents, dirtying a metal watering can and a garden hoe. As I moved farther inside, I detected the pungent odor of fertilizer. It seemed to be coming from the open doors of a built-in cabinet along the back wall of the shed. Careful not to touch anything, my eyes roamed the contents of the cabinet and took in an array of poisons: boxes and jugs of fungicides, herbicides, and pesticides, mostly dusty and old-looking. I was pretty sure it was all standard fare—except for one plastic container that stood out from the rest.

My heartbeat quickened and my palms became slick as I stared at the label of the unusual container. Three phrases, in particular, jumped out at me as if they'd been highlighted in neon paint: "Gopher bait"; "restricted use"; "contains strychnine."

Chapter 14

It would just figure that the afternoon would turn busy, leaving me no time to play detective and follow up on any of the information I'd recently learned. After the shocking discovery I'd made in the toolshed, I immediately ran into the house and rummaged through kitchen drawers until I found a padlock and key. I secured the shed door and was about to call Chief Walden (who *still* hadn't called me back), when Calvin hollered that there was a customer on the phone. I decided to take the call, figuring it would be quick. Silly me. It turned out to be a bride-to-be who wanted to use orchids for her wedding flowers. She had a million questions, which I patiently answered. By the time the call ended, she was 99 percent sure she wanted to hire Flower House for her July wedding. I was so excited about the potential business, I didn't tell her we might not be open. I decided I'd do the job, one way or another. She said she'd get back to me.

As soon as I finished that call, I took care of the roses Calvin had brought in and found him some Band-Aids. Then there was a walk-in customer and after that another order by phone. This caller begged for same-day delivery of a birthday bouquet, even offering to pay extra, so

I agreed. As I put together the bouquet (using some of the fresh roses and carnations, mixed in with some yellow lilies that were nearing the end of their shelf life), I noticed the afternoon was slipping away. I still needed to go to the bank and the post office, so I asked Calvin if he could make the delivery. He punched the customer's address into his phone, as I packaged the bouquet. After gathering up all the recent checks and cash, and a deposit envelope from Felix's desk, I locked up behind us and took Gus with me on the errands.

The whole time I felt a nagging sense of guilt and misplaced priorities. As I sat in my car in line at the drive-up window of the bank, I discussed these feelings with Gus.

"What does it all mean, Gus?"

He perked up, lifting his head from where he reclined in the center of the back seat.

"If the poison that killed Abe came from Flower House, does that implicate Felix somehow? Or Jim?"

Gus laid his head back down, his ears twitching to show he was still listening.

"It just doesn't make sense. Felix had left hours earlier. They both had. For all I know, somebody could have planted that poison in the shed. I never heard Felix mention anything about having a gopher problem."

The cars ahead of me moved up, and I rolled forward, so that I was now second in line.

"And what's the deal with Calvin?" I continued. "He shows up the day after the murder and suddenly becomes a fixture at Flower House. Isn't he just a little too nosy? Why would he take it upon himself to call Jim's ex-wife, Angela? Why should Calvin care where Jim went?"

Was it just me, or was Calvin acting suspicious? Come to think of it, the same could be said for *everyone* caught up in the murder investigation: Bill and Flo, Valerie . . .

I pulled up to the bank window and looked over to see

Richard sitting at the microphone behind the glass. He recognized me and stretched his mouth into a strained, closed-lip smile.

"Hey, Richard!" I said. "Got a deposit for Flower House here." I reached through my car window to drop the envelope into the metal drawer and push the button to send it inside.

"Hey, girl. Nice to see you. At least one person who doesn't suspect me of committing a heinous crime." His voice was tinny and slightly muffled through the speaker on the wall.

"Still?" I said, recalling how he'd said his coworkers had been treating him differently since the murder.

He wrinkled his nose and looked over his shoulder, before leaning close to the microphone. "It didn't help when Chief Walden came in here this morning asking questions about me. I assume he's doing the same with everyone . . ." He trailed off, waiting for me to respond.

"Uh, yeah. Probably."

"Get this. Last night, he and another officer showed up at my *house* and asked if they could come inside. I asked them if they had a warrant, and of course they didn't. So, I politely declined. I know my rights."

My eyebrows popped up at that one. Was that why I hadn't heard from Chief Walden? Because he was focusing all his attention on *Richard*?

"That's crazy," I murmured.

"It's insane. Makes me seriously question the competency of our illustrious police force." Shaking his head, Richard looked down and began tallying the contents of the envelope I'd given him. He typed on his keyboard, double-checked the receipt, then sent it through the mechanical drawer.

Gus pressed his nose to the car's small side window and scratched at the glass. This made Richard smile for real. "Sorry I don't have any treats for the little guy. I assume you don't want him to have a lollipop."

"Probably not a good idea." Another car pulled up behind me, so I shifted into drive and gave Richard an encouraging smile. "Hang in there."

His face fell again, as I drove off. *Why in the world would the cops be targeting Richard?*

At the post office, I brought Gus in with me, hoping no one would kick us out. Luckily, he was a little charmer, eliciting only compliments from everyone we met. I took care of my business as quick as I could, my mind still occupied with suspects and suspicions. By the time we returned to the car, I'd decided I'd better make our next stop the police station. However, before I even started the engine, my phone rang. It was my mom.

"Are you coming home for dinner?" she asked. "I need to know how many rolls to put in the oven. Also, the stew will be ready soon."

I had to hand it to Mom. She knew what to say to distract my attention. Her stew was probably my favorite meal, and I hadn't eaten much today. I should have remembered that today was Wednesday, which meant the gym closed early and Mom would be home cooking. I often made a point to stop by on Wednesday evenings.

"I'm on my way now," I said.

A short time later, I pulled into my parents' driveway, parking along the side so as not to block their access to the garage. Rocky came outside and jogged over to my car. He opened the passenger side door and pushed up the seat back to let Gus out.

"How's my little canine nephew?" he asked, as I got out on my side. "Don't forget to call me whenever you need a dog sitter."

"I would if you weren't at the gym all the time," I said lightly. "Do Mom and Dad pay you overtime?"

"Ha. Good one." Not that he needed the extra cash. He was the most in-demand personal trainer in town. I was quite proud of him, actually.

Mom poked her head out the front door. "Somebody needs to come in here and set the table," she hollered.

"Coming!" said Rocky, before lowering his voice. "Listen, sis, I came out here to give you a heads-up. Mom has been in a snit ever since Granny came down from the mountain yesterday."

"Why?"

"Same as always. I think she just feels guilty and mad and worried—all the helpless emotions. She's started in again on that passive-aggressive thing she does, where she wonders out loud if she'll ever be a grandmother."

"Oh, Lord. Why can't she just be happy we're both in town?"

"She won't be happy 'til there's a house full of family like when she was a kid."

"Well, that's no good. The time to be happy is now."

Rocky shot me an impatient look. As easygoing as he was, he'd never quite gotten on board my positivity train. "It doesn't help that there's a murderer on the loose, and you're still working at the murder house."

"Murder house? Tell me that's not what people are calling Flower House."

"Remind me what the situation is there. You're not by yourself, are you?"

"Uh, no. I mean, yeah, I'm the last florist standing, so to speak. Francie quit, and I just found out Jim Lomack decided to copy Felix and retire without warning. But Calvin is there."

"Calvin. The guy who showed up outa nowhere."

"Not nowhere. He's from Knoxville. And he's really nice. Kind of nerdy, but in a good way. He's always joking around, making up goofy puns." Even as I said it, I realized

I was being inconsistent. One minute suspicious of Calvin, the next kind of liking him. *Do I like him?* Everything was so mixed up right now.

Rocky raised his eyebrows. "Puns? Sounds like Grandpap, always telling us riddles and puns when we were little kids."

"Oh, yeah! I forgot about that. Anyway, Calvin is going to work in the greenhouse in exchange for free rent. At least for the time being."

"Free rent, huh?" Without elaborating, he took a few steps away, as Gus sniffed the bushes.

"Uh-huh." Was Rocky questioning my business sense? I'd thought the arrangement I'd made with Calvin was pretty smart. At this point, Flower House needed workers more than it needed rent money. At least, I was pretty sure that was the case.

Mom stuck her head out the door again. "Come on before the food gets cold!"

"Coming!" I answered.

I grabbed Gus's travel bag (containing food, treats, and poop bags) from the back seat and followed Rocky and Gus inside. My parents' house, my childhood home, was warm and inviting, filled with the scents of home cooking and vanilla potpourri. I kicked off my shoes at the door and headed to the kitchen, where Mom was whipping up frosting for an angel food cake. I washed my hands at the sink before taking four plates down from the cabinet.

"Where's Dad?" I asked.

"He'll be home any minute," Mom said. "He had something to do after closing up Dumbbells this afternoon."

Rocky played with Gus, while I set the table and made small talk with Mom. Contrary to what she'd said, dinner was in no danger of getting cold. Everything was still warming in the oven and on the stovetop. Still, she urged us to hurry up and sit down. We had just said grace and taken our first bites when Dad came in through the back door.

"Good," he said, removing his tennis shoes. "Sierra's here." Gus immediately took off with one of the shoes, leading Rocky on a chase around the house, while Dad filled his plate.

"Nice to see you too, Dad," I said, passing him the salt and pepper.

I expected him to crack a grin, but he didn't. "I have a message for you from Walt," he said.

Uh-oh.

"He said if you want to be a detective, you ought to sign up for the police academy."

Mom dropped her fork, letting it hit her plate with a *clink*. "Police academy? You don't want to be a police officer, Sierra." It was a statement, not a question.

"I don't know what he's talking about," I said.

Dad reached for the butter and tore open a dinner roll. "Something to do with a suspicious comment posted to the funeral home website?"

"Oh. Well, yeah. I tried calling the chief to tell him about it, but he never returned my call."

"He already knew about it," said Dad. "One of his officers was watching the website."

"What comment?" asked Rocky.

"Never mind," said Dad. "The point is, the police know what they're doing."

"Did they trace the IP address?" I asked.

Dad finished chewing the bite he'd taken and swallowed before answering. "As a matter of fact, they did. They traced it to a computer at the public library."

I frowned. That was disappointing. I'd visited the library often enough to know that anyone could use the public computers. You didn't need to show a library card or sign in or anything.

"There were a few other things I wanted to mention to Chief Walden," I said.

"Sierra, you don't need to worry about clearing your name," said Mom. "You're not a suspect."

"But I am, Mom," I protested.

"I thought you were just a witness," said Rocky.

Dad fixed me with a serious look. "You're *not* a suspect," he said firmly. "In fact, Walt told me he's narrowing in on an actual suspect. He expects to be making an arrest real soon."

My mouth suddenly went dry. *Not Richard.* If it was Richard, the chief was making a big mistake. I reached for my glass of iced tea and took a gulp.

Mom noticed my reaction and mistook it for fear. "Why don't you stay here for the night," she said. "I'll clear off the bed in your old room. You can stay as long as you want, at least until the killer is behind bars."

"I need to talk to the chief," I said. "There are things I've learned that he might not know about."

"Things you've learned?" echoed Mom. "What have you been doing?"

Dad shook his head, clearly not happy. "You can speak to any police officer if you have information to share. But you have to trust that Walt knows what he's doing."

I stabbed a cooked carrot with my fork and proceeded to eat in silence. This turn of events put the kibosh on my plans to interrogate my folks. I had wanted to ask them what they knew about Abe and the others who had attended my workshop. Obviously, they wouldn't be very receptive to my questions now.

Mom changed the subject, telling me about a new class she wanted to add at the gym and informing me about Rocky's latest athletic project. He was training for another triathlon.

"You should join me, Sierra," he said, a note of teasing in his voice. I'd tried jogging with him in the past, and he always left me in the dust.

"Yeah, right. Like that's gonna happen."

I cleaned my plate, my appetite unaffected by all the questions swirling in my mind. Mom brought out the angel food cake, which I happily accepted. Feeling pleasantly full, and a little sleepy, I contemplated Mom's offer to stay the night. Besides the comfort and convenience, maybe there was still a chance I could learn a thing or two. I remembered they had a neighbor on the zoning board. If I were to take Gus for a walk around the block this evening or in the morning, I could make a point of stopping by for a chat.

The sound of a ringing cell phone cut through my thoughts.

"Whose phone is that?" asked Mom.

I looked around and grabbed my purse, which I'd set on the counter. "Seems to be mine," I said, pulling out my phone. The display told me it was Calvin. *What now?*

I almost ignored the call, but something told me I'd better take it. With a sigh, I pressed Answer. "Hello?"

"Sierra! Oh, man. Thanks for answering. Are you sitting down?"

I sat up straight, instantly wary. "Yes. Why?"

"Oh, geez. I hate to be the bearer of bad news, but you need to get over here ASAP. There's been another break-in. And this one's a doozy."

Dad and Rocky came with me to Flower House. Mom wanted to come too, but when she realized that meant Gus would be on his own, loose in her house, she decided to stay behind.

"Don't be there any longer than necessary," she'd said to all three of us. "We can go back tomorrow morning to take care of any cleanup."

But "any cleanup," as I was soon to learn, was going to take a whole lot longer than one morning. It would probably take longer than a week.

A uniformed police officer—young Officer Dakin, as it happened—stopped us at the front door. "Wait here," he ordered. "I'll get the chief."

I tried to peek in the window, as Dad gazed across the street and Rocky bounced anxiously on the balls of his feet. Flower House was lit up like a movie set, with all the lights on, plus a police spotlight or two. A minute later, Chief Walden appeared at the front door.

"Hal. Rocky," he said, nodding at the two men, before turning to me. "Sierra, when were you last here?"

I tried to think. "Earlier today. I left around four thirty to go to the bank and post office. Calvin left at the same time to make a delivery. I know I locked the door behind us. Did someone break the lock again?"

"Not quite," said the chief. "I'm going to let you in now, but watch your step. There's broken pottery and glass on the floor."

He stepped back and ushered us through the doorway. I didn't take more than two steps inside before gasping in disbelief. There was a whole lot more than pottery and glass on the floor.

"Dang," said Rocky beside me. "Looks like a tornado came through here."

He wasn't wrong. The floor was littered with debris: loose cut flowers; crushed branches of eucalyptus, dried thistle, and cattails; broken vases; scattered greeting cards. Everything that was previously on a shelf or table was now on the floor. It looked very much like the aftermath of a bad storm.

One glimpse into the events room revealed the same thing. Books, catalogs, flowers, and vases were strewn all over the room. Furniture was once again overturned. The area rug had been pulled up and tossed to the side in a crumpled heap. Even Gus's gate had been kicked over and trampled on.

"I realize it might be hard to tell," said Chief Walden, "but try to notice if anything seems to be missing. We need to know if this is a burglary or straight vandalism."

I nodded, unable to find my voice. Moving down the hall, I stopped at the door to the orchid room. And that's when hot tears sprang to my eyes.

"Georgina's orchids," I whispered. "Why?"

As with the other rooms, all surfaces had been swept, the potted orchids, books, and ceramics pushed to the floor. It was almost as if someone had taken glee in creating the biggest mess possible, making a point to stomp on so many delicate petals in the process.

"It's more than vandalism," I choked out.

"Okay," said the chief, gesturing to Officer Dakin, who pulled out a notebook. "What's missing?"

I swallowed a lump as big as a peach pit and wiped my leaking eyes. "It's property damage. I don't know how much. Probably hundreds, if not thousands, of dollars."

Dakin snapped his notebook shut. "Wait 'til you see the greenhouse."

I turned to him in dismay. "They broke into the greenhouse too?"

"One thing at a time," said the chief. "Let's take a look at the next room."

Fighting the urge to pick up the overturned orchids, I moved along to the office, with Dad and Rocky close behind me. Rocky whistled softly when he peered inside. By this point, I could only shake my head in disbelief. If the office was cluttered before, it now looked as if it had been turned upside down and shaken like a game of Yahtzee. Yet, at a glance, I could see that the computer was still on the desk and the framed posters were still on the walls.

"Nothing obvious is missing," I said.

Chief Walden nodded and steered us to the kitchen workroom. Now I knew how the vandal had gotten in. The glass pane from the back door was lying in bits on the floor.

"We think the intruder entered and exited here and went directly to the front of the shop. They seem to have worked their way from front to back, ending here in the kitchen. They either ran out of time or were scared off before causing much damage in this room."

Looking around, I saw that he was right. The cooler door was wide open, but nothing had been removed. I reached to shut it. "May I?"

"That's fine," said the chief. "We've already been through here." He held open the back door and motioned us to precede him outside. "Watch your step."

Two officers with flashlights approached the chief in the backyard, and they stepped away from us to speak out of earshot. One then spoke into his radio, while the other motioned us to follow him to the greenhouse. Chief Walden fell into step with my dad, murmuring words I once again couldn't hear. I was beginning to feel left out.

Then we entered the greenhouse. I took one look at the extent of the destruction and felt only one overriding emotion: anger. A red-hot, righteous anger at the sheer, wanton cruelty on display. In both sections, housing the orchids and the roses, plants had been uprooted and tossed to the ground. The floor was a carpet of mud, leaves, and blackened flower petals. The sight made me sick to my stomach.

"Unbelievable," said Rocky, standing to the side so

as not to dirty his shoes. "This must have been done by more than one person, huh?"

"There was only one set of prints in the mud," said the chief.

"Footprints?" This was the first I'd heard of a clue, and it gave me a spark of hope. "What size?"

"Average. Probably made by rubber boots. There was no mud in the shop, so we figure they came out here last. Either that, or they changed their shoes."

"I assume they wore gloves," said Dad. "Otherwise, they'd be all cut up from rose thorns."

"This certainly seems planned," said the chief.

The words Deena had overheard surfaced in my mind. *Flower House needs to close.*

I turned to the chief. "You should question Bill and Flo Morrison. They live behind Bread n' Butter next door."

"We've already canvassed all the neighbors. The Morrisons aren't home." He moved toward the exit, and I ran up to his side.

"Wait. I don't mean talk to them as neighbors. I think they might have done this!"

Dad and Rocky stared at me in surprise.

"Why do you say that?" asked the chief.

I hesitated half a second. "I, uh—I have reason to believe they want Flower House to go out of business."

"What reason?"

"Um. A friend of mine heard them say as much."

"A friend?"

"Isn't that hearsay?" said Rocky, unhelpfully.

"We'll look into it," said the chief, turning again to leave the greenhouse.

We followed him out into the yard, where he called over Dakin, before speaking into his radio. This time I heard what he said: he was dismissing his officers. I hated the thought that they were done investigating already. Why didn't they bring their spotlight outside? There could be more clues . . . like muddy footprints leading to the Morrisons' house.

We were walking by the shed when I suddenly remembered the other thing I'd wanted to tell the chief. The outrageous break-in had shoved it from the forefront of my mind.

"Chief! Officer Dakin! Hang on a minute." They turned around, while I fumbled in my purse for the key to the padlock. "I need to show you something in the shed. I found some poison in there earlier today."

Officer Dakin shined his flashlight on the shed door, while the chief glanced at my dad, before answering. "We already searched the shed on Saturday night. You may not have noticed, but officers scoured this whole property, inside and out. There were some fertilizers and herbicides in the shed, nothing out of the ordinary."

"What about the gopher bait?" I said. "The container said *strychnine*."

The chief stared at me for a second, as if I might be spinning fairy tales. "Open it up," he said.

I quickly complied, then squeezed past tools and equipment to get to the back of the shed. "In there," I said, pointing at the built-in cabinet. Dakin shined his flashlight and the chief leaned in to look.

"This wasn't here before," he said. "Dakin, go get a large evidence bag."

"Yes, sir."

With that, the chief gently pushed me out of the shed. Dad and Rocky, who had waited in the yard, were staring toward the back of the house.

"Who's that?" said Rocky. "The new guy?"

I followed his gaze to see Calvin, in cuffed pants, canvas sneakers, and a buttoned-up dress shirt. He was craning his neck and squinting in the darkness.

"Calvin!" I said, waving to get his attention. "Where have you been?"

He jogged over, stopping short when he caught sight of my dad and brother flanking me like a couple of uber-tough bodyguards.

"Um, inside. In my apartment. After I gave my statement, the cops told me to stay out of the way. This is terrible, isn't it?"

"It's more than terrible. Where were you when this happened?"

"I wasn't here. I was at the movies."

Rocky looked like he wanted to ask a question, and I had a few more of my own. But Chief Walden passed by then, caring a large and lumpy brown paper bag marked Evidence. He paused right next to me.

"Sierra, I'll send an officer by tomorrow to check on things. In the meantime, call if anything unusual turns up."

Don't you mean anything else *unusual?* I thought. But I only said, "I will."

"Oh, and you might want to be careful about who you trust. Not everyone is a friend." With that, he nodded at Dad and headed to a waiting patrol car on the street.

"What was that all about?" asked Calvin.

I sighed. "I have no idea."

Chapter 15

I pulled up the quilt on my old twin bed, in what was now my parents' guestroom/overflow closet, and scooched over to make room for Gus. Leaning against the headboard, I looked over at the clock. It was after midnight. I thought about sending a text to Deena but decided against it. It was way too late and, besides, it wasn't like we were best friends or anything.

I ran my fingers through Gus's thick chest and neck fur, which turned out to be more soothing even than the hot tea Mom had had waiting when Dad, Rocky, and I returned from Flower House.

"You can be my best friend, Gus. Would you like to be my best friend?"

He slowly blinked his eyes closed in a gesture of pure trust and relaxation. Sleepiness too. I should have been sleepy, but I wasn't. I was still processing everything that had happened tonight.

After the police left, I'd called Byron to let him know what happened, and he said he would notify the insurance company. A few minutes later, he called back to say an adjustor wanted to meet me at the shop first thing in the morning. That meant we should leave the shop largely untouched. Still, Dad found some boards and patched up the back door, while Rocky swept up the glass in the kitchen. Calvin and I went to the orchid room to see if any of the potted flowers could be rescued. We spoke very little, probably both of us still feeling shell-shocked. In the end, we determined that more than half of the orchids were beyond saving.

"At least they're not all lost," I'd said to Calvin.

"Yeah," he'd agreed, clearly making an effort to look on the bright side. "It's better than I thought."

Now I grabbed my phone from the nightstand and contemplated texting Calvin. I felt bad about leaving him at Flower House. Surely, he must've had qualms about staying in a place where crimes kept occurring. Not only the murder (which was bad enough), but two break-ins in one week! I might be scared, if I were him.

He didn't seem scared, though. He said he'd take inventory of the greenhouse first thing in the morning. "It's probably not as bad as it looked," he'd said. "I bet at least half the plants out there will be okay."

I appreciated his optimism and was grateful for his help. But as I replaced my phone on the nightstand and resumed petting Gus, I began to think. *What was it the chief had said to me? Be careful who I'm friends with? It was something to that effect. Was he talking about Calvin? Or Richard?*

"This whole thing has me very confused," I said to Gus. "Are the break-ins connected to the murder? What was the point of wrecking Flower House like that?"

The chief had said the bad guy came in the back door and went straight to the front of the shop. If they wanted to harm the business, why not destroy all the flowers in the cooler? That would have cost us much more than the mess in the events room.

I suddenly recalled the note someone had slipped

under the door the day after the murder. Where had I put that piece of paper? I shut my eyes and tried to picture what it had said. *You better get out of there if you know what's good for you.* Was it directed at me personally, or the shop in general? And what about the handwriting? It hadn't seemed particularly distinctive to me at the time, but now I wondered if it might match the writing on the death threats Abe had received—assuming those threats were in writing. There was so much I didn't know.

I moved Gus to the foot of the bed and switched off the lamp. As I lay in the darkness, drifting toward sleep, a wisp of a thought circled in my consciousness. *Death threats.* Receiving a death threat would be really scary. The killer didn't only want to get rid of Abe. They wanted to scare him. Was someone trying to scare me too?

Why?

Early the next morning, Mom and I headed to Flower House to meet the insurance adjustor and assess the damage. Dad and Rocky took Gus with them to Dumbbells. Since Rocky would be on front-desk duty, he assured me it would be no problem to keep an eye on the pup. I was grateful for my family's support. As much as they could get on my nerves sometimes, they were the first to rally round in times of need.

Mom and I trailed the adjustor as he inspected the property. He photographed the damage and asked questions as he went. Seeing the destruction in the light of day gave me a hollow feeling in the pit of my stomach. Mom's exclamations of dismay didn't help. I couldn't shake the feeling that I'd let Felix down.

"What do you think?" I asked the adjustor, as he prepared to leave. "Will the insurance make up for any of what we lost?"

He gave me a look of surprise. "Flower House is covered by a comprehensive policy. I can't give you an official determination right now, but I'd say a good portion will be compensated."

"That's a relief." It may have been a setback, but at least it wasn't a total loss.

As soon as he left, we got busy with the cleanup. "Let's start in the front of the shop," Mom said. "It's the first thing people will see, if any customers stop by."

"Good idea." I handed her a trash bag, before grabbing the broom and dustpan. "I can't afford to stay closed any longer than absolutely necessary."

"Mm-hmm," said Mom. "You might as well sell the remaining inventory before closing up for good."

I looked up from the pile of debris I was sorting through. "I haven't decided about that yet. Byron gave me a couple extra days to think about it."

Mom gave me a look of incredulity, as if to say, *Seriously?* Fortunately, there was a tap at the front door, forestalling any arguments.

I unlocked the door and opened it to admit Flo. She handed me a paper-wrapped loaf of bread, still warm from the oven, and a sack of scones.

"Oh my goodness," she said, looking around. "We heard about what happened. Looks like this was more than a smash-and-grab."

I eyed her closely, as Mom came over to take the baked goods off my hands. "These smell wonderful," Mom said. "How thoughtful."

"Where were you last night?" I said, a touch more aggressively than I'd meant to. At Flo's surprised expression, I quickly softened my tone. "The police were asking all the neighbors if they saw or heard anything. I don't suppose you did?"

"No. Bill and I were at a fundraising dinner at our

church yesterday evening. We didn't even know anything had happened until Nell mentioned it this morning."

"Nell?"

"Yes, she stopped by to pick up some cookies and cakes for the diner. She said she heard it on her scanner last night."

"Who has time to listen to a scanner?" asked Mom.

Flo chuckled. "Apparently Nell does, but I don't know how. Running a restaurant is a full-time job and then some."

"Running any business is," said Mom, giving me a pointed look.

"That reminds me," said Flo. "I owe you for Abe's funeral flowers. I didn't have my checkbook the other day, and your credit card machine was down."

"Uh, right," I said. So, that's what Calvin was telling the customers.

"I bought an eighty-dollar arrangement," she said, handing me a check.

"Thanks." I took the check to the cash register, then looked back to see Flo peeking into the events room, which was still topsy-turvy.

"What a mess," she said, shaking her head. "I'd offer to stay and help, but I need to get back to the bakery."

"That's alright," said Mom. "Thanks for stopping by."

"Hey, Flo," I said, as she headed to the door. "I've been meaning to ask you—did Jim Lomack stop by Bread n' Butter on Saturday?"

She furrowed her forehead in thought. "Yes, I did see Jim a few days ago. I think it was Saturday. Why?"

"I was just wondering if he said anything about . . . anything. He decided to follow in Felix's footsteps and take an early retirement, but I didn't get a chance to see him before he left."

"Oh! Well, that's too bad," said Flo. "Now that you mention it, he did seem to be in a hurry. Kind of rude of him not to say goodbye, though." She tilted her head and stuck out her lip, as if to convey sympathy, but there was something in the twitch of her mouth that made me think she was holding back a smile. I narrowed my eyes ever so slightly. It was on the tip of my tongue to ask her how she'd feel if Flower House were to shut down, just to put her on the spot. But she left before I could screw up the courage.

Mom and I went back to our cleanup effort. A few minutes later, Calvin came downstairs and ran up to me, wringing his hands.

"I'm so sorry! I overslept. What can I do to help? Should I start in the greenhouse?"

"Why don't you start with a scone?" said Mom, pointing to the bag on the checkout counter. "You must be Calvin."

"Yes, ma'am. Thank you."

The phone rang and Calvin was closest, so he answered. "Flower House. How can I help you?"

He listened for a minute, then said, "Uh, hold on, please." Cupping a hand over the receiver, he turned to me. "Are we running a flower sale?"

I clapped my forehead and groaned. "I completely forgot about the ad I placed. Go ahead and take the order." I looked around at the mess and realized we'd better clean faster. There were probably orders waiting on the computer as well.

Mom was separating dried flowers into three piles: intact, slightly damaged but fixable, and damaged beyond repair. I left her to that and did the same with the greeting cards. When Calvin got off the phone, he grabbed a scone and went out to the greenhouse. Then there was another tap on the door, and Deena came walking in.

"So, it's true!" she said, taking in the disarray. "Nell Cusley told my mother there had been another break-in at Flower House, and I thought she must be mistaken."

At the mention of Nell again, Mom and I exchanged a glance, and she rolled her eyes.

"It's sad but true," I said. "Somebody really did a number in here. In the greenhouse too."

"Why didn't you call me? We said we'd keep each other posted." It might have been my imagination, but I thought I detected a note of hurt feelings in Deena's voice. *Dang, I should've at least texted her after all.*

"I'm sorry," I said. "It was a late night and kind of a busy morning."

She leaned down to pick up a Mason jar from the floor. Seeing that it was unbroken, she placed it on a shelf. "Do you want some help?"

"Yeah! That would be great."

Mom offered Deena a scone, and I remembered my manners.

"Deena, this is my mom, Mandy Ravenswood. Mom, this is Deena Lee. We went to high school together."

"Oh, yes. Of course," Mom said. "You're Dr. Lee's daughter, aren't you?" Deena's father was a cardiologist at the county hospital. If I wasn't mistaken, her mother was a healthcare manager.

"That's right," said Deena. "Lovely to meet you."

She pulled her long, black hair into a ponytail and rolled up the sleeves of her blouse, and we got busy. Mom finished cleaning up the dried flowers and filled two trash bags with broken stems and merchandise, while Deena and I put the events room back together. Throughout the morning, I was interrupted three times: twice by phone calls and once when a young man stopped in to buy a single long-stem red rose. It wasn't exactly a stampede of customers, but it was turning into one of our busiest days since Felix left.

It was just past eleven o'clock when Mom announced that she needed to leave for Dumbbells.

"I can come back later, if you still need help," she said. "Don't forget to get a copy of the police report for the insurance claim."

"I won't forget. Thanks, Mom."

"And, whatever you do, don't spend any of your own money on repairs or anything else related to this business. Nothing here is in your name. This shop really isn't your responsibility at all."

"I know, Mom."

"The sooner you close the place, the better."

"We'll see." I handed her a partly damaged, but still pretty, potted gerbera daisy. "Take this. It'll look nice on the front desk at Dumbbells."

After Mom left, Deena and I moved on to the orchid room. She swept the floor, while I started marking down the price on books with visible dents or bent pages.

"I gather that the fate of Flower House is in your hands," she said. "It would be a shame if it has to close."

"It *would* be a shame," I agreed. "But, to be honest, I'm not sure I have the skills to keep it going by myself." I filled her in on the situation with Felix and the loss of Jim and Francie. "I feel like I'm holding this place together by the skin of my teeth."

Deena looked thoughtful. "You know, I could use an excuse to get out of my parents' house. Maybe I could help you out for a while. On a volunteer basis, I mean. A few hours here and there?"

"Oh, wow, really? That would be great!" Not only could I use the help, but it would be fun to see more of Deena. In spite of everything, maybe luck was still on my side.

Just then, we heard the jingle of the front door opening. I pushed myself up off the floor and walked up front to greet the customer—who turned out to be Valerie Light.

"Hi, Sierra," she said. "I heard you're having a flower

sale and thought I'd pick up a bouquet for the dance studio. I took my tulips home."

"Wonderful," I said, grabbing an order form from behind the front desk. "Just a basic, cheery spring mix?"

"Something like that. What color roses do you have in stock?"

"Roses? Just about any you can think of. Red, white, blush pink, hot pink, yellow, peach. What did you have in mind?"

She bit her lip. "I like peach. That might be nice with something lavender and some baby's breath."

"That sounds lovely." I made some notes on the form. "Do you want 'em in a vase, or do you already have one?"

"I have lots of vases. I don't need another one." She gazed around the room, then swallowed. "Uh, out of curiosity, do you sell black roses?"

I put down my pen and stared at her in surprise. "Not usually. We might have dark purple."

"Never mind. I was just wondering."

My mind whirred as I connected the dots. The cops who responded to the first break-in had asked if Flower House sold black roses. They'd also mentioned someone filing a harassment complaint. And when I delivered my tulips to Valerie, she'd seemed unduly alarmed at the idea of a flower delivery.

I decided to ask her point-blank. "Is someone sending you black roses?"

Now it was her turn to look surprised. "How did you know?"

"Just a guess. Is there a note with the roses?"

She shook her head. "Not really. Just a blank card with my name on it, and a single long-stem black rose."

Deena came out from the orchid room and joined us near the cash register. She folded her arms gracefully and listened to our conversation.

"You know," I said, "black roses don't occur naturally. They're usually just white roses that have been dyed black."

"Oh," said Valerie. "I didn't realize that. I suppose that will make it even more difficult to figure out who's doing this. I'm sure lots of people buy white roses."

"Someone gave you black roses?" asked Deena.

Valerie nodded glumly. "Six so far. They've been left outside my front door and outside the dance studio. Once on the windshield of my car."

"Weird," Deena murmured.

"They must do it at night," I guessed. "Or sometime when the studio is closed, anyway."

"It's just so unnerving," Valerie said, with a shudder. "I have no idea who it is, or why they're doing this."

I raised my eyebrows, and Valerie uttered a quiet, humorless laugh. "I actually thought it might be Abe. But they continued to come after he died."

"Is that why you were having lunch with Abe at Nell's Diner?" I asked. "To confront him about it?"

Valerie leaned back and gave me a look as if *I* might be the one harassing her with black roses. "What is this? Have you been following me?"

"No! I heard it from Nell. You know how she is. We were talking about Abe, actually."

Valerie glanced at the events room, as if only just now remembering what had occurred in there. Rubbing her arms, she said, "Abe asked me to meet him for lunch last Thursday. I agreed, because I wanted to ask him about the roses. I figured it would be easier in a public place."

"Nell said he looked worried," I said. "Of course, she could have been embellishing her story."

"No, it's true," said Valerie. "Abe told me someone had been leaving threatening notes in his mailbox at home and on his car. He said it might be the same person leaving me black roses. I didn't believe him. He was such a casual liar, I wouldn't have believed anything he said. Now I realize his worry must have been real."

The back door opened with a bang, and a moment later Calvin came clomping up the hall, tracking mud all over the floor. I looked from him to the floor, noting there was one more thing for me to take care of.

He saw my expression and quickly kicked off his shoes. "I'll clean this up," he said. "Then I was thinking I'd go get us some lunch."

Valerie removed a wallet from her purse. "You can deliver my flowers to the studio whenever they're ready."

"No problem," I said, ringing her up. "Thank you for coming in."

The second the door closed behind Valerie, Deena grabbed my arm. "Sierra, what do you make of what she said? Do you believe her?"

I nodded slowly. "Yeah. I think she was telling the truth. I'm just not sure if it was the *whole* truth." I recalled how cagey Valerie had been when I'd spoken with her at the studio—and how paranoid she seemed today. Was she hiding something? Or was she simply afraid?

"You don't think Abe's killer and Valerie's stalker are the same person, do you?" asked Deena. "There were no death threats with the black roses."

"I'm not so sure about that," I said. "There's a reason we sell so many of them at Halloween. Most people associate black roses with scary things: loss, sorrow, hatred, despair. And, above all, death."

Chapter 16

Calvin brought us fast food for lunch, but I had no complaints. I was too distracted to think about food anyway. As Deena, Calvin, and I ate, I was preoccupied with thoughts of crazy killers taunting their victims with black roses, death threats . . . and home invasions. Or business invasions anyway.

"So much for your granny's charms," said Calvin, around a mouthful of French fries.

"What?" I hadn't been listening before, but his last words caught my attention. "What about Granny's charms?"

"The basil and wildflowers, or whatever. They didn't work."

"How do you know they didn't work?" I said, feeling defensive.

Calvin looked confused. "Because of the break-in?"

"No one was hurt, were they? Maybe that's because they *did* work. Maybe it would have been way worse without the charms."

"Gee, I hadn't thought of that."

Deena followed our exchange with amusement. "Maybe you should invest in a security system," she said. "Even one camera might have captured whoever ran amok in here."

"That's true," I said, wondering how much such a thing would cost. "I need to start a to-do list. Or at least a list of things to look into if Flower House stays open."

"You might want to start with a new window for the back door," Calvin suggested. "And a new lock for the greenhouse."

"That sounds like a good job for Richard," said Deena. "He would probably appreciate the work, considering the drop in his handyman business."

"Uh, yeah," I said. I hadn't told Deena about the police showing up at Richard's home, and I didn't feel like putting voice to it now—especially in front of Calvin. "I'll call him later. Right now I need to make a phone call and start fulfilling flower orders." I crumpled up my food wrapper and stood up from the table.

"I'm ready to help," said Deena.

"And I need to get back to my plant-rescue mission in the greenhouse," said Calvin.

I flashed a grateful smile to both of them, then grabbed my cell phone and stepped outside to stand on the front stoop. I had a notion to call Granny Mae.

I watched the clouds float by as I listened to the phone ring. Granny could easily be in her yard or on an errand.

"Hello!" Her warm voice crackled over the line. Instant comfort.

"Hi, Granny! It's Sierra. How are you?"

"Fit as a second-hand fiddle. Sharp as a rusty nail." She cackled merrily. "How are you, hon?"

"Better now that I'm talking to you."

"You still having troubles at Flower House? Do you need me to come down there?"

I hesitated before answering. The last thing I wanted to do was worry Granny. "I think . . . I could just use some advice. There's so much I don't understand. Strange things have been happening. Folks are keeping secrets. Somebody's after something, but I don't know what . . ." I trailed off, not sure if I was making any sense.

"Do you still have that herb bag I gave you?"

"The herb bag? Oh, yeah. I left it under my pillow."

"Well, that's a good place for it at night, but you're meant to keep it with you. Listen, what you need is some confidence."

"I suppose that's true. How am I gonna get that?" I thought it was a rhetorical question, but she had a ready answer.

"Here's what you gotta do. Go out and collect a big handful of pine needles—the kind with a nice, sweet scent—and two or three magnolia petals. Get yourself a square of flannel and some red thread and tie up your gatherings nice and tight. Really squeeze 'em in to release the fragrance. Then put it in your pocket and don't forget it's there. See if that don't make you feel better."

"And that will give me confidence?"

"Confidence, good luck, good feelings. You'll see."

There was a magnolia tree at the end of the block and some pine trees in the park across the street. As soon as I got off the phone, I jogged down the sidewalk to do as she said.

Of course, I didn't totally buy into Granny's superstitions. But I had an epiphany as she was talking. Granny Mae's lucky charms were not unlike the affirmations and other self-help tools I liked to use. They worked when folks believed they did. *What you focus on grows.*

I didn't have a square of flannel or any red thread, but I did find a lint cloth in my purse. I placed my "gatherings" in the cloth and used the corners to tie a knot. It was a sweet-smelling little bundle. Inhaling deeply, I felt better already.

When I joined Deena in the kitchen, I was in a much perkier mood than before. And having her company turned out to be the icing on the cake. She brought a fun, light energy to the place—plus, she was a great assistant. She'd already laid out some flowers and supplies and begun prepping some of the vases.

We had a lot to do. In addition to Valerie's bouquet order, we had eight others that had been placed by phone or online. Fortunately, thanks to Deena's help, we finished much quicker than I anticipated—even with all the laughing and joking around we did in the process. The only problem, as I soon discovered, was that we were running low on certain flower varieties. With all the tulips I'd used in the past few days, there were only a handful left. And, after completing one very specific phone order, we were now completely out of hydrangeas.

"I could stop by the grocery store," offered Deena. "Or check out the florists in nearby towns. I think Manny's is pretty big."

"No way," I said, alarmed at the thought. "At least, not unless we're absolutely desperate. I'll just call our supplier and adjust next week's standing order. In the meantime . . ." I trailed off as I finished tying a bow on a sweetheart bouquet. "I have another idea."

"Oh?" said Deena. "What is it?"

"After we deliver these arrangements, we should drive out to Ranker's Garden Center. They may have some flowers in their hothouse that we can use."

"Good thinking," said Deena, her mouth twitching into a wry grin.

"We can talk to folks while we're there. Chat up the employees. Who knows what we might learn?"

Ranker's Garden Center was on the edge of town, just off Rural Route One between an apple orchard and a dairy farm. By the time Deena and I arrived, it was already late afternoon, and there were only two other cars in the customer parking lot. We climbed out of the Fiat and headed directly to the greenhouse, bypassing a small clapboard building that housed the garden center's business office. Barrel planters filled with spring annuals stood at the entrance to the greenhouse. We went inside, and I inhaled deeply, relishing the damp, earthy scent of growing plants.

Compared to the greenhouse at Flower House, this one was huge. Picking a row at random, we strolled around and took it all in. There were trees and shrubs in plastic containers, houseplants in a multitude of varieties, hanging flower baskets, and trays of herb and vegetable starters. One corner featured outdoor statuary, birdbaths, fire pits, and even a bubbling stone fountain. I gravitated toward a small garden gnome with a jaunty red hat and a mischievous grin.

"I've always wanted one of these," I said, weighing it in my hands.

"Cute," said Deena. "But shouldn't we be looking for flowers?"

"Yep. You're right." I replaced the gnome and patted its head. "Maybe another time, buddy."

"These are pretty," said Deena, pointing to a colorful bush of pale pink peonies.

"They're beautiful," I agreed. "But they're already at the end of their blooming cycle. We should focus on flowers that will last longer."

We wandered up and down a row of flowering plants, pausing to smell sweet lilacs and fragrant hyacinths. As a flower arranger, I was tempted by so many lovely blossoms, from vibrant red poppies to soft, delicate pink azaleas, imagining how I'd showcase them to maximum effect. In the end, I limited myself to a large, potted hydrangea plant, which boasted more than a dozen blue-petaled heads. I picked it up in both arms, and we proceeded to the customer service counter along the back wall of the greenhouse.

The guy behind the counter was tall and lanky, with a mop of hair in need of a trim. He looked young to me, probably in his early twenties. According to the tag on his shirt, his name was Jeffery. As soon as he finished helping the customer ahead of us, I set my plant on the counter and flashed my most dazzling smile. Jeffery barely looked up.

"Find everything okay?" he asked, as he scanned the tag on the hydrangea.

"Yes. Thanks." I cleared my throat and rested my clasped hands on the counter. "I was sorry to hear about Abe," I said.

"Thanks. That'll be seventy-two oh-three."

"Yikes," I muttered, pulling out my credit card. "Have you worked here long?"

"About a year."

I glanced at Deena, who was regarding me with a mixture of encouragement and curiosity. I, too, wondered what I would say next. As I paid for the hydrangea (promising myself I'd heed my mother's advice and ask Byron to reimburse me), I cast about for a conversation starter.

"Um . . . oh! So, I actually work at a greenhouse too. It's much smaller than this one, though."

He smiled politely, but didn't ask me where I worked.

Apparently, I didn't interest him in the least. Undaunted, I chattered on.

"As a matter of fact, one of my coworkers used to work here. Jim Lomack? You probably didn't know him. It was a long time ago."

"No. I don't recognize the name." Jeffery handed me my receipt. "Ben probably knew him, though. He's worked here forever." He nodded in a direction behind us, and we turned to see a white-haired man, with matching mustache, training a garden hose on a cluster of containerized saplings. Water streamed from the container bottoms toward a drain in the concrete floor.

"Abe always told him to do that in the morning, before we open," said Jeffery. "But Ben has his own way of doing things."

"Let's go say hello," I said to Deena. Leaving the plant on the counter, we walked over to the older man.

He looked up and smiled pleasantly. "How can I help you?"

"We just wanted to offer our condolences," I said, "on the loss of your boss, Abe."

"That's nice of you," said Ben, with a slightly bemused expression.

"I think we have some mutual acquaintances," I continued. "We work at Flower House."

"Ah!" he said, brightening. "Give my regards to Felix. I haven't seen him in a while."

I gathered that Ben wasn't one to keep up on Aerieville gossip. All the better.

"Felix recently retired," I said. "Jim Lomack too."

"Well, good for them! I hope they found something to occupy their time. I don't think I'll ever retire. If I'm lucky, I'll die right here among the green leaves and dirt."

"Hopefully, no time soon!" said Deena.

I smiled, thinking how nice it was to see somebody doing a job they actually enjoyed.

"So, Ben, we're actually trying to gather some information about Abe," I said, being purposefully vague. "If it's not too difficult, would you mind sharing your impressions of him? I know not everyone got along with him, but I figure you must have, since you worked for him for so long."

Ben walked over to the faucet on the wall and turned off the water. "I don't mind. I got along with Abe, because I learned how to ignore him. He could be irritating for sure, but he mostly left me alone. He needed me here, especially when Jim left to go work for Felix."

Thrilled that we found someone willing to talk, Deena and I urged Ben to go on. He shared a few stories about times he and Abe had butted heads—and how Ben had always come out on top. I assumed his tales included a fair amount of embellishment, but there wasn't a trace of ire in the telling. Ben apparently harbored no ill will against his late boss.

"I don't suppose he'd fired anyone recently," I said, trying to ferret out any enemies I might not be aware of. Some small part of me still hoped the murderer would turn out to be someone I didn't personally know.

"Nah, not in quite a while. In fact, it seems we're constantly short-staffed—between kids going back to school or losing interest and old-timers passing away."

His last comment made me think of Richard's mother. "Did you know Mrs. Wales?"

"Of course. Barbra Wales was the sweetest lady. She had a greener thumb than me, and that's saying something."

"We know her son, Richard," said Deena.

Ben nodded. "Oh, sure. Richie. He's a regular. Just saw him last week. He and Abe were arguing about something." Ben chuckled at the memory. "Abe was always arguing with somebody. I think he liked to be contrary just for the fun of it."

Deena and I exchanged a glance. "Do you know what they were arguing about?" I asked.

"I couldn't say. Truth is, I don't always have my hearing aids turned on." He tugged on one of his earlobes and winked. "Used to drive Abe batty."

"Do you know Bill and Flo Morrison?" asked Deena. "I'm wondering if Abe argued with them too."

"Sure. I have a passing acquaintance with the Morrisons. Haven't seen them here in ages, though."

"What about Valerie Light or Letty Maron?" I asked.

Ben shook his head. "I don't think so. There *was* a Maron who worked here once. Trent Maron."

"That's Letty's son. I think he worked at Flower House too," I said, recalling the old employee list I'd found.

"He worked here for such a short time, I'm surprised I remember him," said Ben. "Like I said, the younger kids don't stick around long."

Jeffery called out to Ben and asked him to help another customer with her purchase.

"Nice gabbing with you, ladies," said Ben. "You were more fun to talk to than the police investigators. You listened to my stories."

"It was nice meeting you," said Deena.

I thanked Ben, and we returned to the back counter to retrieve the hydrangea bush. On our way out to the car, we were each lost in our own thoughts. Hearing Ben speak about his former boss with such amused tolerance made Abe seem less unpleasant than I'd previously thought. Felix must have liked Abe, too, I realized. At least enough to trust him to take care of Gus.

Deena took the hydrangea from me, so I could open the hatchback and clear out a space. As soon as the plant was safely stowed in the car, I moved toward the driver's side door. But I paused before opening it. Ben and a middle-aged woman were walking our way, he wheeling a dolly holding a small tree. I waited as he placed the tree in the back of the woman's truck.

"Did you want to talk to Ben some more?" asked Deena.

"I do have one more question," I said. As soon as the woman climbed into her truck, I waved at Ben and walked over to him, with Deena at my heels.

"Hi again," I said. "I was just curious. Did Abe have any pets?"

"Not in many years," said Ben. "He used to breed beagles, but he gave that up about seven or eight years ago."

"Ah, that explains it," I said. "Felix was going to ask Abe to take care of his dog. He must have known Abe would have the space and equipment."

"Could be," said Ben. "There's probably still a kennel in the barn. There might be some wire crates or cages too." He gestured to an old pole barn adjacent to the greenhouse. A winding driveway led from the barn to a brick farmhouse in the rear.

"Is that where Abe lived?" I pointed toward the house.

"Yep. A lot of house for a single guy, if you ask me."

"We spoke with his sister, um—"

"Bette," supplied Deena.

"Right. Bette was telling us how she'll be back in a few weeks to go through Abe's things. I might be interested in the dog supplies."

"They'll probably have an auction," Ben said. "You should come back and bid on 'em."

"Yeah, maybe. I wonder . . . Do you think it would be alright if we peeked in the barn? Just to see what's in there?"

Ben shrugged. "It's alright by me. I think it's unlocked."

Deena shot me a look of surprise. As soon as Ben was

out of earshot, she turned on me. "What do you expect to find in the barn—besides dirt and spiders?"

"I don't know. But let's hurry before anyone decides to stop us."

I walked quickly up the driveway, with Deena at my side. In truth, I was more interested in Abe's house. Between the barn and a line of fat pine trees in the side yard, the view from the garden center to the house was conveniently obscured.

As it turned out, the interior of the barn wasn't very dirty at all. One side contained an organized collection of gardening tools and industrial shelves bearing bags of growing medium and fertilizer. The other side resembled a stable, with stalls that had evidently been used as a dog kennel at one time. The space was now used to park a riding lawn mower and a four-wheeler.

After a quick look around, I turned my attention to the house. Deena followed my gaze. "Bill and Flo seemed to think Abe had something they want," she said, putting voice to my thoughts.

"Shall we take a peek?"

With a casual attitude—and frequent glances toward the garden center and road—we circled Abe's house. As might be expected from a professional landscaper, the home was surrounded by ornamental grasses, manicured shrubs, and a path of river rock leading to a wrought-iron bench beneath a willow tree. While Deena played lookout, I ran up to each door just to give the knobs a jiggle. I didn't really expect them to be unlocked, and they weren't.

Rejoining Deena under the trees in the side yard, I shook my head. "No luck."

"I don't suppose you know how to pick a lock," she whispered.

"Why, Deena Lee! I declare." I touched my chest in mock surprise. "I never took you for a law breaker."

She tilted her head at me and scowled. "This was your idea in the first place," she hissed. "I don't even know why I'm here."

"What?" I said, no longer joking. "You and I are in the exact same position. We *both* witnessed Abe's death, and we both want to know who did it and why."

"We are *not* in the same position," she argued. "You're the one in charge of Flower House, and you've been taking the lead on all this investigation stuff."

"You said you wanted to help!" I could feel my face getting hot. Why was Deena turning on me like this?

Deena rolled her eyes. "This is crazy. We're sneaking around like a couple of kids, and we don't even know what we're doing. We should leave this case to the professionals."

"Fine," I said shortly. "If that's—"

I broke off at the sound of a car rumbling up Rural Route One. As one, Deena and I dropped to the ground and ducked behind a lilac bush. We stared at each other with wide eyes, listening as the car seemed to slow down. Would it turn into the lane leading to Abe's house? My mind immediately started formulating excuses for why we were crouching next to Abe's house instead of looking in the barn.

The car kept going without turning in. I breathed a sigh of relief, and Deena stood up shakily. "Craziness," she muttered.

But I didn't stand up right away. Something had caught my eye. From my vantage near the ground, I had a good view of a basement window. And the window was open.

Chapter 17

The western sky laid bare the loveliest shade of tangerine with streaks of pale pink and violet blue as Deena and I drove back toward town, away from Ranker's Garden Center. Willie Nelson crooned a ballad on the radio, and Deena and I spoke little. After a couple of minutes, she pushed her sunglasses to the top of her head and checked her phone.

"My parents will be expecting me for dinner by seven o'clock," she said.

"I need to pick up Gus from Dumbbells and check on things at Flower House."

"It won't be completely dark 'til after nine," she said.

"I can leave Gus with Calvin."

"Maybe we should take my car," said Deena. "This orange thing is bright as a beacon."

I glanced over at her and smiled. "Good idea. Pick me up at Flower House?"

"I'll be there by quarter after nine."

Two and a half hours later, give or take, we were once again on Rural Route One, this time with Deena behind the wheel. The minute I'd told her we actually had a way into Abe's house, her curiosity returned and she was on board with our snoop mission. She'd apologized for snapping at me earlier and said she was only scared. I understood. I was scared too—which was all the more reason, I realized, we should be extra cautious. The last thing we wanted was for nice old Ben to notice my car still in the lot and come looking for us. If we were really going to search Abe's house, we needed to leave and come back after dark.

Part of me expected Deena to back out. Heck, I thought about backing out myself. Yet here we were, dressed in black jeans, dark sweaters, and leather gloves like a couple of amateur cat burglars. Deena pulled her car slowly into the lane leading to Abe's house and parked close to the barn, out of sight of the road. She cut the engine, leaving us immersed in darkness.

"I guess nobody's home," I said, in a lame attempt to be funny.

Deena craned her neck to look around. A glow of outdoor lights emanated from the garden center but didn't reach Abe's property. In the distance, dots of orange light across the fields indicated the nearest neighbors were miles away.

"Let's get this over with," she said.

I pocketed my phone and a small flashlight and left my purse in the car. Deena did the same, and together we ran toward the trees at the side of the house. It was a breezy, moonless night, the only sound the rustle of willow branches trembling in the wind.

With one last look toward the garden center, we scurried to the basement window. Squatting down, I slipped my fingers under the sash and gave it a push upward. It slid open with little effort. Shining my flashlight inside, I saw what appeared to be a laundry room. Directly beneath the window was a dryer, piled high with a jumble of clothes and towels—which would explain why anyone in the house might not have noticed that the window was open.

I handed Deena my flashlight, and she lit my way as I crawled in the window and hopped from the dryer to the floor. She passed me my flashlight, and I did the same for her. She jumped down more gracefully than I had, but we'd both knocked laundry to the floor.

"We'll pick it up on our way out," I whispered.

"Where should we start?" she asked.

"Upstairs. Office, if there is one. Bedroom, kitchen. I don't know. We'll be like the bear who went over the mountain."

"What?" She looked at me as if I were speaking in riddles.

"You know. See what we can see."

There was just enough light for me to see Deena rolling her eyes. I laughed nervously. The adrenaline was making me giddy.

We left the laundry room and took a quick walk around the finished basement. It seemed to consist largely of an unused rec room, dominated by a pool table, which was now being used for storage. I shined my flashlight into an open cardboard box and saw that it contained a tangle of Christmas lights.

Upstairs, the house was messier than I expected, with clothes draped over the living room furniture, shoes jumbled by the front door, and dishes piled in the kitchen sink.

"I guess his sister didn't have time to get started in here," I said.

"And he obviously didn't have a cleaning service," said Deena, her flashlight illuminating a layer of dust on the console behind the sofa.

Finding nothing of interest on the first floor, we made our way upstairs, where we found three bedrooms and a bathroom. The master bedroom featured an unmade bed and matching oak dressers, the tops of which were covered with loose change and assorted men's jewelry. Deena pulled open the folding doors of a closet, while I carefully rifled through the dresser drawers. The only thing we uncovered was the lingering scent of Abe's overpowering cologne, which was simultaneously off-putting and sad.

A faint creak made me pause. I glanced over at Deena, who was looking toward the window.

"It was only the wind," she said, quietly.

"Yeah. I figured."

For some reason, I recalled Granny's theory that Abe's spirit wasn't at rest. What had she said I should do? Bury something belonging to him . . . inside a potato?

My eyes slid to the dresser covered in change. Would a penny be personal enough?

"There's nothing in here," said Deena, moving to the door.

I shook myself. What was I thinking? I knew better than to fall for Granny's superstitions. I followed Deena to the next room, which appeared to be used for storage. It contained a bed covered with miscellaneous boxes and books, an exercise bike covered with a winter coat, and a giant CRT television, gathering dust in the corner.

We continued on to the last bedroom, which was clearly a home office, considering the desk, filing cabinets, and a card table stacked foot high with papers, booklets, and binders. It was also apparent that the police had confiscated Abe's computer, as there was an empty space on the desk and a mousepad with no mouse. As we stood looking around, trying to decide where to start, the room brightened, as a car zoomed down Rural Route One.

"Alright," I said. "You take the filing cabinets, and I'll tackle the table."

Deena nodded, and we continued our search, not knowing what we were even looking for. It didn't take long for me to realize that the table was a catchall. Evidently, it had become a repository for everything from board meeting notes and business proposals to paid bills and junk mail. After a couple of minutes of silent snooping, Deena reported that the filing cabinets contained garden center receipts and statements.

"I'm sure the police have already looked through all this stuff," I said, frustration mingling with disappointment. "But from what you heard, Bill and Flo thought the cops wouldn't think anything of . . . whatever it was they gave to Abe. What could they have given to him?"

"I don't know," said Deena. "But I don't want to be here much longer. I think we're pushing our luck." She moved to the window and peered outside, as another vehicle rumbled down the road past the house.

"This would be easier if I didn't have to hold a flashlight in one hand," I complained.

"I'll help." Deena came over and took my flashlight, allowing me to use both hands to shuffle through papers.

I flipped through binders, keeping an eye out for anything that could be connected to the Morrisons. Picking up the last binder, I uncovered a bulky manila envelope that had been smashed underneath.

"What's this?" I said, undoing the clasp on the envelope.

Deena directed the light as I reached inside and pulled out some of the contents—which turned out to be brochures and pamphlets.

"What are those?" asked Deena, angling her head to see. "Restaurant brochures?"

"Yeah," I said, feeling a twinge of hope. I had a feeling we were finally on to something. I read some of the brochure titles out loud. "'Western Ghost Town BBQ,' 'Fabulous Fifties Musical Soda Shop and Burger Joint,' 'Blue Lagoon Pig Roast and Hula Show.'" I looked up into Deena's frowning face. "They're all theme restaurants."

"Ew. How tacky."

"Or fun," I countered. "They sound kind of fun to me."

I turned over the envelope and dumped the rest of the contents on the table. It was more of the same: informational cards and brochures describing theme restaurants all around the country. But then I saw something else. Caught between two pamphlets was a folded piece of paper. I opened the paper and held it under the flashlight's beam.

"Bingo! Look at the top of this stationery: 'Bread n' Butter Bakery, Aerieville, Tennessee.' This proves Bill and Flo must have given this package to Abe."

"So, they want to build a theme restaurant?" said Deena. "That's their big secret project?"

"I guess so," I said. "But I don't get why it should be a secret."

"Well, not everyone would support something like this," Deena pointed out. "A theme restaurant seems more appropriate for a tourist town, such as Gatlinburg or Pigeon Forge. Or Nashville, even."

"That's true," I said. "If they plan on putting it where their bakery is, that could be kind of obnoxious for the neighbors." I imagined what it would mean for a tourist attraction to open up on quiet old Oak Street. More cars, for sure. Parking would be a nightmare. Suddenly, I gasped, as another realization hit me. Turning to Deena, I said, "They probably want to tear down Flower House and build a parking lot!"

"Could be," said Deena. "So, what does the paper say?"

I held up the stationery and squinted to read the scrawled handwriting. I had to read it twice before I understood. It was the name of the restaurant Bill and Flo wanted to open.

"Oh, Deena," I whispered. "It's so much worse than we imagined."

"What does it say?" she demanded.

I gulped, hardly able to say the words aloud. "It says . . . 'Bill and Flo's Hillbilly Hootenanny: Down Home Cookin' and Jug Band Music.'"

"Oh, no," said Deena, aghast. "Why? Why would they use that word?"

I shook my head, feeling disgusted and betrayed. In Appalachia, the word "hillbilly" was a loaded term. While some folks might own the label as a point of pride, no one would want it exploited. In my opinion, it was derogatory and outdated, representing an awful stereotype so many Appalachians had worked hard to overcome.

"I'd be fine with folk music and down home cookin'," I said. "But it sounds like they plan on exploiting the old unsophisticated, backwoods portrayal of mountain people. No one in Aerieville would ever go for this."

"It might attract out-of-towners, though," said Deena. "People who don't realize how offensive it is."

A loud crash made us both jump. Deena grabbed my arm. "What was that?"

"It sounded like something fell," I whispered. "I think it came from downstairs." I quickly stuffed the brochures and papers back into the envelope and replaced it beneath the binder where I'd found it. Then we tiptoed to the hallway and listened. There was nothing to hear.

"Maybe it was the wind again," I said, keeping my voice low.

"Let's get out of here," said Deena.

When we got to the foot of the stairs, I paused, as a strange feeling came over me. The back of my neck prickled. I turned toward the kitchen.

"What's the matter?" asked Deena.

"I don't know," I murmured. "Does it feel colder in here to you?"

"I may be shaking," she said, "but it's not because of the temperature. Come on."

Ignoring Deena, I crept into the kitchen and looked around. It didn't take long to spot something out of place. A broom lay in the center of the floor, in front of the open door of a closet pantry. We had peeked in the pantry before, but I couldn't remember if we'd closed the door behind us.

"Here's the source of the noise we heard," I said.

Deena came up behind me. "Weird. Should we put it back?"

I picked up the broom and replaced it in the closet, using my flashlight to make sure I propped it securely in the corner. For the heck of it, I then raked my light along the shelves. One row held boxes of cereal and crackers. The next row up held cans of soup and vegetables. The top shelf held paper towels, packages of batteries, light bulbs, and . . . something that made my breath catch in my throat.

"What's this?" I said, reaching for the small object. "A cell phone?"

Deena shined her own light on the phone in my hands. "Abe had his cell phone with him at Flower House," she said. "Maybe this is an old one."

"Or a backup. Or one he used for work." I pushed the power button on the side, and the phone lit up.

"It's charged?" Deena sounded surprised.

"Ten percent," I said. "It could die anytime. Maybe we should take it. We can always buy a charger."

"No way! We can't take it. That would be stealing."

"Don't you want to know what's on here?" I touched the phone's screen, amazed it wasn't password protected.

"Come on, Sierra. Be smart. How would you explain it if someone found out?"

I bristled at the idea I wasn't being smart, but I knew

she was right. "Let me at least look at his most recent messages," I said, touching the email icon at the bottom of the screen.

"Please hurry. We already found what we were looking for, and we've been here way too long."

"Just a minute."

I scrolled quickly through the messages, hoping something would jump out at me. There were a few mundane exchanges with colleagues on the zoning board and some routine appointment reminders. I got excited for a second when I saw Valerie's name, but it was only a brief exchange in which Abe asked her to meet him at Nell's. She replied with one word: "Fine."

I sighed, about ready to give up, when my eyes fell on another familiar name: Richard Wales. It was an email exchange from about a week ago.

"Oh, man," I whispered. "Check this out."

I scrolled to the top and held the phone so Deena could read the messages too.

Abe: It's time for another installment.

Richard: Don't email me.

Abe: LOL. Same time, same place.

Richard: Stop this. Please. You're bleeding me dry.

Abe: I beg to differ. I think you're doing quite well.

Abe: Richard? Please confirm.

Abe: Do I need to remind you of the consequences if you miss a payment?

Richard: No. I'll come up with the money.

Abe: Good boy.

"What the—?" said Deena. "What is this? Did Richard borrow money from Abe?"

"I don't think so," I said. "This sounds like something else."

A roar of wind rattled the kitchen window, followed by the sudden pattering of raindrops. "Jeez!" said Deena, her hand at her heart. "I can't take much more of this."

I closed the email app and turned off the phone, then replaced it where I'd found it in the pantry. I was still tempted to take it, but, as Deena said, I needed to be smart. The police already had Abe's computer and other cell phone—which meant they already knew about these messages. It was probably why they were so interested in Richard.

Spurred on by the sound of pelting rain against the windows, we hotfooted it down the basement stairs and back into the laundry room. We both knew we needed to get out of there before the ground became muddy. We didn't want to leave behind perfect imprints of the soles of our shoes.

Deena grabbed up the clothes we'd knocked to the floor and hastily folded them, before returning them to the top of the dryer. I stood immobile, distracted by the whistling wind—and a nagging question about how in the world I'd found Abe's backup phone. *What made the broom fall?*

"Give me a hand?" said Deena.

I ran over to spot her as she climbed onto the dryer, careful not to disturb the laundry. We had left the window open a crack. She pushed it up the rest of the way and crawled through. I started to follow, then stared for a moment at the laundry. It consisted mainly of towels, undershirts, and handkerchiefs. Once again thinking of Granny Mae, I snatched up a handkerchief and stuffed it in my pocket. *Housebreaker, kleptomaniac. What's next?*

Before I could change my mind, I scrambled onto the

dryer—and then froze. There was a piece of torn cloth, greenish in color, stuck to the inner window frame. Had it ripped from Deena's clothes? Or mine? I hadn't noticed it before, but, then again, it was pretty dark.

"Are you coming?" hissed Deena, her face appearing at the window above me.

I plucked the piece of cloth from the edge of the window and added it to my pocket. Then I accepted Deena's outstretched hand and crawled through the window.

Chapter 18

It was almost midnight when Deena dropped me off at Flower House. Stifling a yawn, she promised to come back the next day to help with flower orders. Given the late hour, I told her to feel free to sleep in.

Oak Street was blessedly quiet. The way things had been going, I always half expected to see the red and blue flashing lights of emergency vehicles on the street. To-night, however, the block was as peaceful as a graveyard. Even the rain had diminished to a light sprinkle.

I let myself in the front door and took off my damp shoes. I had texted Calvin from Deena's car, to let him know I'd be arriving soon. He had said to come on up to his apartment. I padded down the hallway and found the door to the upstairs standing ajar. At the top of the stairs was a small landing and another door, also standing open. I tapped on it anyway before stepping inside.

"Hello?" I called quietly.

"Hey," said Calvin, giving a start. He was sitting in a brown recliner, with Gus on his lap. I gathered that they'd both been dozing. Gus hopped down and ran over to jump on my legs and lick my hands.

"Hey, buddy," I said, petting the top of Gus's head. Glancing around the apartment, I was struck with how bare it looked, with minimal furnishings and no decorations. I'd seen hotel rooms that looked homier than this. I started to tease Calvin for living like a Spartan, but I stopped myself. I was the one who kept telling him this arrangement was probably temporary.

He stood up and raked his fingers through his messy hair. "How was 'girls' night out'?" he asked, which reminded me that was what I'd told him.

"It was, uh, fun. I didn't expect to be gone so long. I'm really sorry it's so late."

"That's okay. It's been a stressful week. You deserve a night out."

Standing near Calvin, with Gus sniffing my legs and feet, I felt a faint rush of wooziness. I was sure it was just nerves and tiredness. But something about Calvin's proximity, and the way he was looking at me, took me off guard. In that moment, he somehow seemed taller and more masculine; more relaxed and less awkward than I'd ever seen him. We locked eyes and, for a split second, something seemed to pass between us.

I looked away and took a deep breath. "Thanks," I said, reaching for Gus's leash, which was coiled on a stool by the door.

"Let me guess," said Calvin, putting on a crooked smile. "Did you go to an art opening? Or was it a poetry reading?"

"Huh?" His comment seemed out of the blue, until I realized he was referring to my attire: black skinny jeans and a turtleneck sweater. "Oh. Not quite." Casting for a change of subject, I asked him how the flower deliveries went.

"No problems," he said. "I found all the addresses and

was able to deliver all the flowers in person. I even chatted with some of the customers. Folks in Aerieville are so friendly."

"Yeah, they do like to talk. Did they try to pump you for gossip?"

"Just a little. I could tell people really like Felix. Everyone seemed to agree he's kind of eccentric but really knowledgeable about orchids and other plants."

Felix. Of course. Calvin's favorite subject. It figured that that's what Calvin would wind up talking about.

"It's funny," Calvin continued. "Everyone I spoke with said they never knew Felix to travel anyplace. They said he never even talked about traveling. All he talked about was flowers, fishing, and geocache hunting."

"That sounds about right," I said, as I tried to attach Gus's leash to his collar. He wouldn't hold still, making it impossible to find the metal ring.

"Of course, it makes sense for him to hunt farther afield, like if he already found all the hidden caches in this area. But how far could he have gone?"

Gus pulled away from me and jumped up onto Calvin's recliner. I sighed. "Look, I know you're disappointed Felix left, after he said you could live here. But I honestly don't know where he is."

Calvin twisted the hem of his untucked shirt. "It's not just that. I was looking forward to meeting him so we could talk shop. We met online on this forum for, um, all things botany. He seemed like an expert on rare plants. I thought I might learn a thing or two from him."

I walked over to Gus and scratched his head and neck, lulling him into complacency. Then I deftly found the ring on his collar and attached the leash. "Gotcha," I said.

Calvin chuckled, and I looked up at him with a grin. The guy really had been a big help over the past few days. A huge help. I knew I ought to do something nice for him.

"Calvin, you're welcome to look through the books in Felix's office downstairs."

"Cool. Thanks."

"And, I suppose I ought to check on things at his cabin. He has lots of books there too. If you'd like, you can come along."

"Awesome! I'd like that."

"I don't think there will be time tomorrow, but we can drive out there on Saturday morning."

Calvin clapped his hands together, like a kid at a birthday party. "It's a date! I mean, not a date. An appointment. A plan. You know what I mean."

And gawky Calvin was back.

I tried to sleep in on Friday morning, but I had way too much on my mind. The strange dreams didn't help—especially the last one, in which I was sharing a bed with Calvin. Or was it Calvin? Maybe it was my cheating ex-boyfriend, Josh, who only looked like Calvin in the dream. Either way, I woke up feeling confused and slightly embarrassed.

To shake off the cobwebs, I threw on a jacket and took Gus for a brisk sunrise walk around the block. My sleepy neighborhood consisted mainly of other small homes, housing a mix of childless young couples and widowed senior citizens. Another dog walker, one of the latter, tipped his hat at me from across the street. Our dogs barked their greetings.

Back home, I started my coffeepot and hopped in the shower. A vague sense of guilt was starting to set in, becoming hard to ignore. After last night, I now knew things I wasn't supposed to know—and I had no good way of explaining how I knew them. What was I going to do?

I got out of the shower and toweled off, then stared at

my reflection in the mirror. I looked paler than usual, my brown eyes big and dark . . . like some kind of sickly Victorian maiden. Laughing at myself, I combed my hair. That was another thing. My bangs had grown to an annoying length—long enough to fall in my eyes, but too short to pull back. At least that was one problem I could fix. I found a pair of scissors and gave myself a trim, catching the clippings in a towel draped over the sink. I'd shake it out later.

That done, I applied a bit of makeup in an attempt to bring some color to my face. Then I dressed in blue jeans and a rainbow T-shirt.

"It's called 'fake it 'til you make it,'" I said to Gus, who was lying in the center of my bed. "Or is it 'dress for the part you want'? Either way, sometimes you gotta start with the external if you want to change your internal state." At the moment, my internal state was verging on anxious and worried. "I'd rather be calm and happy, so that's what I'll project."

For added oomph, I dipped into my collection of essential oils, which I kept in a carved wooden box on my vanity. I perused the little bottles, then selected a "tranquility" blend. I unscrewed the bottle and took a deep inhale. *Ahhh*.

I was feeling better already when I went into the kitchen for breakfast. Making a concerted effort not to rush, I ate my banana-topped cereal and sipped my coffee. *I am calm and collected. I am filled with joy and peace.*

I cleaned up my breakfast dishes and was pulling on my boots when my cell phone rang. It was Byron. Just seeing his name made my calmness level slip a few notches.

"Hello, Mr. Atterly," I said.

"Sierra. Good morning. I know it's early, but I wanted to let you know as soon as possible."

My mind raced with possibilities, each one worse than

the last. *The insurance company denied our claim; he was retiring; there had been another break-in . . .*

"I received a visit yesterday evening from Bill Morrison. He and his wife would like to buy Flower House."

I dropped into the nearest chair and slumped my shoulders. "Really?"

"Yes. They want the building, the property, and all appurtenances. Everything. And they made quite a decent offer. I need to run the numbers, but I believe you would still make a nice little profit even after all debts are paid. We can simply transfer title to you, per Felix's instructions, and then transfer it, in turn, to the Morrisons. Shall I start drawing up the paperwork?"

"Um. Can I get back to you?"

There was a pause at the end of the line, then Byron cleared his throat. "Of course. Think it over. Talk to your parents. I'll check in with you later."

"Thanks, Mr. Atterly."

And just like that, my anxiety was right back where it started. Sensing my change in mood, Gus placed his paws on my knees and tried to cheer me up with his avid attention. I couldn't help but smile.

"You're right, Augustus," I said, sitting up straight and patting his head. "Let's try this again."

I am calm and collected. I feel peace and joy. It's going to be a great day.

Gus and I arrived at Flower House just a few minutes past opening time. Not that it mattered. It wasn't like customers were beating down the door.

I didn't expect Calvin to be up yet, so I was surprised to find him ensconced in the office, surrounded by piles of books and papers.

"Hello," I said, corralling Gus on a doorknob in the

hallway. "Is it just me, or are you making a bigger mess than the intruder did?"

"I'm organizing the books by subject and size first, and then alphabetically in each category. And don't worry. I don't need any help. I can do it all by *my shelf*."

"Great," I said half-heartedly, stepping over a pile of books to get to the desk. "I need to check for online orders."

"Too early for humor?" he asked.

"Sorry." I sat down and turned on the computer. "I'm just a little distracted. Someone offered to buy Flower House."

"Whoa! Really? Think they'll let me stay? Maybe if you and I sign a long-term lease, they'll *have* to let me stay."

"I didn't say I was accepting the offer. There are some things I need to figure out. It's complicated."

"Yeah, sure. Okay." Calvin returned to his sorting, wisely perceiving that I didn't want to talk.

I pulled up the Flower House website and printed out the recent orders—five in all. Then I moved to the kitchen to get to work. Gus followed me with his eyes, before reclining in the hallway. He made sure to pick a spot where he could keep an eye on both me and Calvin.

I started out on automatic pilot. My body went through the motions of gathering supplies and prepping flowers, while my mind wandered to the night before. The biggest bombshell, as far as I was concerned, was the revelation that Richard had something going on with Abe. Of course, it might have been innocent. Perhaps, as Deena wanted to believe, Richard had borrowed money from Abe, and Abe was pressing him to pay it back. But I suspected it was more than that. To me, it sounded like Abe was holding something over Richard, maybe even blackmailing him for some reason. In a way, it didn't really matter. Whatever was going on, the fact remained that Richard had lied. And, worse, it appeared he could have a motive for murder.

I arranged salal greenery in a vase, forming a base for a bunch of fluffy pink peonies and blush ranunculus. As I fed the stems into place, one by one, I tried to look on the bright side. The police undoubtedly already knew about the email exchange between Abe and Richard. Since Richard hadn't been arrested, maybe the messages were no big deal after all.

On the other hand, for all I knew, the cops might still be watching him. Maybe they were in the process of obtaining a search warrant, or gathering evidence, or doing whatever it is police professionals do. *As Chief Walden keeps telling me, he supposedly knows what he's doing.*

"Who knows?" I muttered to myself. "Maybe they'll actually wrap up this investigation sooner rather than later. That would be a good thing."

Only I didn't feel at all good about it. I liked Richard. And I felt crummy for even imagining him as the culprit. Plus, I still had a ton of outstanding questions. Like, why did someone keep trashing Flower House? And why was a product containing strychnine planted in the shed out back? Was it meant to cast suspicion on Felix? Or on *me*?

I put the finishing touches on the peony bouquet, poking in sprigs of sweet pea for an extra-romantic effect. Then I stashed it in the cooler and began the next arrangement: a basket of chrysanthemums, asters, and lilies. For this one, I needed to make a base of chicken wire to fit in the bottom of the basket. As I worked, my thoughts again ran their own course, landing on the other big discovery yesterday: Bill and Flo's theme restaurant idea. *Ugh.*

Of course, poor taste hardly made them murderers, but I wasn't ready to rule them out. They'd started acting weird, all sneaky and secretive and opportunistic, the morning after Abe died. Did that mean he had been blocking their plans? More likely, from what I'd learned about Abe, he was probably demanding a bribe. Maybe he wanted a stake in their business.

Hillbilly Hootenanny. Of all things. The Morrisons must believe there's money to be made in the venture. Abe was evidently in their way . . . and now he's gone. Flower House is in their way . . . and now Felix is gone, and we're having one calamity after another. With Bill and Flo right next door, it wouldn't take much for them to pop over here under cover of darkness. One of them could stand guard while the other wreaked havoc.

I finished the flower basket, then peeled off my gloves and washed my hands. Before starting on the next order, I checked my phone. It was almost eleven and still no word from Deena. I'd told her to sleep in, but I didn't really expect her to be this late. I could have used her help. I was debating whether I should text her when there was a sharp rap on the back door. I jumped and Gus yipped.

With the boards over the window, I couldn't see who it was, but since Deena had just crossed my mind, I figured it was probably her. I unlocked the door and pulled it open to reveal . . . Richard.

"Whew!" he said, examining the lock on the door. "I'm glad to see my handiwork is still intact. When I heard about the second break-in here, I was worried they'd busted right through the lock again. I don't want you thinking I do shoddy work!"

"Um, of course not. They broke the window this time, as you can see." I was so taken off guard by Richard's sudden appearance, I had to bite my lip to keep from babbling.

He came inside and looked around, his eyes sweeping the room. He had a habit of doing that, I realized. What was he looking for?

He walked past me and out to the hallway, where he leaned down to pet Gus. "Hey, little guy. Have you been falling asleep on the job? Neglecting your watch-dog duties?"

"He wasn't here when the break-in happened," I said, moving to the doorway. "It must've been sometime between five and eight thirty on Wednesday evening." I wanted to ask Richard where *he* was during that time, but I didn't have the nerve.

"I ran into Deena at the coffee shop this morning," he said. "She told me everything."

"She what?" If I had been drinking, I would've done a spit take. Surely, Deena wouldn't have told Richard about what we did last night.

"It was a pretty big mess, huh? Lots of damage?"

I let out a breath of relief. *Of course, Deena didn't say anything about last night. I never doubted her for a minute. . . . Not much anyway.*

Richard poked his head in the office and raised an eyebrow. "Wow."

"It's not as bad as it looks," said Calvin.

Gus was sniffing Richard's legs, probably hoping for more attention. I gently pulled him back. "So, uh, did Deena say anything else?"

Now Richard directed his raised eyebrow at me. "Why? Is there something else to tell?"

"No! I just mean . . . I wonder what she's up to this morning. She's been helping me out, and I thought she'd be in by now."

Richard shrugged. "She was getting her coffee to go. Maybe she had shopping to do."

Calvin came out of the office and handed me a piece of paper. "Another order popped up on the computer, so I printed it out for you."

"Thanks." I looked at the paper, then handed it back

to him. "This is for Mother's Day. Can you just put it on the desk, please?"

Richard took a few steps up the hall and peeked in the orchid room. "Do you need help with any repairs?"

"Well, I need new glass for the window in the back door."

He pulled a tape measure from his pocket and came back toward the kitchen. "I can get that for you."

Just then, the front door jingled and Gus let out a bark of warning. Or of welcome. It was hard to tell. Calvin was still standing in the hallway, so he said he'd greet the customer. As Richard and I turned our attention to the back door, we could hear Calvin calling out; "Good morning!" A second later, we heard him say, "Oh, hello, Officer. How can I help you?"

Richard snapped to attention and retracted his tape measure with the press of a button. "Look at the time," he said, without looking at a watch, clock, or phone. "I have to get back to work. I'll come back later."

With that, he dashed out the door and was gone.

Chapter 19

I had to take three centering breaths and repeat a mantra for self-confidence (*I am a responsible adult, I am a responsible adult*), before I could bring myself to face Chief Walden. I felt sure he was going to chide me for continuing to ask people about Abe. Maybe someone overheard Deena and me asking questions at the garden center. There was no way the chief could know about us going into Abe's house. No way.

Wiping my palms on my pants, I swallowed my nerves and came out of the kitchen. I could hear Calvin chatting nonstop in the front of the shop. As I got closer, I gathered he was talking about orchids.

"There are more than twenty-five thousand species! Isn't that incredible? Of course, probably less than a hundred are cultivated as houseplants. Most people are only aware of a few them: phalaenopsis, paphiopedilum, dendrobium, oncidium—"

"I had no idea," said a woman's voice, cutting him off.

I had to round the corner to see who it was, because she was crouched on the floor, scratching Gus's belly. Was there anyone that little dog didn't trust?

"Officer Bradley! Hi," I said, recognizing her from her response to the first break-in. She had been the older cop who had come with the younger Officer Dakin. Her short blonde hair was down this time and pushed behind her ears. I looked around, half expecting Chief Walden to pop out and scare me. "Are you alone today?"

"Yep, it's just me." She stood up, much to Gus's disappointment, and pulled out a pocket notebook. "Chief asked me to check on things here and ask a couple of follow-up questions."

"She wanted to know what we grow in the greenhouse," said Calvin. "So I was telling her about the orchids and roses."

"I know orchids are grown in pots," she said, "but what about the roses? Are they grown directly in the ground?"

"They could be," answered Calvin, "but not here. The roses out back are all grown in containers. The floor is concrete."

"So, I guess you don't have to worry about gophers, then?"

So, that's what this was about. "Not that I know of," I said. "Did you learn anything from that box of gopher bait?"

The officer nodded. "It's an old product and not easy to come by. It's approved for sale to licensed exterminators only. We've been questioning all the pest-control companies in the area. No leads so far."

"I don't suppose there were any fingerprints?"

"No. The box had evidently been wiped down." She held up her hand before I could ask any more questions. "Who had access to the shed?"

"Theoretically, anyone," I said. "I could've sworn Felix used to keep it locked, but, to be honest, I hadn't been out there in ages."

"There was no lock when I went in it the other day," said Calvin. "I was looking for gardening gloves and found the place a mess."

"Either of you notice anyone near the shed in recent weeks? Hanging around or cutting through the backyard?"

"Not me," said Calvin.

"No," I said. "Sorry."

"That's okay." She started strolling around the shop, peeking in the events room and gazing down the hallway. "I'd like to talk to Felix," she said. "Have you heard from him lately?"

"Not since the day after he left, when I missed a call from him," I said. "I can give you his cell phone number, but I think the chief already has it."

"Mm-hmm," said the officer. "Is there anyone else he might be in contact with? Any relatives?"

"The only people I can think of are Byron Atterly and possibly Jim Lomack." I told her about Jim's letter to his ex-wife. Officer Bradley wrote down the information in her notebook.

Calvin snapped his fingers. "What about tracking Felix's credit card transactions? He probably bought a plane ticket and rented hotel rooms. And food, of course."

The officer gave Calvin a look of tolerant amusement. "It's a nice thought, but we can't access financial records without a court order. Felix isn't a fugitive. He's not even a person of interest. As much as I'd like to ask him about his toolshed and the poison, that's not enough to expend all our resources trying to find him. At the end of the day, he's only tangentially connected to the case."

"'Tangentially connected,'" I said, sounding out the words. "That's fun to say." I wished I were only tangentially connected to the murder.

Officer Bradley smiled, then turned the page in her notebook. "One more thing," she said. "What can you tell me about Richard Wales?"

I opened my mouth to respond, but Calvin beat me to it. "The handyman? He was just here."

"How long ago?"

"Like, just a few minutes ago. In fact, I thought he was still here."

"I didn't see his car," she said.

I frowned. *So, she knows what his car looks like.* "He left out the back. He fixed the lock after the first break-in, and he offered to repair the door again."

"Does he often do odd jobs around here?"

"Not at all," I said. "This was the first time. Richard is just a Flower House customer. I mean, I know him from high school and see him around town sometimes. But I hadn't seen him for a while before he came to the workshop the other night."

Gus ran to the front door and sat down expectantly. "Looks like somebody needs to go out," I said. It amazed me how utterly trustful he was. He knew, without a doubt, that someone would notice him and give him what he needed. I wished I had his level of confidence.

"I'll take him," volunteered Calvin. "If that's okay?" He directed his question at Officer Bradley.

"Yeah, sure. The rest of my questions are for Ms. Ravenswood."

Calvin took Gus out, and Officer Bradley moved into the events room and took a seat, leaving me no choice but to follow her.

"About the workshop," she said. "I know you gave a statement that night, but sometimes it helps to go over things again. To the best of your recollection, how was Richard behaving that evening? Did he do or say anything out of the ordinary?"

I shook my head. "No. He was his usual self. Nice, funny, helpful."

"What about with Abe? Did the two of them talk to each other?"

"Not really. But he did—" I broke off, not wanting to make something of nothing.

"He did what?"

"I don't know. It's not a big deal. When the yelling started and food was spilled on the floor, Richard blamed it on Abe. He said something about Abe grabbing at the treats like he was starving. Abe denied it."

"Did you see how the treats ended up on the floor?"

"No. I was talking to Deena and missed how it started."

Officer Bradley stared at the bakery case in the center of the room, as if imagining how it all went down. After a moment, she turned back to me. "Anything else?"

"No, ma'am."

She stood up and handed me her card. "Call us if you think of anything else that might be relevant to the investigation."

"Yes, ma'am."

After she left, I paced through the shop, adjusting dried flowers and straightening decorations. Officer Bradley might not have been as intimidating as Chief Walden, but she still made me nervous. This whole murder business was turning me into a bundle of nerves. Just as I'd suspected, the police were focusing their attention on Richard. I couldn't deny that things didn't look good for him. If he had a motive and an opportunity, did he also have the means? His mother had worked at a landscaping business. For all I knew, they could have had pesticides in their garage for years.

Calvin and Gus came back inside. I called Gus over, so I could pet his floofy head and neck and be comforted by his presence. It worked a little.

"Why were the police asking about Richard?" asked Calvin. "Do they think he's the killer?"

I flinched at the word. "I don't know. I told you from the beginning that it could be anyone."

"Wild."

I laughed without humor. "You can say that again." I walked to the front window and looked outside. Clouds were rolling in again, threatening more April showers. "The thing I still don't get," I said, half to myself, "is why Flower House is at the center of this whole thing. The murder took place here. The poison was planted in the shed here. Someone keeps breaking in. I get that someone wanted to do away with Abe. But why do they want to take down Flower House too?"

Calvin joined me by the window. "Maybe they broke in to get the police to come back and find the poison? And maybe all the activity here is meant to deflect attention off themselves."

I turned and looked at him with curiosity. "Now you're thinking like a bad guy. Smart."

He gave me a goofy grin. "I have my moments. But at *this* moment, I'm feeling hungry." He rubbed his stomach. "How about some lunch?"

I sighed. "Yeah, I guess we should order something."

"Or I could make us some food."

Now I was really surprised. "You cook?"

"I can make mac and peas. I went to the grocery store yesterday."

"Mac and peas?"

"Yeah, it's simple. You just make a box of macaroni and cheese and mix in half a bag of frozen peas. Easy peasy."

I couldn't help but smile. Comfort food for college students, singles, and busy people everywhere. "It sounds delicious."

Calvin took Gus with him upstairs, and I went back to my flower arranging. I was gathering supplies for the next order when the front door jingled again. I walked up front to find that it was Deena. Finally. Dressed in a floral-print wrap dress, dangly crystal earrings, and espadrilles, she could have stepped out of the pages of a fashion magazine. Her glossy black hair formed gentle waves over her shoulders, leading me to wonder how she always managed to look so refreshed.

"Where have you been?" I asked. "The spa?"

"Hardly. I was at City Hall. I'll tell you all about it. Do we have flowers to arrange?"

"Yes, we do. Come on back."

Deena set her purse on the kitchen counter and donned an apron from a hook on the wall. I usually didn't bother with the aprons—which might explain why I wasn't as polished as Deena. I handed her some shears and asked her to clean some yellow roses and pink and white carnations, while I prepared a vase.

"So, what's the scoop?" I asked.

"Do you remember Kate Allen?" she said.

Of course, I remembered Kate. She was another popular girl in high school, and one of Deena's many friends.

"Vaguely," I said.

"Her father is the deputy mayor. I asked for a meeting with him this morning, which he kindly granted. I just had to wait for him to finish up with some other business."

"A meeting about what?"

"Zoning matters."

"You mean—Bill and Flo's zoning matter?"

A self-satisfied grin played at Deena's plum-colored lips. "I didn't bring them up specifically. However, I did suggest to Mr. Allen that all zoning applications should be placed on hold until Abe's murder is solved."

I put my hands on my hips and stared at Deena. "And just how did you explain your reasoning for that?" I demanded.

"He already knew I was a witness to the murder. Everyone knows. I may have also implied that I was privy to certain information about the investigation. In not so many words, I said there's been talk of improprieties in the board's approval of certain projects. As a friend of Kate's, I thought it was my duty to give him a heads-up."

"What did he say?"

"He didn't seem very surprised, actually. But he wondered why the police hadn't said anything about this. I told him that zoning issues aren't their priority right now. And I reminded him that, if it turns out Abe *did* abuse his power on the board, it would look bad for the whole town. He couldn't argue with that."

"Wow. So, you think he'll do it? Put a hold on all pending applications?"

"He said that since the board is short a member anyway, there's a de facto hold. But he also said he could delay replacing Abe, at least for a couple of weeks."

"That's good." I filled her in about the call from Byron and the Morrisons' offer to buy Flower House.

"They don't waste any time, do they?" said Deena. "Well, the zoning hold should slow them down. And it buys us time. We need to figure out how to tip off the police about their scheme to open that hideous theme restaurant."

I shook my head. "I don't think the police are looking at the Morrisons at all." I told Deena about Richard's brief appearance and the visit from Officer Bradley.

Deena's face fell. "The cops are barking up the wrong tree. Whatever Richard is hiding, I can't believe he would resort to murder."

"I'd like to think so too," I said. "But the way he's been

acting—and lying to us—you've got to admit it doesn't exactly smack of innocence."

For a moment, Deena didn't say anything. At last, she nodded. "I know you're right. I just wish there was something we could do."

"Actually, there is. We can talk to Richard. If we're going to help him, we need to know the truth."

After lunch, Deena and I completed the day's flower arrangements and set off together to make deliveries. Once again, Calvin stayed behind with Gus. At least this time I remembered to show him how to operate the cash register and credit card machine. This was the last day of the flower sale, so it was possible we'd have some walk-in customers. He promised to call me if he ran into any problems.

As we drove off in my car, Deena used the visor mirror to touch up her lipstick. "Calvin seems like a good guy," she commented. "He's kind of cute too. Is he single?"

I glanced at her in surprise. "I assume he's single, though I don't know for sure. Do you want me to ask?"

She met my eyes and laughed. "Yes, but not for me. I was thinking of you. I've seen how he looks at you."

I made a face and returned my attention to the road. *Had he been giving me looks?* "He's not really my type."

"Nice and cute aren't your type?"

I waved my hand dismissively without answering. How could I explain the vision I'd created for myself? I dreamed of an exciting, romantic life, with a partner worthy of movie star billing. Calvin didn't exactly fit that image.

"Here's our first stop," I said, pulling in front of one of Aerieville's two elementary schools. It was the head secretary's fiftieth birthday, and we had two separate bouquet orders for her. Deena carried one and I carried the other as we walked up to the school entrance. We had to wait for a security guard to let us in and lead us to the front office.

"Delivery for Carole Webster," I said. "And happy birthday from Flower House."

"How lovely," said the woman behind the counter—Bonnie, according to her nameplate. "Just set them down with the others."

A nearby table held an assortment of supermarket bouquets, flower-filled mugs, a fruit basket, and lots of balloons. It was all cheerful and nice, but none were as elegant or fresh as the arrangements Deena and I had made—if I did say so myself.

"Ours are the best," Deena whispered as we started to leave the office.

"Wait a minute," said Bonnie, walking around the counter. "Steve, the security guard, had to go outside for a minute, so I'll escort you to the exit. Standard protocol."

A line of kids were coming inside from recess, so we had to wait to let them pass. It took me a second to realize the teacher leading them was none other than Letty Maron. As usual, she looked so different when she was in her element as a teacher than she did outside the school.

Deena nudged my arm. "Is that Letty? I've never seen her appear so confident and authoritative."

"I know. She really comes into her own when she's around her kids."

Bonnie turned to face us and dropped her voice. "Are you talking about Letty? She's only nervous when she's around men."

"Really?" I said. That didn't seem quite right to me, but, then again, I wasn't around her that often.

"Oh, yeah. Men make her tense. I'm something of a matchmaker, and I've tried to set her up many times. She always says she's too shy."

"That's too bad," I said, recalling that her husband had died when she was young.

Deena put one hand on her hip. "There's nothing wrong with being single," she said, with a touch of defiance. "Lately, I've started to realize I'm actually happier by myself than with the wrong partner."

I shot Deena a look of disbelief. This from the woman who, not five minutes ago, had tried to set me up with Calvin.

By this time Letty's class had moved on, clearing our path to the door. But Bonnie didn't seem to be in any hurry to return to work. "The right partner is key," she said. "Poor Letty had some bad luck in that department."

"What do you mean?" I asked.

"She told me she used to date a lot," said Bonnie, "because she wanted her son to have a father figure. Unfortunately, all the eligible men in town were either not good enough to be role models—or else they dumped her. After a while, it gave her a complex. Now she can't even be around men without getting spaghetti legs. Her words."

"Maybe she's better off," Deena insisted. "Who are we to say?"

Bonnie pushed open the school door for us. "Well, I haven't given up. I believe there's somebody for everybody."

I thanked Bonnie for walking us out and gave Deena a significant look as we walked away.

"Wow," I said, as we approached my car.

"I know!" said Deena. "Some people just can't stand the thought of a woman taking care of herself. It almost makes me want to stay single on principle."

"I'm sure Bonnie means well," I said. "I was actually more stunned by her willingness to dish the gossip so readily."

Deena chuckled. "That was pretty impressive, even by Aerieville's standards."

As we headed to our next delivery, I kept thinking about Letty and her behavior at the flower-arranging workshop. Was she really just nervous because there were men there? Would she have been equally shy around Bill, a married man; Richard, a gay man; and Abe, a straight single man? Or was all her jumpiness solely because of Abe?

I parked in front of the senior center and sat for a moment, lost in thought.

"What's on your mind?" asked Deena.

"Letty—and the fact that she used to date a lot of men."

Deena rolled her eyes. "That *is* an odd image."

"It's not that. I was just wondering if she ever dated Abe. They're about the same age, and he was single. After his wife died, anyway."

"Hmm. Interesting. So, what are you thinking? She was a spurned lover? Jealous and bitter enough to commit murder?"

I shook my head. "Not when you put it like that. If it's been years since she's dated anyone, killing Abe wouldn't exactly be a crime of passion." I opened my door and went to the rear of the car to take out a wrapped bouquet. Deena joined me on the sidewalk.

"You know," she said, "if Letty did go out with Abe, she might have been the one to end it. He wasn't exactly a catch."

"Yeah," I agreed. "Oh, well. It probably doesn't matter anyway. Even if they did date in the past, it wouldn't necessarily have any bearing on the present."

"Besides," said Deena. "My money's still on Bill and Flo. They had the most obvious motive, and they've been acting super sketchy."

I paused and met her eyes. "The same could be said for Richard. Let's try to track him down next."

After finishing all the flower deliveries, Deena and I drove by the bank to see Richard. Only, he wasn't there. His manager told us he called in sick. He hadn't been in all day.

Back in the car, Deena said, "Now what?"

"Do you happen to know where he lives?" I asked.

"No. We have his phone number, though. Should I call him?"

"Try texting first. Say we'd like to meet for tea again."

She sent the text, and we sat in the bank parking lot and waited. Two minutes later, I was tired of waiting. "Go ahead and call," I said.

He didn't pick up. Deena left a message asking him to call back, but I wasn't holding my breath. I was starting to wonder if he was in hiding.

Outside the sky had cleared, and the afternoon sun streamed through the windshield. Feeling a bit too warm, I started to lower my window, but then I had a better idea.

"It's so nice out. Want to go for a walk?"

We strolled down the sidewalk, past the bank and around the corner onto Main Street. White-petaled dogwoods lined the street, while strains of bluegrass music floated from the window of a bar and grill. I enjoyed the atmosphere, even as I kept hoping Richard would call us back. Before long, we found ourselves standing in front of Tea for You.

"Let's go on in," said Deena. "I have a taste for one of their chai lattes."

"Might as well." I followed Deena inside and perused the menu on the chalkboard behind the counter while we waited in line. School had let out, and the shop was surprisingly busy. "Who knew teenagers would be this into tea? I wish Flower House were this popular."

After we placed our orders, we had to step aside and wait for our drinks to be made. I peeked out the door to see if we could snag one of the café tables along the sidewalk outside. As I did, I spotted my mom walking toward the tea shop. I ducked back inside before she could see me.

"What was that all about?" said Deena. "Who are you hiding from?"

"It's my mom. Dang it. I don't want to talk to her right now."

Deena wagged her finger at me in mock disapproval. "Why, Sierra Ravenswood. Is that any way to treat your mother?"

"I love my mother, but I can't take her excess of concern right now. She'll start asking questions, and I'll have to tell her about Bill and Flo's offer to buy Flower House—and she'll pressure me to accept it. I don't want to deal with that right now."

"Looks like you have no choice," said Deena, nodding toward the door. "She's about to come in here."

"Nope," I said. "You wait for our tea. I'll meet you at the car."

Moving fast, I headed for the exit and startled my mom as she came inside. "Hi, Mom! Have you tried the tea here? It's real good. I gotta go move my car. See ya later!"

"Hi and bye!" called Mom.

I walked down the block feeling slightly sheepish, yet not at all regretting my action. I'd talk to my parents later. Besides, I already knew exactly where they stood regarding my involvement with Flower House. I didn't need to hear it again. What I needed to do was make a decision for myself.

Pausing at a crosswalk, I realized I'd walked the wrong way and would have to turn back to meet Deena at the bank parking lot. Or maybe I'd just go around the block. As I debated which way to go, I looked across the street and saw that I'd come to Light Steps Dance Studio. In fact, Valerie herself was standing outside next to a car along the curb, talking to a man in a baseball cap. Something about the intensity of her expression made me look again. Then the man turned, and I saw who it was: Richard.

What in the world are they going on about? Whatever it was, they both seemed pretty excited. Valerie was talking with her hands, and Richard was leaning toward her and raising his voice, as if he was trying to convince her of something.

The Walk sign flashed on, and I crossed the street toward them. When I was halfway across, Valerie glanced over and saw me, then said something to Richard, and he turned too. Then the strangest thing happened. They jumped into action, as if something had spooked them, hopping into the car and speeding off like Bonnie and Clyde on the run. And I was left in the dust, utterly perplexed.

Chapter 20

Deena and I drove all over town, sipping tea in to-go cups and keeping our eyes peeled for Richard's car. She kept asking me questions, and I kept repeating what I'd witnessed, and it still made no sense.

"You're sure they recognized you?" she asked.

"One hundred percent."

"And you're sure Valerie got in the car voluntarily?"

"That's what it looked like. She could have turned around and gone inside the dance studio. Instead, she got into Richard's car."

"I didn't even know they were friends," said Deena. "I've never seen them together before."

"Me either."

Deena tried calling Richard again to no avail. After a while, we decided to give up and go back to Flower House. It was getting close to dinnertime, and, after all the tea we drank, we both needed a pit stop anyway.

Calvin reported that it had been a quiet afternoon at the shop, though we did have a couple of walk-ins. He was able to sell a pre-made bouquet (my demo from the workshop) and two potted orchids. I supposed it was better than nothing, though not exactly sustainable in the long run. If

I was going to keep the business going, something would have to change.

That evening I tried to practice my guitar, but my attention kept drifting to one central question: *Who killed Abe?* Thinking about everything that had happened today— Richard fleeing when the police arrived, Valerie and Richard driving off in a rush, Deena and me learning of Letty's possible connection to Abe . . . not to mention Bill and Flo's bid to buy Flower House—it was enough to make my head spin.

Is it possible they were all in on it together?

I set aside my guitar and invited Gus up onto the couch. He crouched his backside down for momentum and bounded onto the cushion beside me.

"Good boy," I said, petting his face and head. He responded by trying to lick my face. Laughing, I fended him off and told him to settle down.

"What do you think, Gus? Was there a conspiracy? A big elaborate conspiracy to get rid of Abe and . . . pin it on Felix? Was that the plan?"

Gus stared at me with his soulful brown eyes, imparting doggie wisdom without saying a word.

"I know, buddy. You trust everybody, right? You can't believe anybody would do such a terrible thing. I have a hard time with it too." I sighed and scratched the top of his head. "Actually, I don't really think it was a conspiracy either. No one knew about the bouquet workshop until Saturday morning when Felix hung up the fliers. The decision to poison Abe must have been made that very day. There's no way it was a coordinated effort among five different people."

Then who did it?

I yawned, as the day caught up with me. Come to think

of it, the whole week was catching up to me, bringing a heavy weariness I felt deep in my bones. Dragging myself off the couch, I brushed my teeth, washed my face, and changed into pajamas, barely able to keep my eyes open. By the time my head hit the pillow, I was already well on my way to dreamland.

A jingling ringtone woke me up. Fumbling on my nightstand, I finally put my hand on my cell phone and brought it to my face. It was one a.m.—and the call was from Calvin.

With my heart suddenly racing, I answered breathlessly. "What is it?"

"Sorry to bother you." He sounded perfectly calm, as if this were a casual conversation in the middle of the day. "I just thought I should let you know. Somebody tried to break in again."

Now I sat bolt upright. "You're kidding! Did you call the police?"

"There's no point. They're already gone."

"What? How do you know? What happened?" Gus was awake now, too, and giving me a look that said he also wanted to know what the heck was going on.

"I booby-trapped the back door," said Calvin.

"You what?"

"Since the intruder came through the back door twice, I figured maybe they'd try it again. So, I rigged a trip wire, which I connected to flood lights and a burglar alarm."

Was I still dreaming? I couldn't believe what Calvin was telling me.

"And it worked!" he continued. "There's a window in my apartment overlooking the backyard. As soon as I heard the alarm, I ran over and looked outside. There was a person running away, toward the alley. Unfortunately, I didn't see their face, or much else. All I could tell was that they wore a black stocking cap and a black hoodie."

I frowned, still trying to process what he was telling me. "Are you saying you actually saw the person? What was their size? Tall, short? Fat or thin?"

"I couldn't tell from my vantage upstairs. Plus, they ran fast as a jackrabbit to get out of the light. But the hoodie did seem a little bulky, for what it's worth. Like maybe it was too big or else it was covering bulky clothes underneath it. It's hard to say."

I shushed Gus, who was getting restless at the foot of the bed. "I can't believe they came back," I muttered. "Are you okay, Calvin?"

"Oh, sure," he said. "I'm fine. I don't think they'll come back now."

We hung up, and I fell back onto my pillow. I wished I felt as unworried as Calvin sounded. Instead, I felt quite the opposite. In some ways, the attempted break-in tonight was worse than the others. The last one had occurred when Flower House was unoccupied, at least according to Calvin. He'd said he was at a late movie. And the first time, he claimed he was upstairs sleeping when he'd heard a loud noise. That would have been only his second night in the apartment, so it was a good bet the trespasser thought the place was empty. What about tonight? Did the intruder still not know Calvin was there? Or were they getting desperate?

On Saturday morning, I dropped off Gus with Rocky and called Deena to let her know I wouldn't be opening Flower House until the afternoon. Then I drove to the shop to pick up Calvin. He was waiting for me out front, but I still hopped out of the car to take a look at the back door.

"There's nothing to see," he said, trailing after me. "I figured I better not leave the trap set in the daytime, in case the police come by—or the insurance company or repair guy or anybody else."

"Good thinking," I said, as I examined the ground in the backyard. He was right. There was nothing to see. I made a mental note to call Officer Bradley later to let her know what had happened. For now, I wanted to get out to Felix's cabin, and back, as quickly as possible. I couldn't afford to keep the shop closed all day.

However, as we drove through tiny downtown Aerieville, I caught sight of Coffee Art Café and decided to make a quick stop. "Let's grab some breakfast to go," I said, pulling into the small parking lot behind the coffee shop. "My treat."

It had been exactly one week since I'd been in the artsy little café, though it felt like a year. I glanced at my usual table with a touch of longing. What I wouldn't give to spend a quiet morning dreaming and planning my ideal future. How had things gone so far off the rails?

As we approached the counter, the customer ahead of us stepped to the side and I gave a start of recognition. It was Valerie! She noticed me a second later and looked equally startled.

"Sierra! Um, hello." She seemed conflicted, as if she couldn't decide if she should be polite and normal or run off again.

"What's up, Valerie? Why—"

"What can I get for you?" asked the barista, cutting me off.

"Oh, uh—Calvin, you order first."

I turned around again, but Valerie had moved on to the condiments station and was pouring cream in her coffee. Calvin finished ordering, so I quickly placed mine and paid with a credit card. Then I dashed toward the exit, determined to block Valerie from leaving. She couldn't ignore me now. She didn't look happy as she approached the door, but I didn't let it faze me.

"Hey, Valerie! Do you have a minute to talk?"

Calvin joined me, handing me the cup I'd left behind and addressing Valerie. "I don't think we've met. I'm Calvin."

"Valerie Light," she said, shaking his hand. Then she plastered on a false smile and turned to me. "Sorry I can't chat. I'm on my way to the regatta. Are you going?"

"What regatta?" asked Calvin.

"Is that today?" I said. "I forgot all about it."

Every spring, whitewater-rafting enthusiasts from all over the country converged for the Raft Race, a three-day regatta down the Nolichucky River, from the Unaka Mountains in North Carolina into Eastern Tennessee. Folks in towns along the route joined in the festivities by picnicking along the riverbanks and cheering on the race participants. I hadn't been in a few years, but I remembered how fun it was.

I glanced at Valerie's white canvas tennis shoes. "Are you hiking to the river?" The wilderness could be rugged in places, and trails would definitely be muddy after all the recent rain.

She hesitated half a second before responding. "I'm meeting friends at the lake. There's an Earth Day festival, with music and vendors. We'll be able to see the finish line from the docks."

"Oh, wow," I said, completely disregarding my original purpose for stopping her. "I forgot about that too. And it's so beautiful out today, a perfect day to spend outside."

"Maybe I'll see you there," said Valerie, backing toward the door.

"Yeah, maybe." I turned to Calvin. "We're not dressed for hiking, but the docks aren't far from Felix's cabin.

We should swing by the festival after we do our check-in thing."

Calvin gave me a strange look, then quirked his mouth into a half-smile. "Okay. I'm game."

Not surprisingly, Valerie had slipped out. But I didn't care anymore. The prospect of spending some time by the water, beneath the sunny skies, was immensely cheering. I almost felt like I was embarking on a little getaway, if only for a few hours.

Calvin didn't say much on the drive out of town. He kept checking his phone, as if he expected a message. Once again, I realized how little I knew about him.

"So, how's your consulting project going?" I asked, in an attempt to draw him out.

"Pretty good."

"What kind of project is it?"

"Um, it has to do with plants, if you can believe it. I'm, uh, ghostwriting a book for a guy who grew up in Aerieville. It's part memoir, part natural-history guide-book."

"That sounds cool." I had so many questions, but then he abruptly changed the subject.

"Where's Gus today? I thought you'd bring him along, let him sniff around his old stomping grounds."

"He's with my brother. I figured it would be easier to get in and out of the cabin without having to watch Gus too. Plus, Rocky has the day off and has been wanting to spend time with the pup."

"Is Rocky that big muscular guy you were with the night of the second break-in? Or, one of the two big guys, I should say."

"Yeah. That was my dad and brother," I said. "If you're wondering why I'm not in shape like they are, it's because I choose to spend my time on pursuits other than sculpting my muscles."

Calvin laughed. "I wasn't wondering, but I can relate. I probably haven't set foot in a gym in years."

I gave him a sidelong glance and wondered if he told the truth or not. Beneath the buttoned-up shirts and occasional awkward movements was a pretty healthy physique, from what I could tell.

"Say, Calvin, I have to ask you something."

He shifted uncomfortably. "What is it?"

"How can you stand living at Flower House, considering everything that's been happening? I mean, to be honest, I'm not sure it's responsible of me to let you stay in that apartment."

"Oh, well, it hasn't really affected me. It's actually the perfect situation—a nice location, working with plants and all. Plus, you offered to waive next month's rent. Win-win!"

I shook my head. "You're really not scared? Is it because you're from a big city and more used to crime?" Knoxville might not be the biggest metropolis, but it *was* the third largest city in the state.

Calvin snorted in amusement. "Yeah, that must be it. I'm hard core. Danger is my middle name."

"Right." I rolled my eyes and concentrated on driving, as the road became windier and the surrounding landscape dense with trees. Before long, we pulled into the lane leading to Felix's cabin.

It had only been a week, but the small property already had a look of desolation about it. Weeds had sprouted among the perennials in the front yard, and mail overflowed from the mailbox. Calvin collected the mail, while I unlocked the front door.

Inside, the home smelled musty. I walked from room to room, opening windows and gathering houseplants, which I moved to the round dining table. I planned to bring them back to Flower House.

"Some of this mail looks like bills," said Calvin. "Felix must expect to be back within a month, right? I think you can miss a bill or two before utilities will be shut off."

I opened the refrigerator door and began removing cheeses and other more perishable items. Anything expired, I tossed in the garbage. The rest I bagged to take with us. Might as well not let all the food go to waste.

"I know it seems weird," I said, "but Felix told his bookkeeper he'll be gone indefinitely. That's why he decided to leave the shop to me."

"But he didn't leave you his house?"

"No. At least, not in the message Byron gave me." I closed the refrigerator and reached for my purse, which I'd set on the kitchen counter. "Come to think of it, it's possible Felix could be keeping in touch with Byron. I'll give him a call."

I took my cell phone from my purse and dialed Byron's number. While it rang, I geared myself up for his inevitable question: Was I ready to sell Flower House? No. I still wasn't ready. However, I didn't have to put him off after all, because he didn't pick up. Instead, I found myself listening to Byron's raspy voice on an old-fashioned answering machine. Realizing he probably didn't come into the office on Saturdays, I went ahead and left a message, letting him know I was looking in on things at Felix's cabin.

After I hung up, I flipped through the mail and stuffed the bills in my purse. "I'll take these to Byron on Monday."

Calvin looked up from the coat closet, where he seemed to be rifling through jacket pockets. "Why don't you just call Felix himself?"

"What are you doing?" I asked. "I thought you wanted to look at Felix's books."

He laughed self-consciously. "I do. I just thought we might find extra doggie bags or treats for Gus." He shut the closet door and headed to the bookshelf in the living room.

I followed Calvin with my eyes, then picked up my phone again and stepped out the back door. The truth was, I'd already been thinking about calling Felix again. There was so much I wanted to discuss with him. I wanted to inform him about Abe and all the break-ins, and tell him about Bill and Flo's offer to buy Flower House. And I had so many questions, from day-to-day business matters to the presence of strychnine in the shed.

The call went directly to voice mail.

I sighed. For all I knew, he'd lost his phone or deliberately stopped charging it. I left a message anyway.

"Felix, this is Sierra. Remember me? Your faithful employee? A *lot* has happened since you left, and I really need you to call me back. Please."

I pocketed my phone and gazed into the woods behind the cabin. Many of the trees featured baby-green leaves, while some were flowering—like the red maples, whose tiny ruby-colored blossoms created a splash of color against the deep blue sky. Chirping robins whistled a cheery tune, unconcerned with the trifling problems of humans. *Focus on the positive*, I told myself. *Beauty is all around you.*

Turning around, I noticed some things Felix had left beside the back door: a fishing pole, a tackle box, and a cooler. I decided to bring them inside and clean out the cooler. I could use it to transport the cold food I'd rescued from the refrigerator.

As I leaned down to pick up the cooler, my ears detected a voice drifting from the open bedroom window. It was Calvin, apparently talking on his cell phone. Something in his tone made me hesitate. He sounded different somehow. Moving silently, I crept to the window and crouched down to listen.

"I *am* telling the truth," he was saying. "I had nothing to report before. I just now found my first lead."

There was a pause, before he continued. "If you'd calm down, I'd tell you. Listen. He has a ton of road maps, one for every state—except Colorado. That one's missing. But there's also an atlas. I turned to the page for Colorado, and guess what? He circled Pike's Peak with a red pen. That has to be where he went."

After another pause, Calvin spoke more urgently. "Yes, I'm sure. I have to get off the phone. But first—did you find out anything about the Lomack guy I told you about?"

Whatever the other person said apparently satisfied Calvin. "Good. That makes perfect sense. I'll call you if I learn anything else."

Calvin fell silent, evidently finished with his call. But I could hardly move. I was frozen, wide-eyed and confused. What did this mean?

Then my cell phone rang.

Chapter 21

Spurred to motion, I darted toward the back door before looking at my phone. I hoped it would be Felix, but the display told me it was Deena. *Darn it.*

I let the call go to voice mail and grabbed up the items Felix had left outside. I was bringing them into the kitchen when Calvin walked in from the living room.

"How's it going?" he asked, with a squeak in his voice that hadn't been there when he was talking on his cell phone. Was his whole nerdy persona an act? Why?

"Fine," I said, rinsing out the cooler in the sink. "How's it going with you? Find anything interesting?"

"Yeah." He held up two books, which looked to be scientific texts about rare plants. "Is it okay if I take these back to Flower House?"

"Sure."

Trying to stay calm, I dried off the cooler and placed the bagged food inside. It was somewhat difficult, given that my hands were trembling and my knees felt weak. Thinking back to all my encounters with Calvin, I realized he'd always been fixated on Felix's whereabouts. Why did he care so much where Felix went? And who was he talking to on his cell phone?

Calvin set the books on a chair near the door and returned to the living room. I took a deep breath and tried
to console myself. Just because Calvin was up to something didn't mean it was nefarious. I had no reason to be
afraid of him. *Right?*

Still, I didn't feel comfortable confronting him—
especially alone and in close quarters. Maybe I'd just
keep an eye on him from now on, try to figure him out.

I strolled into the living room and found Calvin rum-
maging through the papers on a writing desk.

"Are you about ready?" I asked.

He looked up, the picture of innocence. "Yeah, I guess.
I was just curious to see if Felix has any more information about rare plants around here. You know, for my book
project."

Before I could respond, my phone rang again. Seeing
that it was Deena once more, I decided to answer.

"Hey," I said. "What's up?"

"Sierra, finally! I've been trying to reach you."

"Is everything okay?"

"I'm not sure. I mean, yes, I think so, but I could use
some help. I was following Richard, but I lost him."

"Where? Tell me everything."

"I went to the grocery store this morning," she said,
"and I saw Richard in the parking lot. He was just getting
into his car, so I decided to follow him."

"Nice," I said. "Did he see you?"

"I don't think so. I assumed he would just drive home,
but instead he drove out of town. I tailed him all the way
to the lake."

"Wait. Douglas Lake? He was going to the Earth Day
festival?"

"Yes, but I don't think he's here to have fun. I saw him
meeting with some guy behind a boathouse. The guy gave
him a rather large package in a brown paper bag."

"What?" I moved to start closing windows as I listened to Deena.

"I know," she said. "It was super sketchy. I tried to keep following him, but he disappeared. He has to be here somewhere. His car is still in the lot."

"Hang tight. I'll be there in ten minutes."

Well, this is a fine mess. Here I was speeding down the road to try and uncover the secrets of one man, and who did I have at my side? Another man with secrets of his own. I didn't trust Calvin as far as I could throw him, but I had no choice. I had to bring him along. I also had to fill him in, to a point. He'd overheard my call with Deena and wanted to know what was going on. I gave him an abbreviated version, naturally leaving out the part where Deena and I had broken into Abe's house and found a suspicious email exchange between Abe and Richard.

"Richard is the handyman, right?" said Calvin. "You think he's running from the police?"

"I don't know that for sure. I just know he ran off when Officer Bradley arrived yesterday, and now he's avoiding me and Deena."

"But he's not avoiding the dancer, Valerie Light. Because you saw him with her?"

"Yeah, that's about it. I don't know what they were talking about. That's one of the things I'd like to ask him."

From the corner of my eye, I saw Calvin squint his eyes thoughtfully, as if he was trying real hard to follow my thought process. "Is that why Valerie seemed scared?" he asked.

"What do you mean?"

"This morning, at the coffee shop. She seemed kind of frightened, like she was treading lightly for some reason."

He broke into a goofy grin. "Ha. 'Lightly.' No pun in-tended."

Ignoring his joke (more so now that I suspected he was a phony), I recalled Valerie's behavior. She clearly didn't want to talk to me. Was she scared? Come to think of it, she'd seemed sort of cautious and uneasy every time I saw her recently. Which was understandable, considering a man had been murdered . . . and someone was sending her black roses.

"She's afraid she's next," I murmured, half to myself.

"Next for what?" asked Calvin.

I didn't answer. We were nearing the lake, and I had to pay attention to the signs directing us to parking for the festival. For many Southerners, Earth Day weekend had replaced Memorial Day as the unofficial start to summer. Of course, it depended on the weather. Some years, we could have snow in April. This spring was on the warm side, and folks were clearly ready to celebrate. The parking lot was packed. I had to circle around to the overflow area and drive a ways before I found an empty spot.

As Calvin and I trekked toward the festival entrance, I gave Deena a call. She told me to meet her at the flag of the world. "It's near the kids' tent," she said. "If you come in the main entryway, go right, past the solar-panel dem-onstration."

In spite of the crowd, we easily found her, sitting on a bench beside the flagpole. She stood as we approached, and when she caught sight of Calvin at my side, she broke into a sly grin. She obviously thought I'd taken her advice to heart.

"Sorry I interrupted your day off," she said. "I didn't realize—"

"It's not a day off," I interjected. "We were checking on things at Felix's cabin. What's happening here?"

She sent me a look to let me know she wasn't convinced.

Shrugging slightly, she held up a multicolored cloth bag that was draped over her wrist. "I snagged loads of goodies: reusable shopping bags, hemp hand cream, hand-stitched cotton napkins, eco lip balm. Oh! And they have sustainable lager in the beer tent. I was thinking of trying it."

I gave her a hard stare, which she waved away. "I walked through the entirety of the festival grounds, looking for Richard. You can't blame me for taking in the sights along the way."

"Still no sign of him?"

"No. However, I did see your lovely neighbors, Bill and Flo Morrison. They were standing in line at a barbecue truck."

"Oh, I know Bill," said Calvin. "Nice guy—even if he is a suspect."

"Richard probably went to the docks," I said. "We ran into Valerie this morning, and she said she was meeting friends to watch the regatta. Maybe she was meeting Richard."

"To the docks, then," said Deena, pointing the way.

"So, we're not gonna try the sustainable beer?" said Calvin. "A cold beer sounds pretty good."

I stopped and faced him. "You don't have to come with us. You should go ahead and get beer and food, or whatever. We can meet up at the car later."

"Oh, that's okay. I can wait."

"No, really," I said. "Go on and enjoy yourself."

Deena gave me a curious look, as Calvin hesitated. Then he shrugged. "If you insist. But I'll find you at the docks in a bit."

Deena grabbed my arm as we made our way down the path toward the boardwalk. "What was that all about? Don't you like Calvin?"

"Calvin is not what he seems," I said. "I don't know what he's playing at. It has something to do with Felix."

"What do you mean?" asked Deena.

"I overheard him on a phone call with somebody. I'll tell you about it later. Right now I'm more worried about Valerie."

We walked past the marina, where small yachts and sailboats were moored in a line. Several empty berths indicated boat owners were out on the water, taking advantage of the clear skies. Near the end of the boardwalk, clusters of people gathered along the railing to keep a lookout for incoming rafts. Whenever one was spotted, the spectators raised their voices in shouts and cheers, drowning out the nearby guitar-strumming street musician and making conversation impossible.

Deena and I kept a lookout, too, but not on the water. We scanned the crowds for any familiar faces. I shared with her my idea that Valerie must be afraid she was being targeted by the killer—and my fear that she might be right.

"You think Richard means to harm her?" asked Deena.

"I honestly don't know," I said. "I can't imagine what motive he would have, unless . . ." I trailed off, my imagination in overdrive.

Deena read my mind. "Abe might have told Valerie about whatever it is he was holding over Richard. The thing Richard was paying him to keep quiet."

"Exactly. Or else—maybe Richard *thinks* Valerie might know, and he's trying to find out for sure."

"Incoming!" shouted a man with binoculars. A wave of hollering followed, muddling my train of thought.

How did the black roses fit in with any of this? Or the death threats Abe had been receiving? If Richard—or Bill and Flo, for that matter—simply wanted Abe out of the picture, why send him death threats? Wouldn't that just put him on guard?

As the cheering died down, I was about to pose these

questions to Deena, but another nearby voice caught my attention.

"Look at that boat," said a woman near the railing. "It's smoking pretty bad."

Others had noticed, and soon everyone's attention was trained, not on the incoming rafts, but on a yacht out in the bay. Deena and I looked at each other, then scrambled to an empty spot along the edge of the boardwalk. I'd just laid eyes on the smoking watercraft when, in the next instant, there was a bright flash and a resounding *boom!* The boat had exploded!

Screams and chaos followed. Half the crowd wanted a closer look, while the other half wanted to get as far away as possible. Deena and I became separated in the ensuing confusion. Festival organizers tried to steer people away from the water, as an emergency vessel approached the floating wreckage.

I tried to stay out of the way, as I looked for Deena. Here and there I picked up on bits of excited conversation.

"I sure do hope nobody was hurt," said an older woman in front of me.

"Are you kidding?" said her companion. "You saw that thing blow up. There wasn't much left of it."

"Well, the passengers could have bailed," answered the first person.

I crossed my fingers, sharing the first woman's hopefulness.

"Whose boat was it?" asked a man walking by.

"I don't know," came the response. "But it hadn't been out for long. I saw it leave the slip just a few minutes before the explosion."

I made my way toward a bench on the edge of the path, thinking I'd have a better chance of spotting Deena if I stood a little higher. I had one foot on the wooden seat when someone grabbed my arm. I whirled around, flailing to keep my balance, and found myself face-to-face with Calvin. His eyes were full of concern. And, I couldn't help noticing, he'd removed his glasses and un-buttoned his shirt collar.

"What happened? People are saying all kinds of crazy things." He still held my arm in a surprisingly strong grip. Part of me wanted to pull away, but I was feeling unsteady. Instead, I leaned into him, glad for his support.

"Um, a boat exploded out in the water. That's all I know."

Above the din arose another shout. "They got some-one! The rescuers are pulling someone out of the lake!"

"We should get out of here," I said. "But I need to find Deena first. Help me look?"

"Of course. Do you want to try calling her?"

"Yeah. But I want to climb up here first." Calvin gave me a hand, as I clambered onto the bench and scanned the crowd. I had a bad feeling about the boat explosion. It could have been an accident, and totally unrelated to all the other weird things going on. But, given my worry about Valerie only seconds before it happened . . . I couldn't help fearing it might be her out there in the water.

Suddenly, the mob parted and I caught a glimpse of Deena, wandering on the sidelines like a lost child. "There she is!" I pointed and waved. "Deena! Over here!"

She didn't hear me, but at least I knew where she was now. I hopped off the bench and pushed my way toward her, with Calvin close behind.

"Wait up!" he said, reaching for my hand.

I waited half a second and let him clasp my fingers be-fore squeezing through the throngs.

What is going on? It was hardly the time for an inner battle, yet here I was, acutely aware of the spark I'd felt at Calvin's touch. Under ordinary circumstances, I'd think he was starting to have feelings for me. And, if I was being honest, I'd have to admit—

No. I wouldn't even let myself think it. He might be a crook, for crying out loud!

This was so the last thing I needed right now.

"Sierra!" Deena rushed over, and I dropped Calvin's hand like a hot cinder. "Did you hear?" she asked.

"Hear what? That they rescued somebody?"

"Not just anybody."

My heart jumped to my throat. "Was it Valerie?"

Deena shook her head. "It was Walt Walden, Aerieville Chief of Police."

Chapter 22

No one could give us any answers. We tried talking to festival organizers, marina security guards, and random bystanders, and no one knew what had happened—or what condition Chief Walden was in when they pulled him out of the water. The one promising note we learned was that he was taken away in an ambulance, hooked up to an oxygen tank. At least he wasn't covered with a sheet.

By this time, the crowds had thinned and the festival felt subdued. It was past lunchtime, so Deena, Calvin, and I made our way to the food vendors to grab some sandwiches. Not that I had much of an appetite, but I knew I'd feel worse later if I skipped a meal. As soon as we settled in at a picnic table, I called my dad. Without going into detail, I told him there'd been a boat accident and the chief was taken away in an ambulance. He said he'd head to the hospital as soon as he could.

When I got off the phone, I noticed I had a missed call and a voice message. I assumed it was Deena or Calvin trying to find me during the commotion earlier. But when I recognized the number, I gasped. The call was from Felix.

"What is it?" asked Deena.

Calvin was eyeing me curiously, so I immediately played it cool. "Oh, it's nothing. I . . . thought I saw a spider. False alarm." I laughed lamely and tossed the phone in my purse. As much as I wanted to talk to Felix, there was no way I'd do it in front of Calvin. The message would have to wait.

Actually, I didn't want to discuss *anything* in front of Calvin. I was dying to talk over recent events with Deena—especially Richard's shady rendezvous and whether or not it could have any connection to the boat explosion. Maybe my imagination was getting carried away again, but I had a hard time believing it was just a coincidence.

I picked at my sandwich and watched people stroll by. Among the remaining revelers was a pack of snickering teenagers, a couple holding hands with an adorable little girl in pigtails, two older women sharing an oversized lemon shake-up, and . . . Letty Maron. For once she wasn't wearing a cardigan sweater. Instead she wore a long yellow T-shirt over purple paisley leggings. The schoolteacher noticed me at the same time I spotted her. She walked over to our table.

"Hi, Letty," I said.

Shooting Calvin a wary glance, she addressed Deena and me. "Hello, ladies. It's a nice day, isn't it? I'm surprised there aren't more people at the festival."

"There were earlier," said Deena.

"Didn't you hear about the accident on the water?" I asked.

"No," she said, looking concerned. "I just got here a little while ago. What happened?"

"Someone's boat blew up," said Calvin. "It was pretty spectacular. And terrible, of course."

"Chief Walden was hurt," I said.

"Oh, my. How awful," said Letty. "I'm sorry to hear that."

"It sort of put a damper on the regatta," said Deena.

"I can imagine," said Letty. "I just stopped by to support some of my students. They created an interactive exhibit to encourage recycling."

"I saw that," said Deena. "They did a really good job."

Letty smiled proudly. "They worked hard on it." She started to leave, then paused and turned back. "Oh, Sierra, I ran into Flo Morrison, and she told me about Flower House. Will you be running a clearance sale?"

"What about Flower House? We had a promo that ended yesterday, but it wasn't really a clearance sale."

Letty appeared confused. "Flo told me Flower House is going out of business. I just wanted to make sure I visit one more time before you permanently close the doors."

I narrowed my eyes and glanced at Deena. Her look matched mine. "Flo is mistaken," I said, through clenched teeth. "Flower House is not going out of business."

"Oh! Alright. Well, good." She scurried off, and Deena looked at me expectantly.

Crumpling my sandwich wrapper into a tight ball, I stood up and threw it into a nearby garbage bin, with perhaps a little more force than necessary. It did little to alleviate my anger.

On the drive back to town, Calvin perused the books he'd borrowed from Felix's cabin, and I stewed about the Morrisons. As if it weren't bad enough that people were getting hurt, a criminal was running loose, and I was rapidly losing people I could trust. Why did Bill and Flo have to be so nasty? *Greed.* That was why. Pure greed.

When I pulled in front of the shop, I half expected to

find another break-in. Luckily, all was calm and intact. The front of the Victorian appeared normal—though the window display needed attention. I should have created a Mother's Day display by now.

Deena parked behind me along the curb. With my focus on the window and Calvin's nose in a book, it was she who noticed the package on the stoop.

"What is that?" she asked. "A return from a dissatisfied customer?"

"What?" I turned sharply. We'd never once had a dissatisfied customer. I couldn't bear the thought.

"Are those dead flowers?" said Calvin.

I ran up the walkway and crouched down to get a better look. "Close. They're black roses."

They were wrapped in plain brown butcher paper and lying on their side. There were six in the bunch. Fully opened, the petals were beginning to wilt and the leaves were slightly crushed. We stared down at the bogus gift, none of us quite sure what to do. Finally, I grasped the edge of the paper and pulled, letting the flowers loosen from one another. There was no note, no ribbon, nothing to indicate where they'd come from.

I looked next door toward Bread n' Butter. The bakery was open and the Morrisons' van parked in front. They must have left the festival shortly before we did.

"How many black roses did Valerie receive?" asked Deena.

"I'm not sure," I said. "But I think it was only one at a time." Could these be the roses Valerie received? Did she bring these here herself? Or was Flower House the new target of Valerie's stalker.

I handed Deena my keys, then grabbed up the flowers, paper and all. Once inside, I took the package to the kitchen and dumped it in an empty bucket. My first inclination was to take it to the compost pile, but I resisted.

Instead, I found Officer Bradley's number and gave her a call. She didn't pick up. Next I tried the main number for the police station, but it too went straight to voice mail. Considering what had happened with the chief, I imagined the whole force was probably busy and distracted.

With nothing else to do, I printed the latest flower orders, heartened that at least there were a few. We spent the rest of the afternoon making bouquets with blooms that needed to be used up. Calvin hovered the whole time.

It was almost five o'clock when Deena announced that she needed to get going. "I still have to pick up groceries for my mom. Seeing Richard in the store parking lot this morning took my day in an unexpected direction."

"For sure," I agreed.

Deena offered to make a home delivery on her way—a sweetheart bouquet for a young girl in Deena's parents' neighborhood. I walked her out to her car.

With a glance toward Flower House, I spoke in a low voice. "I don't want Calvin to know I'm on to him."

She gave me a skeptical look. "I still don't get it. What exactly are you on to him about?"

"He's here under false pretenses! I don't know why, but his whole purpose seems to be locating Felix."

"Why don't you just ask him?"

"I've tried getting him to talk about himself, but he always changes the subject. I'm telling you, he's a—"

"Mystery man?" said Deena, raising her eyebrows suggestively. "Very intriguing."

"I was going to say 'a phony,'" I said. "You're not taking this seriously."

"I'm sorry." Deena laughed lightly. "Calvin just seems so harmless. I'm more concerned about the black roses. At least you know Calvin didn't leave those, since he's been with you all day."

"True," I admitted. "I'd really like to tell the cops about the roses. Maybe I'll try them again."

But when I went back inside I forgot all about the black roses. Calvin was sitting at Felix's computer, scrolling around like he owned the place. I opened my mouth, ready to demand answers and/or put a lock on the office door. Before I could utter a word, he swiveled in the chair and flashed me an eager smile.

"I did it! I figured out how to set up flower-order notifications."

"You mean—like, to an email?" That actually sounded like a great idea.

"Yeah! For the past few days, I kept thinking it was odd that you kept having to check this computer for orders. You should be able to receive orders anywhere."

"I agree, but how?"

"Like this." He turned back to the computer and clicked into the store's website builder, showing me exactly what he did. And, once again, he'd made himself useful. Invaluable, even. Deena was right. It was hard to imagine Calvin as anything other than a friendly, harmless—and slightly enigmatic—guy.

Still . . . I was going to figure out what he was up to. Of that, I was certain. That is, whenever I could find the time.

"By the way," said Calvin, "did you know the Flower House website is set up to receive comments?"

"Sure, I guess. Comments and reviews, right? I haven't looked at it in a while."

"You should really take a look at it now and then, and clean it up. There are a bunch of spam comments."

"Dang, that figures." One more thing to do—reminding me that I still needed to create a flower-shop to-do list. "Feel free to delete 'em yourself, if you're so inclined."

"There might be a way to block some of them," said

Calvin, clicking on the web builder again. "Oh, look! Another one just came in."

I checked my watch, rapidly losing interest as the conversation turned techie. I needed to pick up Gus from Rocky and think about what I wanted to do for supper.

"Huh," said Calvin, still facing the screen. "This is weird. You have to see this."

He stood up, giving me the chair, so I obligingly sat down. It didn't take long for me to understand what he meant. I also felt a sense of déjà vu. There was definitely something familiar in the tone of the message.

Dear Felix,

Your flowers are exquisite, like the rose: a classic
beauty with petals of poison and needle-sharp thorns.
You thought you could leave, escape your fate, but
your house will suffer the consequences of past
mistakes. Proverbs 11:21

"This is more than weird," I said. "It's creepy and sinister and . . . potentially significant. Can you pull up the IP address for the computer where this comment came from?"

While he did that, I grabbed my phone and found the photo I'd taken of the comment on the funeral home website. Just as I suspected, it was the same bible verse. The one about punishing the evil man, and something about the descendants of the righteous. Lovely. And as soon as Calvin brought up the I.P. number, I confirmed it had been sent from the same computer too.

I opened a browser on my phone and began typing in the search filter.

"What are you doing?" asked Calvin.

"I'm checking the hours of the Aerieville Public Li-

brary. Looks like they're open until eight o'clock on Saturdays. Perfect. I'm heading there now."

"Mind if I come along?"

I hesitated, trying to get a read on the helpful man
behind the earnest blue eyes. Finally, I sighed. "Sure. Why
not?"

Chapter 23

The Aerieville Public Library was housed in a low-slung brick building a few blocks off Main Street. I had a library card and, in the past, would check out a pile of books every few weeks or so. But I hadn't been in a while. Consequently, I didn't know the librarians as well as I might have. The young man behind the circulation desk was unfamiliar and, as I soon learned, not very observant.

"So, you can't tell me anything about folks using the computers recently?" I asked again. "Not even a general description? Men, women, younger, older, that kind of thing?"

"Uh-uh. Lots of people use the computers. Unless they ask for help, I don't pay much attention. Sorry."

I should've known better, I thought, somewhat deflated. "Thanks, anyway."

Calvin and I wandered over to the computer carrels, six in all. Three were occupied, all by teenagers. By my sneaky glimpse, it seemed one teen was doing homework, one was playing a game, and the last was watching a TV show—thankfully with headphones on.

Calvin sat down at one of the empty carrels and clicked

on the computer screen. "I should be able to figure out which computer they used."

I handed him my phone, open to the photo of the number in question. A minute later, he said, "Not this one," and moved on to the next computer. A few seconds later, he found a match.

"Bingo! The creepy comment was sent from this computer." He glanced over at the library walls and up to the ceiling. "Too bad there aren't cameras in here."

"Too bad," I agreed.

I sidled up to the kid doing homework, a girl with short green hair. "Excuse me. Sorry to bother you. Did you happen to see who was using the computer across from you in the past hour or so?"

She seemed taken aback by the question. "Um, no. I don't think anybody was there when I got here."

Moving on, I posed the same question to the gamer and the boy watching a show, both of whom gave me the same answer: they didn't see anyone. They were also both quite annoyed at the interruption.

I met Calvin's eyes and shook my head. He gestured toward the other side of the library. "I'll mosey around and see if there are any other patrons or librarians who might have been over here earlier."

"Okay," I said, dropping into the chair he'd abandoned. Part of me wanted to press the teenagers and urge them to think harder. The perp was *just* here, in this very chair, not one hour ago. We were *so* close.

Feeling a bit like Sherlock Holmes, I scrutinized every inch of the small cubicle, lifting the keyboard, peering behind the monitor, and examining the floor. I even closed my eyes and took a deep inhale, hoping for a whiff of lingering perfume or cigarette smoke, even the tiniest clue. I didn't care how silly I looked. I was at my wits' end.

The sound of a raspy cough some distance away made my eyes pop open. Searching for the source, I spotted him near the entrance: a balding gent with a fringe of white hair and a brown houndstooth jacket. He leaned on a tall umbrella like a cane. It was Byron Atterly.

I hopped up and started to approach the old bookkeeper to say hello. I figured I might as well bring him up to speed on the happenings at Flower House. But before I'd taken two steps, Calvin strolled up to me, and I had a sudden change of heart. If Calvin met Byron, he would surely ply him with questions about Felix. And what if Byron *had* heard from my former boss? I didn't want Calvin to have a speck more information about Felix's whereabouts than he already did. At least, not until I could figure out what his motives were.

I'd have to keep Byron from seeing me.

"No luck," Calvin was saying. "Do you want to—"

I darted into the stacks before he could finish his sentence. He followed me. "What's going on?"

"Nothing," I said, backing farther down the aisle. With one eye on the end of the row, I bumped into a shelf, knocking a book onto the floor. "Oops." I reached to pick it up and read the cover: *How to Run a Small Business: All Your Questions Answered.*

I held the book up to Calvin. "I just wanted to check out a book while we're here."

He crinkled his forehead. "That book?"

"Yep. This book." Peeking around the corner, I saw Byron head to a reading nook on the far end of the library. Now I had a clear path to the circulation desk, outside of Byron's view. I took my opportunity and bolted from the stacks, no doubt leaving Calvin bewildered once again. Oh, well.

Stepping up to the desk, I reached into my purse for

my wallet and took out my library card. Then I took another look at the book's title and had to laugh. *How to Run a Small Business.*

The universe sure does work in mysterious ways.

I took Calvin back to Flower House, then headed to my folks' place. By this time, my parents were home from the gym, and Rocky was just getting back from a long hike with Gus. Naturally, the corgi was ecstatic, though tired—not to mention in need of a serious bath. At least Rocky had cleaned off Gus's paws, so he'd be allowed in our parents' house.

Mom invited me to stay for supper, and I was glad to accept—even though it meant I had to endure her questions. Above all, she wanted to know when I planned to call it quits at Flower House. I helped set the table, then sat down across from Rocky and poured myself some iced tea before answering.

"Here's the thing, Mom. I don't really want to quit. I like working with flowers, and I think the shop is worth saving. Flower House is practically an institution in Aerieville. There's nothing else like it."

"It's a lot of responsibility to run a business," she said, once more invoking the "R" word.

I swallowed my impatience. "I know. I admit I have a lot to learn, but I think I can handle it." Now that I thought about it, I realized one thing I needed to do was sit down with Byron and go over the books. If I was seriously going to do this, I needed to know exactly what I was getting into.

"I still don't like it," said Mom, setting down a pan of lasagna in the center of the table. "There's a killer on the loose, and that place keeps getting hit by criminals!"

I couldn't argue with that.

Dad came in, his short hair still wet from the shower. "Hey, little girl," he said, kissing the top of my head.

"Hi, Dad. How's Chief Walden?" I suspected my dad's tenderness might have something to do with his friend's accident.

"He's in critical condition, but stable," said Dad, taking his seat at the head of the table. "The doctors placed him in an induced coma to protect his brain and help the swelling go down. They think he was hit in the head by debris from the explosion."

"So, he wasn't on the boat when it blew up?"

"Must not have been. Of course, we can't ask him 'til he wakes up."

"Even then, he might not remember," said Rocky.

"He's lucky to be alive," said Mom.

"Amen," said Dad. "He'll surely have a long recovery too."

I crunched into a piece of crusty Italian bread and contemplated the odds of the police chief being critically injured in the midst of a murder investigation. "Any word on why the boat exploded?" I asked.

Dad planted an elbow on the table and gave me a serious look. "I spoke with Officer Dakin at the hospital, off the record. It's not public information, since they're still investigating. But they think the engine was tampered with."

I swallowed a mouthful of lasagna, sobered by the news. But not at all surprised.

After dinner, Gus and I went home to the dollhouse, my tiny little haven from all the worries and demands of the big bad world. I gave Gus a proper bath and dried him with my hair dryer. Then I let him have his favorite treat toy, while I cleaned out the tub and took my own silky-soft scented bubble bath. By the time I got out, I was ready to hit the sack. I was pulling a comb through my hair, when my eyes fell on my cell phone resting on the dresser. Suddenly, I remembered my unplayed message.

"Gus! What is wrong with me?"

Gus cocked his head, baffled by the question.

"So much has happened today, I forgot all about Felix's call. Let's hear what he had to say."

I put my phone on speaker and dialed into voice mail. A few seconds later, Felix's voice crackled over the line.

"Oh-ho, 'faithful employee'! Is Flower House keeping you busy? I guess that means you decided to take on the challenge. I had a feeling you would. It's good to have a challenge. Keeps life exciting. Ah, well, I'm sorry we missed each other. Take care now. Oh! Say hello to your grandmother for me. Tell Mae I thought of her the other day. Had a bit of trouble, until I remembered her pine sap trick. Fixed me up right nice." He chuckled lightly. "She'll know what I mean. Bye now."

I stared at the phone, halfway tempted to call him back right now. If this was how it was going to be, communication by voice mail, I'd have to be more specific in the next message I left him. Pacing the floor, I thought about what I should say—until I realized Gus was being awfully quiet. I found him on the other side of my bed gnawing on my house slipper.

"Alright, Gus. That's it. Time for bed. It's probably too late to call Felix right now anyway."

His message had given me one good idea, though. It was time to go see Granny again.

Chapter 24

Flower House was normally closed on Sundays, and I decided now was a good time to stick with the posted hours. I needed a break—as much from Calvin as from the floristry business. After breakfast, I leashed up Gus, grabbed his travel bag, and piled into the car. And to grandmother's house we went.

It was close to ten thirty when we arrived. After parking my car, I took a few minutes to let Gus sniff around the bushes and do his business. The land was bustling with spring activity: chattering birds, scavenging squirrels, and busy bees—but no Granny among them. When she didn't respond to my knock, I let myself in. She rarely locked the door in the daytime.

"Granny!" I called, setting Gus's bag on the floor. "You here?" The living room was dark and quiet. So was the kitchen.

All at once, I understood my mom's constant anxiety about Granny living way out here all by herself. A dart of panic shot through me. I turned toward the staircase, about to holler again and bound up the steps, but Gus gave a bark and tugged me in the opposite direction.

"Okay, Gus. Find Granny!" I let him lead the way.

He took us back into the kitchen and began scratching on the back door. I quickly pulled it open—and there was Granny, on the back porch. She was sitting in a lawn chair with her pants rolled up to her knees and her feet soaking in a big plastic dishpan.

"Well, hello, Sierra," she said with a smile. "Howdy, Gus."

Relief washed over me. I kissed Granny on the cheek, before dropping onto the porch swing adjacent to her chair. I tightened my hold on Gus's leash to keep him from tasting the dishpan water.

"What is that, Granny?"

"It's just oak bark tea," she replied. "It won't hurt the pup."

"Are you feeling okay?" I eyed her carefully, looking for any sign she might be ailing.

"I'm fit as a fiddle," she said. "But I've been up since the crack of dawn. I was just thinking of taking a little nap before lunch. How's everything with you?"

"I'm fine. I had a message from Felix yesterday. He said to tell you hello. He thought of you because he needed to use your 'pine sap trick.' What could he have meant by that?"

She squinted into the distance, deepening the wrinkles around her eyes. "Oh, yes," she said, after a moment. "I remember. Your grandpap and I used to picnic with Felix and Georgina sometimes, way back when. One time we were picking wild berries, and Georgina got caught up in a briar patch n' cut her hand real good. I showed everybody how to make a first aid salve out of pine sap."

"That sounds like a useful skill," I said, thinking I could probably learn a lot from Granny Mae.

"It does in a pinch. Felix musta cut himself, out in the woods someplace. I'm glad he remembered about the pine sap."

Now the worry I'd felt about Granny transferred to angst for Felix. Was he really traipsing around in the Rockies of Colorado all by himself? I hoped Jim Lomack had caught up to him, regardless of what Angela had said about the men being in some kind of competition.

"What's the latest with the flower shop?" asked Granny. "Have things calmed down?"

I hesitated, not wanting to give her a reason to fret. She saw right through me.

"What happened? Did another shelf fall off the wall? Did something break? Or did somebody get hurt?"

"Nobody got hurt. Not at Flower House, anyway. There actually was another break-in and some stuff was broken, but nobody was hurt."

Under Granny's intense scrutiny, I couldn't stop talking. "Well, somebody did get hurt yesterday. Chief Walden is in the hospital. It didn't happen at Flower House, but . . . it's possible somebody tried to harm him because of his investigation into Abe's murder."

Granny nodded her head knowingly, as if none of this was unexpected.

"I don't know that for sure," I hastened to say. "And, like I said, nobody got hurt at the flower shop—except for several plants."

"Did you bury the tater like I told you to?"

"No, Granny. I really don't think that's the answer. It's not Abe's spirit causing all these problems."

She gave me an arch look. "Well, now, how can you know that if you don't try?"

My mouth fell open, but I had no response. There was no arguing with Granny's logic.

"Hand me that towel, will you?" she said, pointing to a pink bath towel draped over the arm of the swing. "I'm going to rest a spell, then I'll make lunch. You stay put and enjoy the fresh air."

"Yes, ma'am."

After Granny went inside, I picked up Gus and set him on the swing beside me. I knew he would have loved to roam the yard and woods, but I was afraid he'd eat something he shouldn't or run off and get lost. He'd just have to be content to keep me company.

I pet his back, as I kicked us into a gentle swinging motion, to and fro, and let my thoughts drift like the wispy clouds overhead. Trilling birdsong and the buzz of insects provided a soothing soundtrack. It was quite pleasant, swaying like that, back and forth. After a while, I closed my eyes, but I wasn't sleepy. It was more like a meditative feeling. If anything, the crisp mountain air and nearness of nature were helping to clear my mind.

Clarity. That was what I needed. As I knew from all the books I'd read on the law of attraction, clarity was the first step in achieving your goals. I needed to shine a light on the muddled events of the past week and try to make sense of it all.

Take the repeated break-ins, for example. What was that all about? Was it meant to harass me? To hurt the business and scare me into closing up Flower House?

I thought about each incident in order. First, Abe had been poisoned in the events room. The next day, I received a note under the door, telling me to get out. Later that night, I'd thought I heard someone outside the window in the orchid room. Was that someone trying to break in?

The next morning, I arrived at work to find that someone *did* break in. That time all the damage (other than the back-door lock) was confined to the events room. Could it have been the killer, looking for something he or she dropped?

There's a flaw in that theory, I argued with myself. All the suspects were present at the workshop. If somebody dropped something—like, say, the button I'd found—it wouldn't tie them to the murder. It would just tie them to the scene, which didn't mean anything.

So, what happened next? The bigger break-in. This time the events room was wrecked once more, as well as the rest of the first floor and much of the greenhouse. That time it definitely felt like someone was trying to hurt the business.

But they still weren't satisfied. The very next night, according to Calvin, they were at it again. A person in a dark hoodie was messing around the back door, until they were scared off—foiled by Calvin's booby trap.

As I thought about it, my mind returned to the idea that someone was looking for something. Maybe the killer lost something more incriminating than a button—like a piece of evidence tying them to a motive for murder.

And just like that, a light bulb went on in my head.

Gus gave a yip, and I realized I'd let the swing slow to a stop. He'd been enjoying the ride. Scratching the top of his head, I used my feet to kick us off again.

"I've got it, buddy," I said. "I know what to do."

After lunch with Granny, plus an hour or so of pulling weeds in her yard and completing any other chores she'd let me do, I headed back to town with Gus in tow. We drove by Flower House but didn't stop. Instead, I parked two blocks away, circled around on foot, and slipped into Melody Gardens from the backside. The small park was a slightly overgrown, but still lovely, flower-filled oasis. There were benches among the mature trees, a crumbling stone labyrinth, and even a small trickling water fountain. It was the perfect place for a secret meeting. I'd shot Deena a text asking her to meet me there, so I could fill her in on my plan.

She found Gus and me strolling the narrow brick path between flower beds. I had to grin when I saw her. She was wearing a mini-trench coat, a silk headscarf, and oversized sunglasses.

"Is that your spy get-up?" I asked.

"You said this was a top-secret rendezvous," she said, giggling a little. "I figured it would be fun to dress accordingly."

"Well done, then." I could've told her the outfit was quite the opposite of discreet, and bound to attract more attention than less. She would have been better off in jeans and a windbreaker like me. But there was no one around to see us anyway. We moved to a secluded picnic table beneath a stand of trees and sat down.

"Here's the deal," I said. "I believe the killer has been looking for something at Flower House. So, the way to catch them is to make them think I have what they want."

"Ooh, like, set a trap, you mean? Lure them with the spurious bait, lie in wait, and see who bites?"

"Exactly."

"Where will all this take place?" she asked. "And how will you get the word out to all the suspects?"

"I haven't worked out all the details yet. I was hoping you could help with that."

For the next several minutes, we put our heads together and brainstormed a few ideas.

Deena removed her scarf and pushed her sunglasses to the top of her head. "Okay, so we tell people you found something incriminating, and then . . . wait to see who comes after you?"

"Um, let's keep thinking." As much as I wanted to draw out the culprit, I didn't relish the thought of making myself a sitting duck.

"Oh! We should bring your brother in on this. He's already built like a bodyguard. He can stick with you and keep you safe—and tackle the bad guy when they show up."

"Nobody's tackling anybody," I said, feeling protective of my little brother in spite of his muscles. "I don't really want to confront the killer at all. I was thinking maybe I'd leave a small box or a briefcase someplace and see who comes for it. Something like that."

"Like at Flower House? We'll have to bring Calvin into the fold," she said. "Maybe we should anyway. Strength in numbers and all that."

I shook my head. "Not Flower House. It's too confined. Somewhere out in the open would be safer." I gazed around the park, wracking my brain for a solution. I needed some plausible reason why I'd be bringing the thing—*Thing X*—to some outdoor location.

As if on cue, the wind gusted, turning a rusty weather vane that someone had stuck among the flowers. I watched it spin back and forth with a lonely, creaking sound, and my skin began to prickle. That and the lengthening afternoon shadows lent a ghostly feel to the empty park. It called to mind Granny's superstition about Abe's restless spirit— and her insistence that I bury something at his gravesite.

And there was my answer.

"What are you thinking?" demanded Deena. "You have a glint in your eye like you've solved the mystery."

"Not quite," I said. "But we're getting closer."

With another glance around the park, to ensure we were alone, I leaned in. "Here's the story we need to spread: I found something at Flower House. I don't understand the significance of it, but I think it's related to Abe. He's been haunting me."

"Haunting you?" said Deena, with a trace of doubt. "Will anyone buy that?"

"They only need to believe that *I* believe it. And I'm the granddaughter of Granny Mae, folk healer and mountain storyteller." I grinned, warming to the idea. "So, yeah. Un-explained things keep happening at Flower House. Abe's spirit is restless. Therefore, I think I need to get rid of this thing that I found."

Deena shivered, whether from the cool breeze or my ghost story, I couldn't say. "How are you going to do that?" she asked.

"There's only one thing to do. I have to bury it, at mid-night, in the cemetery."

"Brilliant," Deena whispered. "Then you'll hide nearby and watch to see who comes for it."

"*We'll* hide nearby." I had no intention of doing this by myself.

Dusk began to fall, as we continued hatching our plan. The tricky part was figuring out how to get the word out to our main five suspects—and no one else. We talked about staging a conversation between the two of us at Bread n' Butter, but we didn't know how to ensure anyone would overhear us, let alone all five targets.

"What if we tell Nell?" suggested Deena. "She can spread news faster than the Associated Press."

"That's for sure," I said. "But the problem is, she'll tell *everyone*. I don't want the whole town showing up at the cemetery out of pure curiosity."

"Good point." Deena frowned, stumped again.

Gus whimpered, letting me know he was bored of sniffing around the picnic table.

"Let's walk," I said, standing up and heading toward the brick path. "I think you're on to something with the Nell idea. Only, instead of the town gossip queen, we need someone else to strategically flap their lips about me and my 'silly superstition.'"

"Like me?" asked Deena. "I can do it."

"Hm. I'm not sure that would be believable." I stopped walking and faced her, suddenly feeling a tad insecure.

"Would it? I mean, people have probably noticed us pall-ing around town by now. As my friend, it might not seem realistic if you're the one casually dropping talk about this crazy thing I'm gonna do in the graveyard." I smiled self-consciously. *We* were *friends, weren't we?*

"That's true," she agreed, causing me to relax. *Of course, we're friends.* "Then who?" she asked.

I sighed. "I hate to say it, but I think we need Calvin's help after all."

Chapter 25

Deena and I wasted no time. As soon as we agreed we'd hit on our best course of action, we hurried to Flower House to talk to Calvin. He was a bit dubious at first, understandably. But it didn't take much convincing to bring him around. As we explained, Deena and I would make special "thank you" bouquets for the Morrisons, Letty, Valerie, and Richard—ostensibly thanking them for their support of Flower House during this challenging time. Calvin would deliver the bouquets, giving him the perfect opportunity to drop the deets about the "fanciful notion that had taken hold of my boss, Sierra."

"Do I have to say 'fanciful notion'?" asked Calvin.

"No," I said. "You need to be as natural as possible."

"Try to come off as amused, but curious," advised Deena. "Like you're wondering if everyone in Aerieville is as superstitious as Sierra."

"Got it." Calvin grabbed a potted orchid from a shelf and held it in front of him, while affecting a casual, innocent pose. "Hey, you'll never believe what Sierra's going to do tonight. Tell me if you think this is normal." Then he grinned at us. "How was that?"

"Terrific," said Deena, clapping her hands together.

"Yeah, terrific," I said, with less enthusiasm. I wasn't sure what bothered me more: the fact that it was so easy for him to lie—or the thought that he might really believe I wasn't quite normal.

Not now, Sierra, I told myself. I needed to focus on the mission at hand. I'd worry about Calvin and his secrets later.

The next day we reconvened at Flower House to set our plans in motion. Deena and I made the thank-you bouquets—cheerful arrangements with pink and peach roses, bright orange lilies, and green poms. Then Calvin headed out to make the deliveries, starting with Bread n' Butter. We watched through the window, on pins and needles, until he emerged from the bakery. When he finally came out, he glanced our way and flashed a thumbs-up before getting into his car for the next delivery. *One down, three to go.*

Calvin's next stop was going to be the bank, in the hopes that Richard would be back at work. As he reported by phone, Richard wasn't there—but the branch manager didn't mind sharing his home address.

"Why didn't we think of asking for Richard's address?" Deena asked.

"It's just as well," I said. "Maybe it wasn't such a good idea to confront him about Abe anyway."

Calvin told me his next stop would be Light Steps Dance Studio, followed by the school where Letty taught. He planned on intercepting the teacher as she left the building at the end of the school day.

In the meantime, Deena, Gus, and I took a brief excursion to the cemetery. I wanted to find Abe's grave and scope out a good hiding place. I also wanted to get a head start on the digging part of the plan, so I brought along a shovel and a small rose bush. With Deena playing lookout while holding onto Gus's leash, I dug a largish hole and planted the roses loosely, thus making my job easier that night—hopefully.

We decided to go on home after that and try to get some rest. Deena said she'd come to my house at eleven, and we'd proceed in one car from there.

Of course, it was difficult to rest. I was too keyed up. Every time I tried to nap or meditate, my mind would roil with a jillion different scenarios for how the night might go—each more distressing than the last. Finally, I decided to expend my excess of energy by doing housework. I scrubbed my sinks, mopped the floor, polished the furniture, and folded laundry. The dollhouse had never been so clean.

At dinnertime, I made myself a loaded baked potato smothered in cheese and chives. After eating, I selected another potato, the largest Idaho in my pantry. With a sharp knife, I sliced it in half and cut a hollow in the center. Then I took the handkerchief I'd snagged from Abe's house, folded it real small, and placed it in the hollow. I set the other half of the potato back in place, pinned it shut with toothpicks, then slipped the whole thing in a plastic bag and put it in my purse.

"This is for you, Granny Mae."

At around eleven thirty, Deena and I took our places in Aerieville's lone graveyard, a sprawling, tree-dotted acreage abutting a Christmas tree farm on the edge of town. I'd dropped Deena at the tree farm, then proceeded to the church parking lot next to the cemetery, where I left my car—in clear view of anyone who might be watching. My plan was to bury the potato, return to my car, then drive around the block and join Deena in her hiding place among the trees.

Now, as I walked along the narrow asphalt road that wound through the cemetery, I was struck by how pitch dark it was. Clouds blotted out the stars and the moon, and the cemetery had no street lamps. That made sense, I realized, since no one was supposed to be here at night. I was lucky the gate was easy to hop. I just hoped my luck would continue, and I wouldn't get caught.

As I neared the plot where Abe was buried, I left the road and picked my way through the grass, trying not to bump into any tombstones. The air felt damp and cool. Every little sound seemed amplified in the silence: the squish of earth beneath my boots, the rustle and chitter of nocturnal creatures moving about in the darkness. A twig cracked somewhere behind me.

My heartbeat quickened, and I began to second-guess the entire plan. We had formulated it so quickly. Maybe we should have slept on it before taking action. For one thing, why was I alone right now? There was no reason why I couldn't have had Deena at my side for this part of the show.

I slipped my hand into the purse slung over my shoulder and curled my fingers around my phone. I hadn't wanted to use a light more than necessary, for fear of attracting attention and being arrested for trespassing. But that fear was quickly being overtaken by more primal fears: of the darkness, of boogeymen . . . of killers.

Another stick cracked in the stillness, and I sensed a motion out of the corner of my eye. Suppressing a shriek, I spun around and found myself face-to-face with a dark-clad figure. He clicked on a flashlight and held it under his chin—revealing the shadowy, grinning face of Calvin.

"Boo!" he said quietly.

I punched him in the arm.

"What are you doing here?" I hissed. "You scared me half to death." I glanced toward the thicket where I'd left Deena and wondered if she was seeing this.

"I didn't want to miss the fun," he said. "I thought you were gonna come by the shop first. When I realized you weren't, I had to drive here myself."

"Hold your flashlight down," I grumbled, moving on to find Abe's grave. I was irritated that he'd snuck up on me, but not too mad. In truth, I was grateful not to be alone.

"Here it is," I whispered a moment later. "Can you shine your light for me?"

"At your service," he said.

I pulled on a pair of gardening gloves, kneeled down, and removed the rose bush. Then I took the potato from my purse and out of the plastic bag and placed it in the hole.

"What is that?" asked Calvin.

"I can't tell you, remember?" I said. "Bad luck."

Before he could respond, I set the rose bush back in place (making a mental note to come back tomorrow and plant it properly), then stood up. "Let's go," I said, taking off for the entrance.

A short time later, Calvin and I climbed into my car, took a short drive, and parked again on a side street. Moving quickly, we slunk into a patch of trees on the property bordering the cemetery. We found Deena dancing in place in our designated hiding spot.

"Finally!" she said softly. Then, "Calvin?"

"The one and only," he said, with a little bow.

"You didn't see him jump out at me?" I asked.

She looked sheepish. "Sorry. I guess I was watching my own back." She darted a wary eye toward the darkness behind her.

"Never mind," I said. "I guess there's safety in numbers, right?"

She started to say something else, but I held up my hand in warning and pointed. I'd spotted a pinprick of light bobbing in the cemetery. It appeared our prey was falling for the bait.

The light winked like a firefly as a person drew near Abe's grave, then stopped and crouched down. That was when I realized we had a problem.

"Who is it?" Deena whispered in my ear.

"I can't tell. It's too dark, and we're too far away."

The clock was ticking on our one chance to unmask the villain—so to speak. If I didn't make a move now, this whole endeavor would be for nothing.

"I'm going in," I said. There was no time to hesitate. Creeping into the cemetery, I darted to a nearby statue and hid for a second, then ran to take cover behind a large tree. I moved from one hiding place to another, like some kind of cartoon character. I had to bite my lip to keep from giggling out of sheer nervousness.

At last, I was close enough to see the person straighten up and stare at an object in their hand—the toothpick-pinned potato. Then he spoke, and I knew who it was.

"What is this? This isn't the bank statement."

It was Richard. And he seemed annoyed, more than anything. He tossed the potato back into the hole and brushed his hands together in disgust. With a huff, he stalked off in the direction from which he'd come.

I remained in my hiding place until I saw two shadows materialize from the edge of the cemetery. Deena and Calvin were heading my way.

At the same time, I heard a noise from the opposite direction. Turning, I thought I saw another shadow flit among the graves, then disappear.

Deena ran up to me, her flashlight bright in the blackness. "Who was it?" she asked breathlessly.

"Richard," I said.

"Oh no," she groaned. "I was hoping it wouldn't be him."

"Me too," I said. "Me too."

Chapter 26

Granny always said it was bad luck to walk over a grave. Then again, she was the one who told me to come out here in the first place. At midnight, no less, to help Abe's spirit cross to the other side. Did one superstition cancel out the other? I was quite sure we stepped on more than one burial plot as we scurried out of the cemetery. Between the deepening shadows and the mysterious night sounds, we kept picking up the pace. At one point, Deena stumbled and grabbed my sleeve to keep from falling—which made me bump into Calvin. It's a wonder we didn't all topple down. After that, we fairly ran out of there, stifling nervous laughter the whole way.

As far as I was concerned, the fact that we weren't caught was pretty darn lucky in and of itself.

We made it to the street and stopped outside my car. Then we just stood there, uncertain what to do next. Deena rubbed her arms, while Calvin kicked mud off his boots.

"Whew!" I unbuttoned my jacket, feeling warm from the run and the excitement. Adrenaline still coursed through my veins.

"Hey," said Calvin. "I have some beer in the fridge

at my place. Want to come over and talk things through? You know, next steps or whatever?"

Deena and I looked at each other. Was she thinking what I was thinking? There was certainly a lot to discuss, and a cold brew sounded mighty tempting. But I wouldn't go without her. In spite of all Calvin's help, I still had qualms about being alone with the guy.

Happily, we were on the same wavelength. Deena gave me a slight nod.

"That sounds great," I said, turning to Calvin. "How about bringing the beer to my house, though? I'm a little worried about leaving Gus on his own for so long."

"Sure! Good idea!" Calvin seemed even more enthusiastic now than he had been earlier. I wondered if it was the prospect of hanging out with Deena and me or the fact that he was going to see where I lived. On second thought, he was probably just looking forward to seeing Gus.

First, we drove by Flower House, where Calvin ran upstairs to grab a six-pack from his apartment. Then he followed Deena and me to the dollhouse.

That turned out to be a good call. Gus had been asleep earlier when I'd slipped outside to meet Deena in the driveway. He was awake when we returned and about as worked up as a worried parent: happy I was home yet not above letting me know about the angst he'd been through. There were newspaper shreds all over the living room floor.

"Hey, little buddy!" said Calvin, kneeling down to accept Gus's affection. "Were you bored here all alone? Had to find something to entertain yourself?"

"Sure, take his side," I joked, as I cleaned up the torn newspaper. Deena excused herself to wash up, then came back and rummaged through my kitchen for snacks.

"Cheese and crackers okay?" she asked. "Or apples and pears?"

"Yes to everything," I said. "Suddenly, I feel famished."

Calvin washed and sliced the fruit, while I popped some popcorn. Then we settled around my kitchen table for beer and snacks.

Calvin took a swig of beer and fixed me with a questioning gaze. "So, are you gonna let me in on your game, or what?"

Are you gonna let me in on yours? I met his eyes for a lingering second. Blinking, he pushed up his glasses in a gesture of nervousness I didn't quite buy.

Oblivious, Deena answered for me. "It's not a game. We laid a trap, and Richard took the bait."

Calvin looked from me to Deena and back again. "But why would he care about a potato? That is what you buried, isn't it? You asked me to tell everybody you found something connected to Abe. How is—"

"The potato was a decoy," I explained. "I figured whoever is breaking into Flower House must be looking for something that ties them to the murder."

"Richard took the bait," said Deena, glumly placing a piece of cheese on a round cracker. "I wonder what he thought he was going to find buried in the ground."

"A bank statement," I answered. Deena and Calvin each looked at me in surprise. "I guess you couldn't hear him," I said. "When he picked up the potato, Richard said, 'This isn't the bank statement.'"

"How would a bank statement incriminate him in the murder?" asked Calvin.

Deena snapped her fingers. "The blackmail. This statement must somehow prove Abe was blackmailing Richard. Maybe it shows suspicious withdrawals or something."

"What blackmail?" asked Calvin. "You gals gotta catch me up."

"Um, never mind that," said Deena, glancing my way. She clearly didn't want to tell Calvin about our clandestine operation at Abe's the other night. I was with her there.

"What matters is that Richard took the bait," Deena continued. "That must mean he's the killer. Right?"

"I'm not so sure," I said. "Something's bothering me about this whole thing." I crunched into an apple slice and chewed thoughtfully. *If Richard is the killer, then why are there still so many loose ends?*

"You know, he may not have been the only one," said Calvin.

"What do you mean?" asked Deena.

"I'm not positive, but I might've seen someone else out there in the cemetery. After Richard left."

"You saw that too?" I said. "I thought maybe I imagined it."

"What?" said Deena. "Who was it? Did they see us?" She shuddered and called Gus to sit at her feet. He indulgently let her scratch the top of his head.

"I feel like we're missing something," I said. "I wish I had a giant whiteboard or . . ." I trailed off, as I caught sight of the notebook I'd left on the kitchen table. "I need to take notes. Hang on."

One of the self-development tools I'd learned was the "mind map." It was a great way to pull thoughts from my head and take a good look at them in some kind of organized fashion.

I grabbed a pen and opened the notebook to a clean page. As Deena and Calvin watched, I wrote "Abe" in the center of the paper and drew a circle around it. From there, I drew lines connecting Abe to other names I wrote: "Richard," "Bill and Flo," "Letty," "Valerie," "Felix" and

"Flower House." I stared at the names for a minute, then added more words to the paper. Next to "Richard," I wrote "bank statement" and "blackmail."

"Don't ask," I said, as soon as Calvin opened his mouth. "It's just a theory, anyway."

"Add 'mysterious package,'" said Deena. "Remember, I saw him pick up something at the Earth Day festival?"

"Right." I did that and continued to the other names. Next to "Valerie," I wrote "history with Abe" and "resentment." Next to "Letty," I wrote "personal issues" and "possible history with Abe?". Beside "Bill and Flo," I wrote "theme restaurant."

"What does that say?" asked Calvin, tilting his head to get a better look. "Theme restaurant?"

"Yeah," I answered. "The Morrisons are the ones who offered to buy Flower House. They want to open a hillbilly theme restaurant."

Deena and Calvin both made a face at that. "So, it would be in their interest for Flower House to shut down," said Calvin.

"It was also in their interest for Abe to be out of the way," said Deena. "He could have blocked their plan or forced them to pay for his approval."

"Compelling," murmured Calvin.

I tapped my pen on the table and made a few more notes. I wrote "black roses" and connected it to both "Valerie" and "Flower House." Finally, I wrote "Chief Walden" in a circle of his own, floating on the side.

Calvin leaned in to get a better look and whistled. "How do you *know* all this?"

I couldn't help smiling a little. "I'm just really observant, I guess. And I've had a lot of help from Deena."

"We have been busy, haven't we?" said Deena, opening her second beer.

"Wait, there's more." I picked up my pen again. "Flower

House is connected to 'break-ins,' 'damage,' and 'gopher bait.'" I added these words to the diagram.

Deena pointed at Abe's name. "For Abe, you can write 'garden center,' 'zoning board,' and 'poor reputation.'"

"Right," I agreed, making the additions. Then I began doodling on the paper, as I tried to identify some sort of pattern. What did it all mean?

Calvin finished off the popcorn and crinkled his eyes as he regarded both me and the diagram I'd drawn. I wondered if he realized I was onto him. If I ever had the time, I'd have to make a mind map about him. *Wouldn't that be interesting?*

"What do you make of it?" asked Deena. "It looks pretty messy."

"It *is* messy." I had another bite of fruit as I studied the convoluted map I'd made. After a moment, one observation did float to the surface. I gestured toward the pencil jar on the counter. "Could you hand me that red pen?" I said to Calvin.

He obliged, and I uncapped the pen. Slowly, in red ink, I circled "Abe," "Valerie," "Chief Walden", and, finally, "Flower House".

"There are *four* victims," I said. "Four targets. Abe, obviously. But also Valerie, with the black roses. Walt Walden with his sabotaged boat. And Flower House with all the vandalism." *Not to mention being the scene of the crime.*

Calvin and Deena waited for me to go on, but that was all I had. I reached for my beer and took a sip.

"Four targets," echoed Deena.

"Four targets," repeated Calvin.

"I wonder—" I began, but Deena spoke at the same time.

"Any word—sorry."

"Go ahead," I said.

"Any word on Chief Walden's condition?"

"Last I heard, he was still in a coma." I relayed what my dad had told me. "I think I'll go to the police station in the morning and see if I can speak to Officer Bradley or someone else. Somehow I'll try to share the things we've learned about Richard." How I'd do that without sounding like a criminal or a crazy person, I had no idea.

"Good luck," said Deena.

I looked down at my notebook again and yawned, suddenly feeling the lateness of the hour. Whatever significance I'd thought I'd uncovered was now gone, slipped into the recesses of my mind.

Deena closed the cracker box and stood up. "I should get going. It's way past my bedtime." She gave Calvin a pointed look.

He took the hint and hopped up. "Me too." Then he glanced at Gus, who sat expectantly next to the back door. "Would you like me to take him out before I go?"

"Yeah, that would be nice. Thanks." I shut my notebook. Maybe my scribbles would make more sense in the morning.

As soon as Calvin and Gus went outside, Deena peeked through the blinds at them, then turned to me with a grin. "Sorry if I overstepped my bounds. I can leave now, if you want."

"What are you talking about?" I took the beer bottles to the sink, rinsed them out, and tossed them into the recycling bin.

"You know," said Deena. "So you can say goodbye to Calvin in private."

I turned swiftly to face her. "*What?*" Then I saw the teasing glint in her eye. "Very funny."

"I'm only half kidding," she said. "You can deny it all you want, but there is definitely something going on between the two of you."

I opened my mouth but couldn't come up with a suitable retort.

"Mm-hmm," said Deena. "I'm always right about these things. You'll see."

"I'm just too tired to argue right now," I protested.

"At least he isn't a protein-powder salesman."

At that, I laughed out loud. Deena winked at me and laughed too. We were still giggling when Calvin and Gus came back inside.

"What'd I miss?" asked Calvin.

"Nothing," I said quickly.

"More secrets, huh?" said Calvin.

"For now," said Deena.

I rolled my eyes and ushered them both to the door.

The next morning, it was my phone that woke me. The bright sun probably would have done so, sooner or later. Not Gus, though. After the late bedtime, he was content to sleep in like me. I was tempted to ignore the phone, but it wouldn't let up. Finally, I grabbed it from the bedside table and pressed Answer.

"Hello?" I mumbled.

"Wake up, sleepyhead," said Calvin. "The flower business needs you."

"Why? What's going on?" I sat up and rubbed my eyes, before squinting at the clock. It was almost ten o'clock. *Jeesh*.

"The phone keeps ringing. The last call was an office manager looking for orchids. She asked for a dozen plants and wants them delivered today, if possible."

Now I was definitely awake. "That's great!"

"Also, someone stopped in to ask about a corsage for prom next month. I didn't know what to tell them."

That was a good question. I still didn't know if I'd

be in business next month. "I'll be there as soon as I can."

I took a quick shower and pulled on a cotton peasant top over blue jeggings. If I was going to be the face of Flower House, I decided I ought to start dressing the part. Then I scarfed some cereal, poured my coffee into a to-go mug, and set off with Gus.

"It's going to be a great day," I said to the pup—and to myself. "I am a capable individual who attracts all the help I need. Yes, indeed."

When I arrived at Flower House, Calvin was bringing orchids to the kitchen and lining them up on the worktable for my inspection. I helped box them and load up his car.

"I'd assist you with the delivery," I said, "but I still haven't made it to the police station."

"No worries," he said. "I got it."

As Calvin was leaving, Deena called me on my cell. She said she had some "business to attend to," and she'd come in later this afternoon. I thought she was being oddly vague, but I didn't press her. She could tell me later what kind of business she had.

"Okay, Gus," I said, as soon as I got off the phone with Deena. "It's time we take a little drive downtown."

Only I didn't leave right away. Instead, I puttered around the shop, dusting the shelves and setting out a fresh bucket of single-stem flowers. The truth was I was reluctant to go to the police. I hadn't figured out exactly what I was going to say to convey my concerns without incriminating Deena and me in multiple crimes and misdemeanors. Plus, I still felt I was missing an important piece of the puzzle.

I was still in the front of the shop when I heard the sound of the back door opening. Gus erupted in a string of excited barks and zoomed to the kitchen. I figured Calvin must have forgotten something. Then I heard a voice that wasn't Calvin's, and I froze in place.

"Yoo hoo! Anybody here?"

I swallowed hard. Then I forced my feet to move and copped a friendly smile before poking my head through the kitchen doorway.

"Richard! Hey! What are you doing coming in the back door?" *And why didn't I lock it behind Calvin?*

Richard was patting Gus's head. He looked up with his usual deadpan expression. "I have your glass."

"My glass?"

"For the back door. I bet you thought I forgot."

"Oh, yeah. No. I just—uh, I heard you've been sick. You alright?"

"Peachy." He reached for something right outside the door, then turned back to me. "Actually, I was a bit under the weather, but I'm better now. The bank has a strict stay-at-home policy, even if you've got the slightest sniffle, so I had to miss a couple days of work. Thanks for the bouquet, by the way. It was gorgeous, as always."

"You're welcome." I leaned against the counter and watched as he began prying boards off the back door—using a rather large crowbar. I caught my breath when I saw it. It appeared heavy and well-used. It was probably a tool like that that had been used to break the lock on the door in the first place.

Then something else grabbed my attention. Richard was wearing an olive green denim shirt—with a missing brown button. I didn't remember him wearing that shirt on any of the recent days he'd been here. The shirttail was ripped too. It was missing a piece of material in what looked like the exact shape and size of the cloth I'd found in Abe's window. Richard must have climbed into Abe's basement just like Deena and I had done. He was probably looking for whatever it was he'd thought I buried in the cemetery. A "bank statement" was what he'd said.

All at once I had a flash of insight. If Abe was blackmailing Richard, he must have been holding something pretty serious over Richard's head. And if it had to do with a bank statement . . . could Abe have discovered a discrepancy implicating Richard in some funny business at the bank?

Suddenly, Richard turned around, holding the crowbar aloft. "Say, Sierra. There's something I've been wanting to ask you."

"Oh? What's that?" I inched along the counter, putting a little distance between Richard and me.

"It's about Abe." Richard took a step toward me, and I flinched.

"What about him?"

"He really wasn't a very nice man. But you already knew that, didn't you?"

Huh? I had no idea what Richard was talking about. All I knew was that he was coming toward me with a heavy tool and a weird glint in his eyes. My heart gave a panicky flutter. Thinking fast, I reached for the basement door.

"Oh, hey!" I said. "I just remembered. Can you do me a favor? There's a problem with the hot-water heater. Can you take a look?"

He lowered his arm, a look of confusion passing over his features. "Now?"

"Yeah, sure. It'll just take a minute." I pulled open the door and waved him toward the stairs. "Please?"

"Okay." Still holding the crowbar, he headed downstairs, flicking the light switch along the wall.

When he was almost to the bottom, I hollered down. "Someone's calling me! I'll join you in a minute."

"M'kay," he replied.

Quietly, I shut the door and locked it. Then I ran to the front of the shop, where I'd left my purse. As I fumbled for my phone, Gus ran excitedly for the front door. I looked through the window and saw Granny Mae walking up the sidewalk.

Oh, jeez. *Not now, Granny.*

I slipped outside, leaving Gus inside, much to his displeasure. I intercepted my grandma on the front porch.

"Hi, Granny! I was just on my way out. What brings you here?"

She was laden with cloth bags, draped over both arms. She set them down and reached into one, producing one of her flannel herb bags. She handed the lumpy pouch to me.

"I'm delivering medicine bags to my customers. I made one for you. It has rosemary, basil, fennel, and some other things. It's my clear-thinking recipe."

Lifting it to my nose, I smelled an earthy, spicy aroma. "Mmm. This is great, Granny. Thank you."

"You're welcome." She glanced toward the door behind me, where Gus was scratching and barking on the other side. "I hope you're not going to leave him loose in there. He'll tear the place up."

"Oh, no. I—I'm just gonna leash him up and then get going on some errands."

"Alright, then. I have a lot of stops to make. Better get going." She picked up her bags.

I leaned in and gave her a quick hug. "Be sure to stop at Dumbbells and say 'hi.'"

"If I have time," she said, then turned to leave.

Back inside, I ran for my purse to look for my phone once more. Then I realized Richard was knocking on the basement door. Gus's barking had drowned it out before.

"Hello!" he said. "What gives?"

I sprinted to the kitchen and yelled back. "Oh, uh, sorry about that! The door is stuck. Just give me a minute."

With my purse in one hand and the herb bag in the other, I slipped into the office and fell into a chair. I needed to call the police before Richard decided to break down the door. I set the herb bag on the desk, giving it another quick sniff before doing so. Suddenly, I remembered something: another herb bag, still in my purse. It was the one Gus had found after Granny dropped it in the events room. I should've returned it to her while she was here.

Or did she drop it? I pulled the flattened bag from my purse's outer pocket and stared at it as the strangest feeling washed over me. *What if someone else dropped this bag?*

My mind reeled. Someone wanted desperately to find something they'd lost in the events room. Could this be it? Was this what the killer was looking for all along . . . because it contained the poison they'd used to kill Abe?

I dropped the bag on the desk like it'd bitten me. If there were traces of strychnine inside, the police technicians would be able to tell. I'd let them figure it out.

At last, I located my phone at the bottom of my purse. But I hesitated before calling. I couldn't stop wondering exactly what had happened the day of the murder. Did the killer have the pouch of poison in their pocket? I imagined somebody sprinkling the powder on Abe's plate while everyone else was distracted by the scene between Abe and Valerie. But how did the killer—Richard?—happen to have one of Granny's herb bags? They were distinctive, homemade. Only Granny's customers would have one.

The front door jingled. Gus hopped up from his perch at my side and bolted to the front of the shop. I followed him, noting that Richard was being suspiciously quiet. Maybe he'd called for backup.

I half expected to see Valerie, but it was Letty standing in the foyer. She held a foil-covered pie plate out of Gus's reach. "Sorry, pup," she said. "I didn't think to bring treats for you."

"Hi, Letty," I said. "What do you have there?"

"Sugar cookies. My way of saying thank you for the lovely bouquet."

"That's sweet." I reached for the covered plate, but Letty swiveled toward the events room and opened the doggie gate with her free hand.

"Are you busy today?" she asked. "I thought you might want to have some cookies now, if you have the time."

"Oh. Well, um." Flustered, I couldn't think of a coherent response. What was Letty doing here on a Tuesday morning? Shouldn't she be at school teaching?

"Do you have the kettle on in the kitchen? A cup of tea would go well with the cookies."

I stared at her, at a loss. This seemed so out of character. And how did she know we had a tea kettle in the kitchen? For all most folks knew, there was only a florist workroom in back.

Letty set the plate on a table and removed the foil. Then she joined me in the front room. "Can I help you make the tea? I don't want to put you out. I was just recalling our visit, when you stopped by last week for tea and cookies."

"Mm-hmm." I remembered that visit too. I also remembered seeing one of Granny's herb bags on Letty's coffee table.

Letty was a customer of Granny's.

She was looking at me expectantly. "Sierra? Are you okay?"

"Yeah! Sorry. I was just thinking." I spoke slowly now, formulating my thoughts as I voiced them. "Your son, Trent, worked at Flower House, didn't he? Years ago?"

Something flickered in her eyes, and a tiny crease appeared between her eyebrows. "Yes. I don't think you worked here then."

"He worked at Abe's garden center too," I said.

"Briefly, yes."

"Why briefly?"

Now her face darkened. I'd clearly struck a nerve.

"Abe fired him. Unfairly, I might add. I asked him to give Trent another chance, but he refused."

"That's too bad." I watched Letty closely, trying to fathom what she wanted. Gus wasn't paying us any attention. He was busy trying to figure out how to reach the cookies.

"It was the last straw for Trent," said Letty. "Abe was his last hope. Felix had already given him the boot. When Abe let him down too, Trent started running with a bad crowd—and they got him involved with drugs."

"That's too bad," I repeated. "You must have been upset with Abe after that."

"Yes," she said, with a coldness that made me shiver.

I forced myself to remain calm, even as my heartbeat quickened. All along I'd struggled with the idea that any of my friends or acquaintances were capable of murder. As obnoxious as Abe was, I couldn't imagine how he'd provoked someone enough to end his life. The motive would have to be really powerful, I thought.

Standing here now, face-to-face with Letty, as she talked about her son's raw deal, I thought I saw that powerful motive. It was the protective instinct of a mama bear.

"Why don't you have a seat?" I said. "I'll make us some tea." *And call the cops while I'm at it.*

I turned around and started down the hallway.

"Hold it," said Letty, in her strict schoolteacher tone.

Startled, I turned around—and felt my stomach drop like lead. The teacher held a handgun. And she was pointing it right at me.

Chapter 27

I was definitely going to take Gus to obedience school the first chance I got. If I knew how to tell him to attack on command, I might have been able to get away from Letty and her deadly pistol. As it was, he was oblivious to the fix I was in, still more interested in the cookies in his midst.

Then again, if anything were to happen to the little guy, I'd never forgive myself.

I inched backward, toward the rear of the shop, forcing Letty to move forward with me.

"What are you doing?" I squeaked, raising my hands in the air. "I don't understand."

"I think you understand perfectly," she said. "I was hoping it wouldn't come to this, but you leave me no choice." With her left hand, she pulled a flannel bag from her sweater pocket and held it up for me to see. "I'll just put this in some water, and you'll drink it, and then there won't be anything else to worry about, for you or me."

Now I knew she'd really lost it. How could she think I would willingly swallow the poison that had killed Abe? I'd just as soon let her shoot me. . . . But if I could keep her talking, I could buy myself some time. Calvin would be back soon. Maybe I could even dash out the back door.

"I'll shoot you if I have to," she said, shaking my last shred of confidence. "It's messier, but it will work just as well. Either way, I'll make it look like you did it yourself. It was the remorse you felt for poisoning Abe."

My eyebrows popped up. "Why would I poison Abe? He never did anything to me."

Letty laughed at that. "He did something to everybody. In this case, I suppose it was your loyalty to Felix. As Abe's business rival, he was supposed to take the blame. It was the perfect way to punish both men at the same time."

Punish both men. That sounded like the language used in the anonymous Internet comments. Letty must have believed she was punishing those who had wronged her son—a "descendent of the righteous."

I was at the threshold to the kitchen now. I needed to keep her engaged, focused on the past—instead of her present plan to do me in.

"So, what happened with Trent?" I asked. "I don't get how Abe or Felix are solely responsible for his winding up in prison."

She scowled, and my breath hitched. I needed to be careful not to make her too mad.

"No, they weren't *solely* responsible. The hooligans who got him mixed up in drugs are all in prison too. But it was the adults in his life who failed him: Abe and Felix, who wouldn't let him keep a job. Valerie Light, who called the police on him for loitering outside her dance studio. Walt Walden, who arrested him. And the district attorney, who filed the charges." Letty saw my surprise and offered a grim smile. "The attorney is already deceased. His justice is outside my hands."

I tried to comprehend Letty's warped reasoning. Apparently, she felt she was doling out consequences to the level they were deserved. Valerie's role earned her the stalker treatment; while Abe and Walt's role warranted their bodily harm—or death.

"Get a glass," Letty ordered, waving the gun toward the cabinets near the sink.

Dang it. I needed to keep asking her questions. I wracked my brain. "Oh! That day at the funeral home, you were washing black dye from your hands, weren't you? Was that from the black roses you made for Valerie?"

She narrowed her eyes but didn't answer.

"Uh, what about the death threats?" I said quickly. "Was it just to scare Abe?"

"You answered your own question," said Letty. "I wanted him to suffer, while I worked out the details. I didn't know exactly how I'd have access to his food or coffee. I thought it might happen at Bread n' Butter—Felix and Abe both ate there often enough. Then you provided the perfect opportunity with your little workshop."

"But how—"

"Stop stalling!" Letty barked. "Get a glass *now*, and fill it with water."

In slow motion, I reached for the cabinet. *This is not happening, this is not happening.* I took down a glass, moved to the sink, and turned on the faucet. Water flowed into the glass, reached the brim, and overflowed onto my hand, yet I didn't stop it. Wild ideas rushed through my mind. *I could throw the water in her face. I could bolt for the door and hope she's a bad shot.*

Suddenly, a loud crash came from behind me, followed by a grunt and a thud. I shrieked, dropping the glass, and spun around to see the basement door lying on the floor—and Richard standing before it, sweaty, dusty, and fierce as a tiger. He held the crowbar in one hand and a screwdriver in the other. But his snarl soon turned to confusion, as he gaped at Letty, crumpled on the floor with a handgun by her side. The heavy door must have knocked her over.

"What in the name of Lady Gaga is going on here?" he demanded.

"Letty killed Abe!" I said.

Richard regarded me suspiciously. "*Letty* did? I thought *you* did."

"You thought *I* did? I thought *you* did!"

Richard and I stared at each other for a moment, at an apparent impasse. I tried to grasp how he could possibly suspect me, until certain events started to come back to me. "Wait," I said. "Did Valerie think so too? Is that why the two of you ran from me the other day?"

"Of course. You're the one who orchestrated the workshop. And then we heard you had access to some heavy-duty pesticides."

"But why would I do such a thing?"

"Valerie told me how Abe had taken advantage of her when she was younger. We figured he must've done the same to you. He was a lech, after all."

I glared at Richard, offended that he could think such a thing of me. Then I remembered all the evidence stacked against him.

"*You're* the one with a real motive," I said, pointing at him for emphasis. "Abe was blackmailing you, wasn't he? Something about a bank statement?"

Richard turned pale and leaned against the counter for support, as he set down his tools. "What do you know about that?"

"I know enough. The police must know something too. Why else have they been dogging you? And why have you been avoiding them?"

He slumped his shoulders. In spite of everything, I suddenly felt sorry for him. "What did you do?" I asked, in a softer tone.

"I was desperate," he said in a small voice. "My mom needed care I couldn't afford. I asked Abe if he could help, as my mom's employer, if not as a friend. He refused—unless I gave him my car as collateral and agreed to an exorbitant interest rate."

"Wow," I murmured. Abe really was a rat.

"So, I said, 'no thanks.' And then—I'm ashamed to say—I took the money out of his bank account anyway."

"Uh-oh." That sounded serious.

"I thought I could pay it back before he ever missed it, but no such luck. He checked his balance and noticed right away. I took out a fast-cash loan and replaced the funds, but he still had the statements showing the discrepancy."

"And he threatened to report you?"

"Yep. How's that for poetic justice? I wound up owing him forever anyway, on top of the loan I took out. That's why I had to take on the handyman work, for the extra cash."

Richard's confession had taken only a minute, but, in the back of my mind, I was acutely aware I should be calling the police. And perhaps help Letty, who seemed to be out cold. Still, I had one more question for Richard.

"Who did you meet on Saturday, behind the boathouse at the lake?"

He gave me a look like I might be a witch. "How did you know about that?" Then he held up his palm. "Never mind. It doesn't matter. It was—" He broke off with a gasp. At the same time, I gave a yelp of surprise. Letty was on her hands and knees, reaching for the gun!

"No!" I yelled. And without thinking, I stuck out my foot and gave her hand a rough kick—sending the gun flying through the air. It landed with a clatter on the other side of the room.

With a crazed look in her eyes, Letty made a rush for

the back door. Like a goalie, I blocked her way. And, before I knew it, she spun on her heels and was out the other door, running for the front of the shop.

"Get her!" I said.

Richard raised his eyebrows, as if to ask why we should bother. But he soon rallied and scrambled after Letty, with me at his heels. All the running drew Gus's attention, and he started barking madly. Before Letty could reach the front door, Gus nipped at her ankles. She tried to pull away, moving toward the events room—and tripped right over the doggie gate.

"Sierra, catch!" said Richard, tossing me a decorative garden stake he'd grabbed from a shelf. I caught it in both hands, then quickly stepped into the events room and pointed the sharp object at Letty.

"Stay where you are!" I ordered.

Richard hopped over the gate to join me, holding a heavy vase like a weapon.

And that's how we stood when the front door opened and Calvin entered with officers Bradley and Dakin.

Thank goodness, I thought, relief washing over me. To Officer Bradley, I said, "Hello, ma'am. I've been meaning to call you."

Chapter 28

The police took Letty away in handcuffs. As they exited the flower shop, I stared down at the cookie crumbs sprinkled across the floor of the events room and was reminded of the scene here after Abe's death. It seemed we'd come full circle.

Then I glanced at Gus, who had run to the window to see outside, and again at the crumbs. He had eaten most of the cookies. A horrible thought popped into my head. I raced to the front door and ran outside.

"Wait! Letty!"

The officers paused, and she looked up at me with a haggard expression.

"Was there poison in the cookies? Gus ate them!"

She met my eyes, making me wait for a second that felt like an eternity, then shook her head to tell me "no." The cops urged her into the back of their waiting patrol car, and then they were gone.

I became aware of Flo standing outside the bakery, shielding her eyes from the noonday sun. I waved at her cheerily, before returning to the shop. *Nothing to see here*, I thought. Just another ordinary day at Flower House.

I believed Letty was telling the truth about the cookies, but I would still watch Gus carefully to be sure. So far, he was acting as lively and frisky as ever. Calvin was playing with him, keeping him occupied as he'd done while the police took statements from Richard and me. They'd also taken a peek at the kitchen and, thankfully, bagged and removed Letty's gun.

After that, Richard said he wanted to go home, take a shower, and "collect my nerves." He said he'd come back later to fix both doors in the kitchen, if I wanted him to. I assured him I did. I apologized for locking him in the basement, but he wasn't angry. In fact, he felt guilty and embarrassed about what he'd done at the bank, and he promised he would come clean.

Now I slid into a chair in the events room and watched Calvin and Gus. Calvin looked different, I realized, than when I'd first met him. He wore an open-collar button-down shirt and jeans that actually fit. His manner was more easygoing too, less stilted. As if feeling my eyes on him, he looked up and grinned.

"Richard told me how our buddy here saved the day," he said. "Attacking Letty's legs and making her fall over the gate?"

"Ha! Sort of," I said, with a smile. "Hey, how did you know to bring the police to Flower House anyway?"

Calvin walked over and pulled out a chair across from me. Gus followed him, still wanting attention. "After dropping off the orchids, I tried calling you to ask if you'd like me to pick up something for lunch. I went ahead and stopped off at Nell's Diner, tried calling again, and still no answer. Then I started thinking about that stunt in the cemetery. I got this crazy notion that Richard, or one of the others, might try coming after you. I actually bumped into the officers at the diner and decided to say something."

"It's a good thing you did. Letty was trying to escape

when you arrived, but she was pretty unstable. Who knows what she might've done next."

Calvin nodded soberly, no doubt conscious of how differently things could have turned out. In that moment, I regarded him with a mixture of gratitude, curiosity, and something like affection.

Impulsively, I reached over and squeezed his hand. "Thank you."

His eyes flickered with surprise, before he quirked his mouth into a slight smile. "Of course."

A cell phone buzzed nearby. I let go of Calvin's hand, so he could reach into his pocket and look at his phone.

"Excuse me a minute," he said, standing up. Gus and I watched, as Calvin walked to the front door and stepped outside, while saying, "Hey, what's up?" into his phone.

Hmm. I got up too and went to the kitchen to fill Gus's water bowl. After he had a drink, I coaxed him into the office with a chew toy and sat down at the computer.

Now that Abe's murder was solved, I finally had the bandwidth to focus on the other mystery that had been nagging at me: Felix's sudden departure and Calvin's convenient arrival.

I pulled up a web browser and clicked on the history tab. I knew Calvin had been freely poking around in here. He could very well have erased the computer's history and cleared all past search results—but apparently he didn't. I scrolled down to see what websites Felix had visited in the days before he left. From what I could tell, the site names pretty well reflected his interests: Geocaching Today, Fishing Poles for Sale, River Water Levels, Geocaching, Botanical Names of Plants, Geocaching.

I opened the link to a geocaching forum, which Felix seemed to frequent on a daily basis. It didn't take long to see that my old boss went by the handle "Flower Man."

"How original," I said. I was talking to myself, as Gus was still engrossed in his chew toy.

Evidently, Felix participated in conversations on a number of topics, but the one that came up the most was the "Arwin Treasure."

"Treasure, huh? Didn't Angela say Jim Lomack was on a treasure hunt?"

I'd assumed she was referring to the pretend *treasure* that made up a cache in a geocaching game. However, as I soon learned, legend told of a real treasure. Years ago, an anonymous rich man, known only by the moniker "Arwin," reportedly hid a cache of jewels worth upwards of a million dollars. He'd also hidden a series of obscure clues all over the country, in increasingly hard-to-find places. Some of the clues used the botanical names of plants marking the hiding place for the next clue.

Interesting. I gathered that the treasure hunters had been stumped about one particular clue for years. Apparently, it involved a riddle about a rare plant.

A soft sound behind me made me look up. Calvin was standing in the doorway.

"Whatcha doing?" he asked, glancing at the computer screen.

I leaned back in the chair and crossed my arms. "Tell me the truth. Why are you really here?"

"What do you mean?"

"Okay, then. How about if *I* tell you why you're here. You're trying to figure out where Felix went, because you think he solved the clue to the Arwin Treasure. And you're working with someone else, who's trying to follow Felix. Is that about right?"

He opened his mouth to respond but evidently didn't know what to say. All he managed was, "Uh."

I frowned. "Is anything you told me true? Are you

really a botany teacher ghostwriting a book? Did Felix really agree to rent you the apartment? Or are you a complete fraud?"

"I'm not a fraud!" Calvin insisted. "I mean, I'm not actually writing a book. That was a fib. But pretty much everything else is true."

I gave him a skeptical look. "So, you're really a klutzy, pun-loving plant nerd?"

At least he had the grace to blush. "Okay, I admit I acted a bit nerdy and awkward at first. I thought I'd have better luck ingratiating myself here with a more, I don't know, *innocent* persona? I thought I needed a cover to explain why I was so interested in Felix's books and papers. But then you turned out to be so trusting, and I realized I didn't really need the act."

Now I was irked. He might as well have called me "gullible and naive." I narrowed my eyes, about ready to kick him to the curb. But then he hurried to my side and dropped to his knees so we were eye level.

"You were right to trust me," he said quickly. "I'm not a bad guy. Look." He reached over me to move the mouse and click into another exchange on the geocaching forum. "This is a conversation between Felix and me. See how far back it goes? Way before I even learned about the treasure."

I glanced at the computer screen. "You're 'Plant Prof'?"

"Yeah, that's me. See? Felix and I bonded over our shared interest in both botany and geocaching. I mentioned I needed a break from Knoxville, and how nice Aerieville sounded, and he offered me the apartment above his shop."

It appeared he was telling the truth. But I wasn't entirely satisfied. "What about your partner? What will he do if he catches up to Felix? Try to steal the treasure?"

A shadow of concern passed over Calvin's face. "That's actually a good question. I don't know this guy that well, and I'm starting to suspect he might not be as chill as I'd thought."

"What do you mean?"

Calvin shook his head. "I'm afraid Felix might be in danger—and not just from my partner. There are others out there trying to find him."

Alarmed, I sat up straighter. "You need to throw them off the trail then! Tell them Felix went someplace else."

"Yeah. I guess you're right." He scratched his head thoughtfully. "The good news is that there are supposed to be several more clues. Felix probably won't find the treasure anytime soon. Anyone following him will probably leave him alone, so he can lead them to the next clue."

"Well, I'm going to warn him anyway," I said, looking around for my phone. "Let him know he might be in danger."

"He probably already knows to be careful," said Calvin. "He's aware of all the interest in the treasure."

I supposed Calvin was right. But knowing Felix, and how absentminded he was, he could have a parade of followers and be none the wiser. I'd still give him a call sometime soon.

Gus gave a bark and ran out of the office.

"Someone must be here," I said.

A moment later, we heard Deena's voice. "Hello! Anyone here?"

Calvin stood up and I swiveled my chair away from the desk as Deena came in. "There you are," she said. "What did I miss?"

A bubble of laughter escaped from my lips. "So, so much," I said. "I don't even know where to start."

"Sorry I'm so late," she said airily. "I had some phone calls to make and things to take care of."

"Oh, right," I said. "You had 'business to attend to.'" I found myself slightly miffed at her vagueness. Didn't she want to confide in me?

"Yes. I had to speak with my doctoral advisor and purchase a plane ticket for Chicago."

Now she really had my attention. "What? You're going back to Chicago?"

"Just long enough to close out some accounts and get my stuff. I've decided to move back to Aerieville for good."

"Oh!" This rollercoaster of emotions was leaving me slightly breathless. In the past half hour, I'd experienced worry, fear, disappointment, relief, and hope. What next?

"Yes," she went on. "And I've already found a cute little apartment on Main Street. I can't keep living with my parents." She gave me an eager smile. "I'm definitely going to need a job, though. Is it possible I could work here, with you, full time?"

"Me too," chimed in Calvin. "In case you were wondering, Sierra, I'd like to stay on. For real."

Deena cocked her head curiously. "I've clearly missed something here."

"So, so much," I said again. Then I looked from Deena to Calvin, and I realized I'd already made up my mind days ago. But now I was ready to make it official.

"Yes," I said. "You can both stay. And I'll ask Byron to put you on the payroll. I've decided to keep Flower House going, as long as I can."

In the following days, the flower shop had more visitors than ever before. It seemed the whole town was grateful and relieved there was no longer a murderer at large. Go figure.

In fact, so many folks stopped by to offer congratulations and well wishes, I decided to run another flower sale. I was excited about the future of the business. Between Mother's Day, prom, and the upcoming wedding season, I had a feeling we would be very busy in the coming months. As I mentioned to Deena, I also wanted to plan more flower-arranging workshops. She'd raised an eyebrow at that. "Crime free, of course," I'd assured her. I was positive Aerieville had seen its last murder for a long time. Odds were certainly against it.

My family dropped in too, on the day of the grand reopening. Truth be told, I was a little nervous to face my mom. Memories of my stint in Nashville were resurfacing like sharks' fins. I couldn't forget her disappointment and worry when I'd left college and struck out on my own, followed by her begrudging acceptance when things seemed to go my way—until they didn't anymore. Given my history, could she ever see her way to supporting my decisions?

"Sierra! Come here and let me hug you, Ms. New Small Business Owner!" Mom pulled me into a strong embrace right there in the foyer of Flower House. "I brought you some information about the Chamber of Commerce. There's a meeting tomorrow evening. You can come with me, and I'll introduce you to everyone."

I chuckled at her exuberance. "Okay, Mom. Sounds good. Thanks."

Dad and Rocky each clapped me on the shoulder as they breezed past, on their way to the hors d'oeuvre table. I caught Granny's eye over Mom's shoulder. She gave me a subtle wink, before glancing up at the basil still tacked above the doorway—probably gauging whether it needed

replacing. In that moment, my heart swelled with gratitude. My family was there for me, no matter what. I truly
was one lucky woman.

Of course, the Morrisons were not thrilled when I told
them I didn't plan to sell Flower House. They were even
more disappointed when they learned who the mayor appointed to replace Abe on the zoning board: one Valerie
Light. Valerie shared the news when she stopped by to purchase roses (white, yellow, and lavender). She also told
me she was a big proponent of public participation and
transparency in government. There would be no more
board approvals without community input.

Deena was as relieved as I was to learn that Bill and
Flo's plans had been thwarted—especially considering
how sneaky they'd been. In truth, I wasn't entirely opposed
to the idea of a theme restaurant. If done right, it could
be a boon for the neighborhood. But I was definitely glad
we would have a chance to hear the details and offer our
opinions when the time came.

With all the lingering mysteries solved, I felt as if a
huge weight had lifted off of me—heavier than anything
I'd ever lifted at Dumbbells. There was a lightness to my
steps I hadn't felt in a while. Moreover, in spite of all the
recent troubles, I realized I'd actually gained quite a bit
over the past couple of weeks.

I thought about this one morning while walking Gus
through Melody Gardens. I'd found a new friend in Deena,
a joyful new companion in Gus, a brand-new business
venture. And, with Calvin, a new . . . well, let's just say
another new friend. At this point, I couldn't be sure of my
feelings toward him. After all, I still needed to get to know
the real Calvin Foxheart.

I did know one thing for sure, however. I now understood I didn't need to move to some far-off exotic locale,
date a movie star, or become a famous singer in order to

be happy. I'd learned it was possible to make the life of my dreams right here, in little ol' Aerieville.

"Right, Gus?" I said. "As the saying goes, 'Happiness comes from within.'"

He gave a bark and jumped on my legs, clearly in agreement.

Acknowledgments

I owe a huge debt of gratitude and tons of admiration for all the folks who helped bring this book to life. This includes my awesome agent, Rachel Brooks, who provided so much encouragement and excellent advice—and who found the perfect home for this series; my amazing editor, Nettie Finn, who not only advocated for this project and guided it to fruition, but who also boosted me with her irresistible enthusiasm; and my talented and super-sharp beta readers, Cathy, Tom, and Jana, who offered the most helpful feedback (and who also happen to be part of my loving and supportive family). As always, I'm eternally grateful to my husband/partner/BFF, Scott, and our beautiful, incredible kid, Sage, for their love, laughter, and unconditional support.

Last, but not least, I have to thank "Aries," the real-life inspiration for Gus. This sassy corgi has brought more joy to our lives than we could have ever imagined.